THE SIOUX RAISED THE TOMAHAWK...

I knew he was already counting coup on me and would brag in his lodge tonight of my fresh scalp lock hanging at his belt. I feinted to my left as if to dodge again, but at the last possible instant, leapt to the right in front of his running pony. One flying forefoot caught me in the thigh and spun me down in excruciating pain.

But the Indian had gone by me leaning to the other side. I rolled to my feet, ignoring the pain. As he wheeled his pony for yet another try, I half ran, half crawled to my rifle. I dove for it and rolled over, levering a fresh cartridge into the chamber just as he charged down on me for the third time. From a sitting position, I only had time to raise the rifle and jerk the trigger. The rifle jumped and crashed and I flinched, waiting for the impact of the ax as the painted, glistening body came hurtling off his mount to land on me....

Summer of the Sioux

Tim Champlin

BALLANTINE BOOKS • NEW YORK

Library of Congress Catalog Card Number: 81-67836

ISBN 0-345-34277-1

Manufactured in the United States of America

First Ballantine Books Edition: January 1982
Third Printing: March 1987

For my wife, Ellen, and my mother, Elizabeth

CHAPTER
One

THE trip had been going badly from the start, and for the tenth time that morning I asked myself what I was doing there. But it was too late to turn back now, as I sat shivering in the unheated Union Pacific passenger coach that was slowly being dragged across the monotonous Nebraska prairie.

Covering General Buck's upcoming campaign against the Sioux didn't promise to be the safest or most comfortable way to spend the summer, and the discomforts had started early. When I boarded a Northwestern train in Chicago two mornings ago, May 6, I was drenched by a torrential thunderstorm being driven horizontally under the passenger sheds by a high wind. Once aboard, I had to sit for four hours in wet clothes as the start was delayed by locomotive trouble. Due to the delay, I had missed my connection with the Union Pacific in Omaha but had taken advantage of the situation to stop and meet the famous General Daniel Buck.

Even though it was Sunday, I had found him at his headquarters, poring over reports from his officers in the field. He saluted me curtly as I was shown into his office. I handed him the letter of introduction my newspaper had instructed me to get from his superior, General Phil Sheridan in Chicago. As he scanned the letter, I caught a quick impression of a man in his middle for-

1

ties whose square frame made him appear heavier than
he probably was. His close-cropped blond hair and
forked beard were liberally tinged with gray, and the
slightly beaked nose gave him a rather fierce, hawkish
appearance. He looked every inch the soldier in spite of
the fact that he wore no uniform.

"Well, Mr. Tierney," he smiled, rising and extending
his hand. "I'm glad to have you with us. This promises
to be a tough campaign. Can you ride and shoot?"

As he came around the desk, he moved with a barely
discernible limp—the result of an arrowhead he carried
in his right hipbone as a souvenir from an earlier campaign in Arizona. I could feel his piercing blue-gray
eyes sizing me up.

"I can ride fairly well, General, and I'll bet I can
probably hit a haystack at a hundred yards."

He laughed. "Very well, you'll ride with the cavalry.
I'm going with my aide, Mr. Burke, to the agencies to
get some friendly Indians to ride with us. I'm afraid
we'll have to rely on the Crows and Snakes since the
Sioux, Cheyenne, and Arapahoes are disaffected, and
may all join the hostiles.

"You'd better go to Fort Sidney or Fort Russell
where the expedition is being formed. You'll need an
animal and can probably buy one at Cheyenne. I'll be
at Fort Fetterman about the middle of the month."

I had thanked him and headed back to my hotel
room. When he mentioned that it would be a tough
campaign, I knew he wasn't just making conversation
or trying to impress me. General Buck had a reputation, even among seasoned cavalrymen, of being a hard
driver who spared no one, not even himself. His words
had echoed ominously in my head the rest of the night,
and as I stepped aboard the westbound Union Pacific
early this morning, I began to have second thoughts
about this whole affair. Yet when Mr. Storey, the Ver-
monter who publishes the Chicago *Times Herald*, had
asked me to take this assignment I had jumped at the
opportunity eagerly. I guess what really underlay my
decision was the unexciting prospect of reporting social

events and politics in the stifling city heat. Sweating on the trail as a war correspondent at least was preferable to sweating out a deadline in a city room with the editor breathing down my neck.

But sweating was one thing I definitely was not doing at the moment.

"Natives call it blackberry winter," the portly conductor remarked when I complained about the unseasonable early May chill. "Not cold enough to fire up the heaters, though," he continued, shaking his gray head slightly as he handed back my ticket. I decided a layer of fat must be insulating him against the cold as I watched him sway his bulk on down the aisle with an air of unconcern. It looked as if his black coat would split if he took a deep breath.

I muttered some uncomplimentary things about the U.P.'s management as I turned away to stare morosely out the grimy window at the dull brown prairie crawling past under a leaden sky. The day promised to be cold and bleak, with a brisk north wind. I shivered and pulled my corduroy jacket closer around me, feeling the cold air seeping in around the window. Might as well get used to it, I decided, since being in the field for about three months was sure to bring more discomforts than this, and more danger, too.

The coach I rode in was about half-empty. Those passengers headed for points farther west—Cheyenne and the West Coast—were ensconced in the Pullmans. And that's where I wished I was at the moment. But the money had not been available. Even if my paper could have spared the extra funds, I probably would have saved it to help outfit myself for the trail at Cheyenne.

With nothing to read and only gloomy thoughts to go with some fresh hunger pangs, I settled my hat over my eyes, twisted into a more comfortable position, feet on dunnage, and closed my eyes for some much-needed sleep.

I was able to doze only intermittently during the rest of the morning.

* * *

Following the supper stop at Kearney, I stood out on
the rear platform of my car to get some fresh air. The
northerly had finally blown the cloud cover away to the
south, leaving the air clear and crisp. The setting sun
was softening the humps and hollows of the barren
landscape. It appeared that the whole Platte River valley must be honeycombed with the burrows of prairie
dogs, since these rodents abounded by the millions.
They looked like small, brown rocks until the passage
of the train alarmed one of them, and the "rocks" suddenly came alive as they all rushed for their holes.

The twilight deepened into dusk and I remained on
the platform, in spite of the chill breeze, smoking a cigar and enjoying the sight of the moonrise over the
countryside. As I watched its silvery reflection flashing
along the shallow Platte, I thought of the millions of
buffalo that had overrun this area only a few short years
ago and the tribes of Indians who had freely hunted
them before the advent of the railroad and white civilization. Now both Indians and buffalo had been nearly
driven from this region of Nebraska. There was no telling what the passage of the next few years would bring.

I forced myself to stand and pace and think in the
cold draft until my body and brain were fatigued. When
I finally popped open the case of my Waltham, the bril-
liant moonlight showed me it was nearly midnight. So I
retired to the relative warmth of the coach, stretched
out in the double seat with my coat over me, and immediately fell asleep.

"Sidney! Sidney! Next stop! We'll have a forty-five-
minute breakfast stop here."

The fat conductor went out the end door of the car,
and I sat up, rubbing my gritty eyes, feeling as stiff and
cold as a corpse. The clicking of the wheels was already
slowing as I looked at my watch. It was 7:05.

When I stepped down onto the platform, a brisk
wind hit me in the face, clearing the cobwebs from my

brain. The platform was crowded with both civilians and soldiers. Nearly all of the military wore the yellow facings of the cavalry, since the barracks of the post were located close to the town.

By the time I was seated in the spacious depot dining room smelling the delicious odor of coffee, I was wide-awake. It was bacon and eggs, fried potatoes, and flapjacks, and I did justice to everything in sight. I was halfway through my second helping before I looked up long enough to notice a blue-coated cavalry officer who, for some reason, looked familiar in this crowd of strangers. Then I realized I had just seen him debarking from my train. He was too far away down the table for conversation, but as soon as I had stuffed myself and paid my bill, I accosted him as he stretched his legs.

"Pardon me, Captain, didn't you just get off this train?"

He gave me a quick, curious look.

"Yes, I did," he replied, turning away.

"You wouldn't by any chance be heading for Cheyenne, would you?"

"Yes. I'm rejoining my command there."

"General Buck's command?"

A pair of brown eyes regarded me quizzically from under his blue hat brim. He was slightly taller than my own five feet nine inches. Unlike many of the soldiers I had seen, he was clean-shaven and his lean face was slightly tanned by wind and sun.

"Are you a reporter?" he finally asked.

"Yes, but not local. I've been assigned to cover General Buck's campaign for the Chicago *Times Herald*."

He turned to resume his walk. "In that case, you and I are headed for the same place."

I knew the upcoming campaign was no military secret and that it was generally known in the East, so I was curious as to why he had wanted to know if I was a reporter.

"Based on many of the accounts I've read in the papers about previous campaigns," he replied to my query, "I've almost come to the conclusion that most reporters, or editors, will write and print any type of sensational tripe that will help circulation."

He made no apologies for present company. But, after all, I was the one who had started this conversation. "Well, that's one of the reasons my publisher wanted me to come along on this campaign—on-the-spot accuracy and detail."

At this he seemed to soften a little. He paused again in his stroll.

"My name's Curtis Wilder, Mr. . . . ?" He thrust out his hand.

"Matt Tierney, Captain Wilder." I gripped his hand in a firm handshake.

"All aboard! All abooooorrrdd!" The conductor's call came faintly on the wind from the other end of the crowded platform.

"If you're traveling alone, Mr. Tierney, would you like to join me? It's been a long ride and I'd appreciate the company."

"My pleasure."

We filed aboard with the other passengers, and a few minutes later Sidney was behind us as our train continued chuffing along the wide, flat Platte River valley. The train was moving slower now on the long, gradual upgrade toward the Rockies.

I retrieved my luggage and brought it forward to the next coach. Even though Captain Wilder had invited me to share his car, he didn't seem disposed to talk. I was cudgeling my brains for some remark to break the ice when he unexpectedly spoke.

"Beautiful country," he remarked, almost to himself, staring out the window at the undulating prairie that was streaked with a greening carpet of spring. "I like the wide-open spaces."

I was not inclined to agree, but said nothing.

"Have you been out this way before, Mr. Tierney?" he asked, apparently remembering my presence.

"No. This is my first trip."

"Going to be great ranching country before many more years," he mused. "Look at those antelope."

I followed his pointing finger and could just make out several dun-colored pronghorn bounding along the plains, about two miles distant.

We rode in silence for a few minutes.

"Where is your home, Captain?"

"Philadelphia, but I haven't really lived there in about thirteen years—since I enlisted at nineteen."

"Civil war?"

"Yes."

"Been in the army ever since?"

"Just about. When I was mustered out in the summer of sixty-five, I managed to get an appointment to West Point and started in sixty-six. Graduated in seventy and was ordered directly to the Department of the Platte as a second lieutenant in the cavalry."

"So you've served in the West for about six years."

He nodded.

"You've advanced pretty quickly. Going to make it a career, I guess."

"Plan to. But then, nothing is certain."

I glanced sideways at him and wondered what was behind that preoccupied stare. "Weren't you part of the strike against the Sioux on the Powder River in March?" I asked.

"Yes."

"Pretty tough campaign, from what I've read."

"The weather was. Below zero every night, and the snow was deep."

"What about the Indians?"

"Well, from my point of view, it was a very frustrating expedition."

"Oh . . . ?"

"We didn't really accomplish what we set out to do. It was somewhat of a standoff."

"How do you mean?"

"We took them totally by surprise, burned their village and set 'em afoot. But later that night they stole back most of their horses we had captured. Very few casualties. The scouts indicated it was Crazy Horse's village, but we found out later he wasn't even there. We proved they are not safe even in their remote winter encampments. Other than that we didn't do them much damage except waste a lot of good buffalo meat we couldn't carry off, burn their tepees, and butcher a lot of good Indian ponies we couldn't herd."

"I heard General Buck brought charges against Colonel Reynolds, who headed the raid. What was that about?"

"Well . . ." He paused as if reluctant to air the army's dirty laundry in front of a civilian. "There was a little internal dissension about the way the battle was conducted."

"Any opinion about it yourself?"

"Not if you're planning to report any of this to your paper."

"No. All of this is past history. My paper would only be interested if or when the court-martial is held. I'm just trying to get the lay of the land, because I'm sure some of these same men are going to be involved in this upcoming expedition. Just want to know what attitude to expect from the men I'll be bivouacking with."

"I think Colonel Reynolds did everything that could be reasonably expected from a commander under the circumstances. There were charges brought by two or three of the company commanders against each other and against Colonel Reynolds. Professional jealousy and personality clashes, in my opinion. Also, under fire, small slights and small mistakes take on exaggerated importance. Human nature is such that when things don't go perfectly under stress, then people have to look for someone to blame."

He smiled ruefully.

"Colonel Reynolds was blamed for leaving the body of a dead soldier behind on the field to be scalped and mutilated and for allowing the Indians to recapture the pony herd. He was also criticized for burning up several tons of buffalo meat when our command was in need of food. Actually, we couldn't have carried it all away without wagons and plenty of time to load them. And besides, the Indians were firing at us the whole time from the hills just beyond the village, and darkness was coming on. Even though it was bitter cold, the men had taken off their overcoats so they could fight unencumbered, and through some mix-up, about half of the coats were left behind."

"As fast as things seem to be moving with the Indian problem, the court-martials may be moot by the time the army gets around to holding them."

"You could be right."

He brightened up, as if shaking the whole thing from his mind.

"By the way, have you made arrangements to mess with anyone?"

"No."

"Well, I'll be forming a mess with two other junior officers I know. You're welcome to join us if you like."

"Thanks. I appreciate that."

He grinned slightly. "The army feeds its enlisted men but lets the officers forage for themselves. Maybe they feel I can afford it on two thousand dollars a year."

CHAPTER
Two

In the early afternoon we passed through the long snowsheds. As we emerged from them we could see Long's and Gray's peaks in the distance to the southwest—our first view of the Rockies. And, less than an hour later, we were steaming into Cheyenne. Again the depot was crowded. Captain Wilder and I shook hands and parted company for the time, as he headed for Fort D. A. Russell, only three miles from town. I hired one of the loafers on the station platform to help me haul my luggage to the Savoy Hotel where the rooms came cheap, if not luxurious.

It was a second-floor room with an iron bedstead, washstand, and window that overlooked the street. There was little else but a straight-backed chair and a peg for my clothes. The thin wooden walls screened only against prying eyes; they admitted every noise from the adjoining rooms and hall. And there was plenty of noise to be heard.

After checking in, I went to look over the town. My first stop was a barber shop and bath house a block from the hotel. After a shave, haircut, and a good soaking in one of their wooden tubs, I felt like a new man. It was four-thirty when I emerged on the sidewalk, ready for an early supper.

Cheyenne looked as if it had been set down at random in the middle of nowhere. The wind blew unchecked off the treeless plains. Even though the air was fairly warm now in the late afternoon sun, the streets were a quagmire from the recent spring rains. Only about half the buildings were painted; the rest had weathered to a dull gray. Many of them had the usual false front.

As I clomped along the boardwalk, searching for something that resembled a restaurant, I thought that uninviting as this place appeared now, it must be doubly dreary during the long winter months.

Finally I ducked into a surprisingly large, clean eating place. The supper crowd had not yet arrived, and I ordered a big steak with potatoes. The buffalo meat was delicious, and well worth the rather steep price.

When I stepped out onto the sidewalk again, toothpick in hand, I noticed several soldiers going in and out the batwing doors of a saloon about a block away on the opposite side of the street. Just what I needed to settle my dinner, I thought—a beer.

I had to push my way into the Eagle Saloon. The place was only one average-sized room, hardly big enough to accommodate the amount of business it was getting. Yet for a frontier town, the Eagle Saloon had some pretensions to elegance, with a huge, ornate mirror behind the mahogany bar, stacks of glittering glasses, two heavy, oil-lamp chandeliers suspended from the tall ceiling, and even a piano player keeping up a steady pounding over the general din.

As I eased up to the bar and ordered a beer, I noted the crowded room was made up of about half civilians, half soldiers. The balding bartender drew off my draft, and before I could even get the foamy mug to my lips, a familiar voice at my shoulder startled me.

"So we meet again sooner than expected, Mr. Tierney."

I turned quickly and found myself staring into the bronzed, clean-shaven face of Curtis Wilder.

"Well, hello, Captain. Didn't expect to see you here. Figured you'd be with your troops tonight. Aren't you camped just north of town?"

"Just had to report in. Then I was free for now. And I wouldn't miss a chance to get one of these good steaks Murphy fries up. Best in Cheyenne, if I do say so. Have you eaten?"

"Just finished."

"Too bad. Maybe tomorrow."

He jerked his head toward one of the tables. "C'mon over and meet a couple of your messmates."

"You gentlemen are liable to be making your last trip if you're going out after the Sioux," a voice interrupted.

The eavesdropper standing in front of me straightened up from leaning heavily on the bar. When he looked up with bloodshot eyes, I saw a man who appeared to be in his late twenties. Under the wide hat brim, his handsome, youthful face was flushed. "But, I suppose one time or place is as good as another for dying."

Inebriated as he was, he interpreted my look of curiosity correctly. "Wiley Jenkins is the name, sir, at your service." He attempted an elaborate bow. "Late of Kentucky. And I would be there now instead of swilling in this godforsaken hole on the edge of the world if it were not for the fact that I have become 'persona non grata' in that land of bluegrass and smooth bourbon due to some unfortunate marital and uh . . . financial affairs. A soldier, or rather civilian, of fortune, you might say."

Wilder nudged me and motioned to get away and head toward his table. Without a word, I turned away, but Jenkins caught my arm.

"You may think I'm drunk, sir, and you wouldn't be far wrong. But I'm not trying to cadge the price of a drink from you. You're not in the military. I don't know if you're working for them in some civilian capacity, but if you are, heed my advice—there are safer and more enjoyable ways of making a living in this part of the country. You'd better think twice about it, if you're not tired of living. Those Sioux are mad as hornets, especially since all those gold hunters invaded their sacred Black Hills."

Wilder was already weaving through the tables, but I hesitated, my reporter's curiosity aroused. "Everyone else I've heard talking in town seems to believe just the opposite," I countered. "They're saying the army won't have much trouble running the Indians out of the Black Hills country and holding them out long enough for the miners and settlers to move back in and get established. In fact, the talk is, their resistance will be broken and they'll all be back on the reservations by winter."

"The army may be able to keep 'em on the run for a while, but they can't keep it up indefinitely. The Sioux and northern Cheyenne won't stand and fight any pitched battles. That's not their style. It's hit and run with them all the time. The army'll never catch up with 'em in the field."

I leaned on the bar and regarded his elegant figure in the scrollwork of the mirror.

"How come you pretend to know so much about this? Thought you said you were new to this part of the country."

"You mistake my meaning, sir. I said I was lately from Kentucky—not that I'd never been here before. I just find it convenient to come here when it's necessary to absent myself from my native state for a period of time, and I don't care to have anyone know where I am." He paused to toss off a small jigger of whiskey and pour himself another one before he continued.

"My father, God bless his larcenous soul, is a mining engineer and a major partner in the New Hope Mining and Milling Company. You've heard of it, perhaps? It was organized about ten years ago at Cincinnati, and he's been traveling all over the West ever since, testing and investing in mining properties for them. Since he's the mineral expert, the company directors invariably act on his recommendations. Naturally, his services come high." He laughed harshly. "And, as if he needed more money, he's also busily engaged in helping his partners fleece the stockholders of the New Hope." He turned around, leaned his back against the bar, brushing cigar ashes from his camel-colored vest, and hooked a booted heel over the brass rail.

"But the point of all this is, I've traveled a good deal, some of it with my father, but mostly on my own, so I'm no stranger to this part of the country or what's been going on here. In fact, my father's here in town someplace now with my sister, just waiting to head for Deadwood on the heels of this expedition to look into grabbing up some o' that gold-strewn real estate for himself and the New Hope Company. He was up there earlier, but the government ordered the army to run 'em out last year. Guess the government has now changed its policy to 'if you can't whip 'em, join 'em' in regard to keeping whites out of the hills. But I can tell you there's going to be hell to pay before it's settled. The Indians are not going to take the breaking of this latest treaty with the traditional savage stoicism."

"If you think the Black Hills are all that dangerous for whites right now, may I ask what your sister's doing traveling with your father—whatever her age?"

"Oh, Cathy?" He turned toward me, removed his hat and placed it on the bar, wiping the beaded perspiration from his forehead. "To tell you the truth, I'd almost quit thinking of her as a girl. She's twenty now—a woman by chronological age—but she's been a tomboy all her life. Never took to dresses and frills. Can ride and shoot better than most men. She's been making these sojourns with Dad for years."

I noticed Wilder looking in my direction from a back table. As I waved an acknowledgement, one of the saloon girls sidled up to Jenkins from the opposite side.

"Buy me a drink, honey?" She flashed him a pretty smile, as her dark eyes flickered from his wavy brown hair to his tailor-made suit to the half-eagle he had just laid down to pay for his drinks.

"Sure." He swept the bottle up by the neck, encircled

the girl's waist with the other arm, and lurched away, without so much as a backward glance in my direction.

I ordered a fresh beer and quickly joined Wilder at his table.

"Was that drunk trying to bend your ear or your pocketbook?" Wilder greeted me.

"My ear, mostly." I grinned without elaborating. But my reporter's instinct told me there was something more to Wiley Jenkins than just another loquacious drunk, and I filed away the chance meeting in the back of my mind for possible later use.

"Matthew Tierney, I'd like you to meet Lieutenant Ludwig Von Bramer."

I hooked a chair up with one foot and sat down, reaching across the table to shake hands with a man of sallow complexion and rather sunken cheeks, whose hooked nose was counterbalanced by a huge, blond mustache.

"Lieutenant."

"Goot to know you," he greeted me without removing a curved pipe from his mouth. "Velcome to da 3rd Cavalry."

"And this is Lieutenant Brad Shanahan, Matt."

"How do you do, Mr. Tierney."

"It's Matt."

I gripped the hand of the youthful third officer at the table as I looked into a friendly, intelligent face. He wore the stylish mustache and goatee. His hair was black and contrasted with the kind of pink-white skin that flushes easily.

"Has your regiment got the route for the front yet?" I inquired of the group.

"Some of it," Von Bramer replied first, pushing his chair back and crossing his legs, revealing the huge dragoon boots he wore. He seemed to move with a nervous energy. "Our battalion should have it already, but 'tis alvays da vay! Got tamn da luck! Ve ought to have moved a veek ago. Dey're alvays slighting da 3rd Cavalry at headquarters." Heavy clouds of smoke billowed from his pipe as he fidgeted with his beer mug and re-crossed his legs.

"Well, maybe it won't be long now, Lieutenant," I ventured. "I saw General Buck in Omaha and he said he'd be at Fetterman by the fifteenth."

"You don't zay zo? Den ve get off. Vell, dat is goot."

Just then Wilder broke in as he caught sight of some-one in the crowd nearby.

"Colonel! Colonel Wellsey. Over here!"

A slightly built soldier worked his way over to our table.

"Colonel, there's someone here I'd like you to meet."

I stood as Wilder introduced me to Colonel Guy Wellsey, a battalion commander of the 3rd Cavalry. He was a somewhat pale, but pleasant-looking officer. A sweeping trooper's mustache was topped by a straight nose and gray eyes that had just a trace of shadowed circles under them.

The colonel drew up a chair at Wilder's invitation and joined the conversation.

"Any news about the campaign, Colonel?" Shanahan inquired.

"Nothing official yet. But I have it on sufficiently good authority that we'll march from the railroad here in two columns. One will form at Medicine Bow, ninety miles or so west of here, and will cross the North Platte at Fort Fetterman." He nodded gratefully as Wilder slid a whiskey and water in front of him. "The other will march from Fort Russell to Fort Laramie, cross the North Platte there, and march by the left bank so as to join the other column in front of Fetterman. From Fet-terman we'll march north until we strike the Indians. In brief, that's about the program."

"By the way, I'm in need of a horse. Anyone know of a good place to buy one?" I inquired.

"Yes," Colonel Wellsey replied. "I've got a friend in the business. I can see that you get fixed up with a good mount."

"Might see if you can get a bay to match the horses in my troop as long as you're riding with us," Wilder

said, tilting back on his chair and reaching for his pipe.
Crash!

A tray of drinks went flying across the table behind
us as Wilder bumped into a saloon girl who was just
passing behind his chair. Even before the glass stopped
shattering, there was a clatter of chair legs scraping and
voices cursing. Wilder's chair came forward with a
thump. A bulky figure shoved the frightened girl aside
and leaped over to grab the back of Wilder's collar.

"Wilder, you stupid, clumsy bastard!" the voice
rasped.

He yanked Wilder over backward and swung his free
hand in a wild punch at the side of Wilder's head. The
punch missed and the big man lost his balance, and the
two went down in a crash of breaking chairs and tables.
About half the room jumped to its feet, anticipating a
fight. But the men at the two tables quickly dragged the
two apart and pinned the big man's arms. His face was
livid and the front of his shirt was splattered with beer
and liquor.

"No, Major, no! It was an accident!" one of the
men yelled urgently. "C'mon. Forget it. Let's get outa
here."

I had hold of one of Wilder's arms, and I could feel
him relax slightly. Just as I started to let go, he lunged
and broke loose, diving for his assailant with something
like a growl. Von Bramer, Shanahan, and I grabbed
him again. The four men, two of them in cavalry uni-
forms, who held the other man, were hustling him toward the door, knocking people out of the way as they
went.

"It's okay, Murph," Colonel Wellsey said as the bartender came up with a shotgun in hand. "Just a little
accident. We'll take care of the damages."

The bartender retreated and we picked up the chairs
and sat back down at our table.

"That damn Zimmer. Drunk again," Wilder gritted,
brushing off his uniform. "Sorry, Colonel, but I wish I
could've gotten in just one good punch," Wilder said.

"I know, but you'd have regretted it later," the colonel replied, coolly smoothing the ends of his mustache. "I'll take care of this back at the fort."

He nodded to us, got up and left.

"Who in the hell *was* that?" I asked, since everyone else seemed to know.

"Major George Zimmer, second-in-command of the 3rd Cavalry, hard drinker, and self-styled ladies' man," Wilder replied sardonically.

No one seemed too surprised by the incident. Shanahan had signaled to a girl for a fresh round of drinks, and Von Bramer was calmly refilling his pipe.

"He's your superior officer?"

Wilder nodded.

"Well, nothing like serving under a real officer and gentleman. He was certainly way out of line. Has he got something particular against you?"

Wilder nodded reluctantly. "I guess he's still steamed up over a clash we had awhile back. About two months ago we really got into it when I refused to sign a falsified report he drew up on one of my sergeants."

"Oh?"

"Yeah." Again he hesitated, then shrugged. "For some reason he liked this sergeant—a man named Cooney—and wanted to get him promoted, based on his action at our fight in March. Cooney exposed himself foolishly to enemy fire against my orders, but Zimmer chose to interpret it as bravery. Cooney was a dullard, in my opinion. Don't know how the man ever got beyond Private. He certainly wasn't officer material. Anyway, Zimmer was furious when I wouldn't sign this glowing report he wrote. But, as it turned out, Cooney was invalided out of the service with a stomach disorder in April. Defused the issue, but Zimmer hasn't forgotten."

Over his pipe Von Bramer remarked, "It iss bad enough dat a zuperior offizer iss foolish. Bud it iss even more foolish to point it out, my friend."

Wilder looked uncomfortable. "I can't stand the man," he muttered.

"Yah. Vell, nobody can. And there's lots of odder tings ve can't stand neither. But ve do, no?"

Wilder swallowed his drink. "Let's order some food," he said.

I got the distinct feeling they had said something to one another that had passed right over my head.

CHAPTER
Three

"MESSAGE for you, Mr. Tierney." The desk clerk reached into the pigeonhole and handed me a slip of paper, as I approached the desk in the lobby of the Savoy Hotel to pick up my key three days later. I unfolded it and read:

Matt—
    The command is under orders. Better check out and meet me at Fort Russell as soon as possible. We'll probably be moving out soon.

Curtis W.

I stuffed the note into my pocket and headed up to my room to pack. Word had passed through town yesterday that General Buck had arrived at Fort Russell, but this morning I heard that he and his staff had already left for Fort Laramie to the north.

I'd spent my time getting acquainted with Cheyenne and buying my arms and gear. I had gone with Wilder while he bought food and supplies for our mess, and I had picked up a good poncho for myself. In the matter of arms, I'd taken a little more time. I had left my twelve-year-old Henry rifle at home, and I'd finally selected a new, 1873-model Winchester with a blued metal receiver and octagonal barrel. As a side arm, I'd bought an 1872-model single-action Colt revolver, holster, and cartridge belt. The heft and balance of these two weapons was superb. And they had one great advantage over the many other models—both used the same .44-40 cartridge. So I stocked up with about a thousand rounds of this ammunition.

I also invested in a good, used McClellan saddle that was just comfortably broken in.

I rented a spring wagon to haul my stuff, and a newly made friend named Duffy, a burly, red-faced Irishman who operated a bookstore in Cheyenne, insisted on driving the wagon out to the fort for me that afternoon while I rode alongside on the strong, deep-chested bay Colonel Wellsey had helped me find. I had met Duffy while browsing through his bookstore. When he found out that I had been born in Ireland, even though my parents had brought me to the United States in 1851 when I was only eight, he embraced me like a long-lost son. He himself had fled the old country during the great hunger of the forties.

Just as we entered the fort parade grounds, something startled the team and they bolted wildly. The wagon lurched, throwing Duffy out. He sailed through the air in an arc, landing squarely on the top of his head. The only thing that saved him a broken neck or concussion was the high-crowned Stetson he was wearing. He staggered to his feet, cursing and puffing, as I rode up.

"You hurt, Duffy?" It was all I could do to keep from laughing, when he turned around and I saw him struggling to pull off the hat that had been jammed down over his face and ears.

"A damn foine way to start a campaign," was all he said when he finally got it off.

The team finally stopped about 200 yards away and were grazing quietly, while my luggage was strewn all over. Several orderlies were detailed to pick it up.

I was quartered in one of the barracks overnight and the next morning several troops of the 2nd and 3rd Cavalry started the march toward Lodge Pole Creek, about eighteen miles north of Fort Russell. It wasn't until the next day, May 18, that I got started, however, since Captain Wilder was ordered to hold up until then.

The fort was all orderly confusion as hundreds of soldiers, wagons loaded with supplies, and a pack train of mules handled by civilian packers assembled and moved out in line of march.

"Curt, I've got a couple of things I need to take care of in town before I leave. I'll catch up with you later today," I yelled at Captain Wilder as he swung into the saddle shortly after sunrise.

"Okay. We'll be camping on Lodge Pole Creek, just a few miles out. The road is easy to follow. We'll see you there tonight." He touched the brim of his hat and wheeled his horse toward the waiting column.

I had purposely waited until the last possible moment to send a wire to my newspaper, because I knew it would be some time before I would be able to get a dispatch by courier to the nearest telegraph office once we marched away from civilization. I had sat up the night before writing a short summary of my trip to date. There was another motive for my desire to delay joining the march, I admitted to myself as I rode back to Cheyenne. I had not been accustomed to riding for several years now, and I wanted time to myself to get toughened up to it before I made a fool of myself in front of seasoned horsemen.

However, at the telegraph office I was glad I had held back for yet another reason, for I ran into another newspaperman, a seasoned veteran, Robert McPherson, representing the Los Angeles *News Sentinel*. He was a gray-haired man of about fifty, whose constant cough advertised him as a consumptive if I ever heard one. Why he would be joining such an expedition I couldn't figure, but since he was also late getting started, I waited until he had secured an outfit, and we rode out together about midafternoon. Since it was a fairly warm day and he was as out of practice at riding as I was, we lounged along on our horses, sitting on one cheek and then on the other. The road was clear and the country undulating and treeless, with very little vegetation of any kind.

Finally, along toward sundown, we urged our horses to a trot and about twenty minutes later, came over the brow of a hill into sight of the white tents of the camp spread out along the banks of Lodge Pole Creek in a shallow valley. Some horses were grazing among the standing wagons. Several troopers were taking care of their mounts, and a few cooking fires were being kindled.

Since most of the other messes were full, McPherson was invited to join Wilder, Von Bramer, Shanahan, and me for now. In no time we were all seated in Captain Wilder's spacious whitewall tent, putting away our first meal on the trail—and with plenty of food for everyone.

"I see you two have had your hair cut short," Wilder said. "What're you trying to do—cheat the Sioux out of some decent scalps? They'd be laughed out of the village if they hung those trophies in their lodges."

I just grinned. McPherson wiped his mouth and coughed his slight, hacking cough before he replied.

"Captain, I, for one, propose to see that that does not happen. But in case it should, I sure won't be in any position to laugh at some brave's embarrassment."

"Speaking of braves," Shanahan said around a mouthful of meat, "I believe a lot of people have underestimated the strength of the Indians we're going after."

"Don't you think General Buck knows pretty well from the scouting reports what their force probably numbers?" McPherson asked from the head of the folding camp table.

"Hardly. More and more of them are slipping away every day from the agencies to join the hostiles. Unfortunately, they've been well fed during the winter and are well armed. Whatever sketchy reports General Buck may have received are surely out-of-date by now. Not only that, but General Buck has been fighting the southern Plains tribes. These northern Plains tribes are all somewhat related and can forget their differences to join forces against a common enemy."

"Well, I guess we can speculate from now 'til doomsday, but I believe what we're liable to encounter is going to be a surprise to everyone, including the general," Wilder said.

The discussion rambled on in that vein for a time, and shortly after we finished eating, a bugle sounded, and the horses were led up and put "on line"—tied by their halters to a strong rope stretched between wagons—curried, and fed.

While we sat around the camp fire, smoking our pipes in the cool of the evening, the mules set up their usual daily braying chorus. Just after full dark, the sentries were posted and we returned to Wilder's tent, stretched out on buffalo robes and blankets, and went to sleep. The last thing I was aware of was Wilder's snoring and McPherson's eternal cough.

My dreams were suddenly shattered by the blast of the bugler sounding reveille. It was still dark when I stumbled out of the tent, stuffing in my shirttail and trying to get my eyes open. "What time is it?" I asked Wilder as he shoved a tin cup of black coffee and a piece of hardtack into my hands. I could barely make out his form in the low firelight.

"A little after five."

"Why in the hell does the military always have to keep such ungodly hours? This time o' year there's plenty of daylight." I sipped tentatively at the scalding coffee.

He chuckled, squatting on his heels and poking at the fire. "Tradition and discipline mostly. But there is a practical reason, too. Sunrise is a favorite time for Indian attacks."

My knee joints were so stiff and sore from my previous day's ride that I could hardly mount my horse.

"Let me see your stirrups," Wilder said when I mentioned my trouble. "Ah, there's your problem. Lengthen those stirrups and you'll be okay. Indians usually ride with short stirrups like that for long distances, but I don't know how they do it. It would cripple me. Not only that, but I can get a better grip with my legs."

I complied and got some relief as we swung out of camp by six o'clock.

By the time the sun was well up, we were riding through desolate, powder-dry sagebrush country. The suffocating dust churned up by the feet of the animals in the windless air was coating all of us and sticking to our sweaty skins.

Wilder rode up to me about midmorning, just as I was finishing the last of the water in my canteen. "Pretty dry, huh?"

I nodded, squinting in the glare despite the hat shading my eyes.

"Try holding a small pebble in your mouth. As long as you're not completely dried out, it'll trigger enough saliva to keep your mouth wet."

"Thanks."

The command was halted several times during the day to give the horses a chance to graze and the new soldiers to get some of the soreness out of their bones. Even though I never let on, I was profoundly grateful for every stop. About sundown we went into camp at a place called Bear Creek, where there was plenty of wood, water, and grass. It was almost a repeat of the first night's camp. We were up before daylight again next morning and pushed hard, making few stops, to catch up with the column that had started a day ahead of us.

About noon the column was halted as a horseman came galloping down toward us from a ridge in front. It was a Lieutenant Otto bringing word that Colonel Peterman's command was only a few miles ahead.

We pushed our horses to a trot, leaving the wagons behind, and in about two hours caught up with the rear wagons of Peterman's advance column. The colonel was getting ready to make camp, but decided, because of the combined force, that there wasn't enough water and grass and pushed on for several more miles before camping. By the time we finally stopped, I was so galled and saddle-weary and hungry that, when I unsaddled my horse and turned him out to graze and roll, I wouldn't wait for supper but went to chewing on a piece of raw army bacon and hardtack, washing it down with a tin of very bad water. Then I spread my saddle blanket on the ground and went sound asleep under a tree.

It took Von Bramer's foot in the ribs to rouse me up an hour later to eat supper. But, in spite of my nap, I turned in and slept soundly through the night.

I awoke the next morning to the sound of rain drumming on the tent and an orderly came by to tell us that if the rain didn't stop by eight o'clock, the battalion would stay put for twenty-four hours since the heavy wagons would mire down in the mud. That day, at least, we had cause to be grateful to the rain. Most of the day I spent resting, getting acquainted with the soldiers, and starting on a dispatch for Chicago. Late in the afternoon I was walking along the creek bank about a hundred yards from my tent when the sound of a familiar voice stopped me. It was coming from a group of teamsters huddled out of the rain under a shelter tent, playing cards. I walked toward them and peered under the canvas that was propped up to admit some air. The voice came again and there was no mistaking it.

"Wiley Jenkins, is that you?" I asked. The voices stopped as the mule packers and teamsters looked up curiously.

"Well, if it's not my old friend from the Eagle Saloon. How've you been? I don't believe I ever did catch your name." I was surprised that he remembered me at all, but perhaps he had not been as drunk as he appeared. The man who thrust out his hand bore little resemblance to the man I remembered from the week before. He was sitting cross-legged on the ground, dressed in a pair of buckskin breeches and boots, and a coarse, red cotton shirt. But it was the same wavy hair and sardonic smile. And this time he was sober.

"Matt Tierney, here," I said automatically, still bewildered to find him here. He gripped my hand, pulled himself up, and stepped outside with me. The men inside resumed their card game as we walked a few steps away under the trees.

"What the hell are *you* doing here?" I managed to get out.

"Working as a mule packer. What else?"

"But I thought you were really against this expedition. And besides, I had you pegged for one of the spoiled, idle rich who could sit back and offer commentaries on the world without having to work to change it."

He grinned. "Well, I do have some money, but it's fast running out, so I needed some kind of employment. And I wouldn't accept money from the old man even in the unlikely event he were to offer it. As for joining this expedition, well . . . I'm still young enough to be foolish, I guess. Besides, my curiosity got the better of me. It's one thing to study about wars in the history books and newspapers, but quite another to be an eyewitness to man's inhumanity to man. The better to criticize and comment, as you say." He stepped back to avoid some water dripping from the overhead branches.

"Besides, I've had a little experience throwing a diamond hitch, so . . . here I am. But don't get me wrong. Even though there's likely to be some fighting, you're not going to find me in the middle of it. I'll find a way to stay out of range. Civilian packers are under no obligation to help tame the savage hordes."

I made noncommittal noises while privately deciding to keep an eye on Jenkins, if only because his views provided some perspective on the military.

* * *

The rain stopped that night and we finally dragged ourselves out of the camp mud the next morning at ten. It was only a short march to Fort Laramie where we arrived about one P.M. A few more troops joined us there. Since Fort Fetterman was still some ways off, Colonel Peterman moved us out with only an overnight stop. In the early morning the entire command crossed the Laramie and North Platte rivers in the face of a raw northeast wind. The weather was a pleasant break from the earlier heat.

Our seven companies of cavalry were an imposing sight, as I watched the columns ride up and away from the river, their accoutrements rattling. The various companies were differentiated by the colors of their horses—Company K of the 2nd was Lieutenant Hogan's gray-horse troop, Captain Butler's Company C of the 3rd was a white-horse troop, and so on down the line. My own bay matched the bays of Captain Wilder's Company B.

Most of the men were fairly young, lean and athletic, wearing the broad, felt hats of various styles and colors, with either blue or buckskin pants and blue shirts. The majority of the noncoms and officers were distinguished by the yellow leg stripe. Since the standard-issue dark blue uniform trousers weren't known for their durability, some of the men had sewn leather across the seat and down the insides of both legs. No uniform code is strictly enforced on an Indian campaign. Each man carried sixty rounds of fixed ammunition in his belt for the single-shot, breech-loading Springfield carbine he carried slung across his back or in his saddle loop. Each had a supply of revolver cartridges as well. Sabers had been left behind as useless encumbrances.

The first ten miles we marched that morning was through undulating grassland not far from the North Platte. We paused about nine for a few minute's rest in a little natural amphitheater and from there on, the march was sheer hell, as we entered a labyrinth of bluffs and canyons. Some of the cuts were so narrow that it was single file in the twisting and turning trail. Then up and down hills, some of them so steep that we were forced to dismount and lead our horses, as they slipped and slid on the loose rocks.

Even though Colonel Peterman attempted to keep scouts out ahead and on both flanks, it was nearly impossible, since the bluffs were perpendicular in the cut-up terrain and the scouts were forced to follow the only trail there was—the one the column was on. I noticed several of the officers nervously sweeping the tops of the bluffs with their field glasses—and with good reason. Had any Indians chosen to attack us there, we would have been helpless. A small force could easily have trapped the command and wiped us out. Fortunately, no Indians appeared. A lone elk was the only living thing I noticed, watching us from the top of a distant cliff.

After two hours we finally untangled ourselves from this endless gorge and came out into red-clay country that couldn't even support enough grass to feed our horses, so we wound up pitching camp in the early afternoon in a bend of the Platte. Because of the road we had come over, we had left our wagon train about five hours behind, but they caught up to us by dusk.

We were on the move by six the next morning, and I was beginning to get toughened up to the trail. In order to find a road decent enough for the wagons to travel, we were forced to strike away from the river across a searing desert of blinding sand and rocks. Some of the men with weak or sensitive eyes were forced to wear tinted goggles to protect them from the dazzling reflection off the white sand. And not a drop of water was to be had for the entire day's march of thirty-five miles. Everyone's face was scorched by the striking glare. Even though the officers cautioned against it, the men stampeded for the water and drank to satiety when we struck the river again that afternoon. I was among them.

As I lay flat on my stomach, my face in the shallow,

murky water, Captain Wilder moved up beside me. He led his horse into the scant shade of a mesquite bush and dropped the reins as his mount thrust his muzzle into the water. "Why in God's name the U.S. government keeps a standing army in the field to take away this kind of land from the Indians is beyond me." He splashed some water on his reddened face, then made a cup of both hands and drank. "Lukewarm and full of silt, but it's the best stuff I've tasted in a long time." He grunted.

"Try straining it through your teeth. Takes some of the grit out."

"Are you sure this beats big-city reporting?"

"Don't ask me that now." I rolled over on my back and blew out an enormous sigh.

CHAPTER
Four

"Boots and Saddles" put us on the trail again the next morning, and we found ourselves right back in hilly country of red sandstone, cut up by hundreds of ravines, some of them terrifically deep.

Since our company led the march the day before, we formed the rear guard and marched a little more at leisure. The terrain was beginning to have a bad effect on the mules. Their legs were swollen and their backs were galled by the constant rubbing of the heavy packs. While watching the mules, I began to wonder about Wiley Jenkins. I had not seen him since our chance meeting a few days before. But, since our battalion was strung out for several miles, it was not surprising. He seemed to have the ability to adjust to any type of company and play any role, from dandy to mule skinner, so maybe he was blending in like a chameleon.

We'd had the snowcapped landmark of Laramie Peak in sight in the distance on our left for a couple of days, and it appeared to be changing positions due to our twisting and turning course.

"I'm going to try a short cut," Wilder announced, riding up to me about eight. "Want to join us, and explore a little of the country?"

"Sure."

I spurred my horse after him and three of his men, as

31

they headed straight across country in the direction of Fetterman. Curt was an excellent horseman and took on some ravines so steep I would have bet no man could climb them, much less a horse carrying a man. I was bringing up the rear and assumed they would dismount and lead their animals. But no. When I saw them leap straight up the steep banks, their horses lunging and clawing, I dared not do any less. I followed their example by letting the reins go, giving my horse his head and leaning my weight forward, holding my breath. Somehow we made it. But coming down was just as hair-raising. The horses nearly stood on their heads. One slip, and horse and rider would have cartwheeled to the bottom with broken necks and backs. But, given free rein, these horses were as surefooted as mules.

I eventually lost count of how many of these gulches we climbed in and out of, but Wilder finally paused on a high ridge and we spotted a long, low white building on a bare bluff off to the northwest—our first sight of Fort Fetterman. We paused for a few minutes to let our horses blow, and one of the men with us, a Sergeant Killard, pulled a long twist of tobacco from the wide top of his boot and bit off a chew. "Damnedest place I ever saw," he observed, working the quid into his cheek. "I was garrisoned there for a year some while back. It's the Sahara in the summer and Siberia in the winter. Oughta give it back to the Indians—exceptin' they wouldn't have it."

When we rode through more gullies and finally joined the high wagon road again, we could see in a valley far below us the rows of white tents blossoming like even rows of mushrooms all over the plain on this side of the river opposite the fort. That, and the swarms of cavalry horses and mules, told us that the column from Medicine Bow had already arrived and gone into camp. From where we sat we could also make out a cloud of dust and the flash of sun here and there on a carbine barrel, as the first of our own column entered the camp nearly four miles ahead of us. I was having trouble getting accustomed to being able to see objects at such vast distances in the clear air of Wyoming. It threw my depth perception off. I had to keep reminding myself that a vast herd of horses several miles away in a valley was not, as it appeared to the naked eye, a swarm of insects a few feet away on the ground.

"Some 'shortcut'," I remarked to Wilder.

He grinned. "A rough ride helps to let off steam." I wondered why he needed to let off steam but made no comment.

The teamsters whipped their animals to a trot downhill, and a half-hour later we were on the valley floor and into the camp. If possible, the sight of Fort Fetterman was even more bleak and desolate close up than it had been from a distance. Except for a few cottonwoods and willows along the banks of the river, there was not a tree in sight. The painted, one-story adobe buildings were set on a bluff, commanding a view of the river but also exposed to the merciless sun, wind, and blizzard. It looked to me like Sergeant Killard's succinct description was probably accurate.

"I just got word the ferry's out, Matt," McPherson greeted me, as I emerged from Wilder's tent with a packetful of papers.

"What? But I've got to get across to get these dispatches sent."

"I know the feeling. My paper would like to know what I've been doing to earn my salary lately."

"Let's walk down and take a look."

At this point the normally placid Platte, swollen by upstream spring rains, was running bank-full and muddy, the swift current spinning huge whirlpools into the murky surface.

"I wouldn't advise tryin' to swim it," the leathery, laconic Sergeant Killard remarked, as he walked his horse up and saw us staring at the disabled ferry where several men were working. "They ain't but damn few men and no horses atall thet'd be that dumb. Ferryman told me that a wagon driver, a sergeant, and two privates tried swimmin' their horses across a few days ago. All of them drowned."

While we discussed our next move, a cheer went up from the crowd around the ferry.

"Looks like they've got'er patched up. Let's get aboard while we've got the chance."

Mac and I clambered on, along with a group of men who had been waiting.

"Whoa! That's enough. That's all I can take at a time. Wait your turn." The burly ferryman cut off the flow of eager customers. Then he and two of his assistants began pulling on a rope that passed through a set of pulleys overhead of the flat-bottomed wooden craft. We lurched out into the river, and the current helped push us at an angle downstream toward the far bank.

Just as we neared the opposite shore, the frayed rope suddenly parted and the ferry swung broadside at the mercy of the current. There was immediately a lot of shouting and waving of arms from the shore, but no one did anything as we were swept off downstream.

"Look, Matt!" McPherson shouted in my ear. I turned and saw the head and shoulders of Sergeant Killard and his horse lunging out into the river from the shore behind.

As the straining horse swam alongside, eyes wide and nostrils flaring, someone heaved out a short length of thin cable from the ferry. It was a perfect shot that fell just in front of Killard and behind the horse's neck. The sergeant grabbed it and we could see him taking a turn around the pommel of his saddle underwater. The horse never broke his swimming stride as he pulled straight ahead for shore. It was almost as if it were an act that had been rehearsed. The slack was taken out of the cable; the ferry swung slowly back on course. Killard slid out of the saddle to ease the burden of weight his horse was now struggling with. But it was only about twenty yards to shore, and a few seconds later the horse stumbled as his feet struck bottom and he lunged up the muddy bank, streaming water, with Killard clinging to the saddle. He unwound the cable and threw it to some waiting men, amid the cheers.

A few seconds later McPherson and I and the rest of the passengers stepped off, dry and safe. Killard was trying to disengage himself gracefully from the crowd that was slapping his back and pumping his hand. His hat was gone and his hair was plastered down and his boots squished water every time he took a step.

"Hey, Sarge!" He glanced up sharply at my yell. "What was that you said about damn few men and no horses being dumb enough to swim that river?"

Under the stubble of beard and the tan, his face flushed a deep red. I grinned, and Mac and I headed up to the fort.

We found General Buck in the commandant's quarters, a square building with a wooden porch running around all four sides. He was dressed in a tan canvas field outfit, still not in uniform. He laughed at our dirty, unshaven appearance and our sunburned, peeling noses, as the officers and reporters crowded into the room.

"That was a pretty rough road we just came over, General," McPherson said, coughing slightly.

"Only a prelude, gentlemen," he replied, rubbing his hands together briskly, his blue eyes twinkling. "There are many rougher roads in Wyoming, and I'm sure we'll have to travel some of them before it's over and we bring those damned Indians to heel. We have to . . ."

A back door slammed open and a commotion interrupted him. We all turned to see the sentry struggling to hold someone out.

"What is it, Private?" General Buck's voice cracked like a shot. The sentry snapped to attention, dropping his hold on a lone Indian who stood still in the open doorway. "Friendly Cheyenne, sir. He don't speak no English. But he's tryin' to get in here for some reason."

"Anyone here speak Cheyenne?" One of the halfbreed scouts stepped forward. "Ask him what he wants," the general ordered.

The scout spoke in the Indian's native tongue, using some sign language to help.

The Indian replied in a deep, slow voice, apparently pausing for dramatic effect, even though we didn't know a word he was saying. He punctuated his speech with emphatic gestures and signs. Finally he stopped and the scout hesitated, trying to get his translation straight. "He says the great Sioux chief, Crazy Horse, sends a message to the white chief, Buck, not to bring his pony soldiers north of the Tongue River."

"Or what?" the general demanded.

"War," the scout replied, simply.

"Well, that insolent . . ." The general stopped and collected himself.

I looked toward the Indian, but he was gone. He had delivered his warning and then slipped quietly out the open door. The general's expansive mood was gone, and he dimissed the civilians with a brusque word or two and called his officers aside for a briefing.

Mac and I went out through the compound. The parade ground of the garrison was bare and dusty and devoid of any kind of shade and most grass.

"What's that thing, Mac?"

"Where?"

"In the corner over there."

"Looks like a big box or chest of some kind. Maybe they keep rifles or gunpowder in it. It's padlocked and they have a guard on it."

"Not likely they'd keep arms or ammunition outside in the weather like that. A wooden box would leak rain. Anyway, that stone building is the magazine."

"But it's got tin over most of it."

"Say, Private, what's in the box, there?"

The blue-uniformed soldier came to attention, perspiration trickling down his face from under his cap. "A sweatbox, sir. Got a man in there."

"A *man*? That thing's only about three feet high and four wide."

"Yessir."

"What did he do?"

"Drunk on duty and insubordinate, sir."

"A man could die in there in this heat."

"Possible, sir." The private stared straight ahead, never changing expression.

"Damnedest thing I ever saw," Mac said, shaking his head as we walked away. "I thought we were out to subdue the savages; didn't know we had become the savages."

We had our dispatches telegramed to our respective newspapers, and as we emerged onto the parade ground again, General Walsh's briefing had apparently just ended and we saw Captain Wilder wave as he came toward us in the dusty sunshine.

"Going over to the sutler's store. Care to join me?"

We did. On the way we mentioned having seen the sweatbox.

"Another hallowed army tradition," Wilder said bitterly. "Only one of many along this line. Just before we came across the river, I saw a couple of soldiers from the Medicine Bow command marching around camp, carrying knapsacks full of rocks."

"What for?"

"Fighting. The theory is that if they have extra energy to burn off, they can march until they drop from exhaustion. This is supposed to take the fight out of them."

"And does it?"

"Well, commandants of these remote forts and posts have a tough discipline problem. There's just not enough for the men to do. And not only in time of peace. Even in wartime, these soldiers see relatively little action. And it's usually over quickly. Boredom is the main enemy. Routine drill and housekeeping chores don't begin to use up all their waking hours. There are usually only a limited number of books to read, and gambling is discouraged. The officers sometimes have their wives and families with them for a little civilized society. But most enlisted men can't even afford wives, and no quarters are provided for dependents anyway.

Add to that the fact that quite a few of these recruits are tough kids from the streets of New York and Boston who enlisted to escape the police, and you can see the officers in charge of a fort like Fetterman have their work cut out for them. Especially if any alcohol is available."

"Speaking of alcohol, what's this Hog Ranch some of the soldiers were talking about?"

"It's a saloon, dance hall, restaurant, and hotel just a half-mile north of here, across the river. Caters primarily to the enlisted men. The place is notorious for shootings, stabbings, bad whiskey, and worse women. There are the usual blowouts around payday, and then it's the guardhouse and boredom again until the next time. I've actually seen men jump up and cheer when told they were going into action against the enemy. It's just a matter of having something positive to direct their energy toward. Seldom have any trouble with men on the march."

"Yes, but don't you think that some of the punishments like that sweatbox are a little extreme?" I asked.

"Of course," Wilder replied, giving me an odd look, while he added a half-dozen bars of soap to the writing paper and tobacco he had selected from the sutler's stock. "What's more—and very much off the record, Matt—it's strictly against regulations. There are a lot of rotten things in the army, but it's common practice, and the regulations are ignored. In fact, for relatively light offenses, I've seen bucking and gagging, men spread-eagled, dunked repeatedly in a stream, and hung by their wrists or thumbs. A friend of mine, Captain Albert Barnitz, told me about an incident back in sixty-seven when he was serving under Custer at Fort Hays, Kansas. Two enlisted men went out of camp without permission to the post a half-mile away to buy a can of pears from the sutler because of so much scurvy in the camp. They were gone only forty-five minutes, missed no musters or duties, but Custer ordered that half of each man's head be shaved and they be paraded all over the camp to humiliate them before they were confined in the guardhouse."

"No wonder nearly a third of all enlisted men desert," McPherson said.

"That figure, if it's anywhere near right, probably includes all the 'snowbirds' who enlist for the winter months just to have food and shelter and then hightail it to get good-paying jobs in the mines or on the railroads in the warm weather."

"All of 'em should be shot for desertion," a voice snorted behind us.

The three of us glanced up at the big man who had interrupted. He was a heavyset officer of florid complexion. The thinning, ginger-colored hair on top and the bushy, muttonchop side whiskers made his head appear unusually wide. He wore a major's bars on the impeccably neat blue uniform coat. The insolent blue eyes were slightly bloodshot, and as he leaned heavily on the counter near me, I caught a faint, sweetish odor of bourbon. His face was vaguely familiar; then I suddenly connected it with the scuffle in the Cheyenne saloon.

I glanced back at Wilder. His face had gone white, and his eyes narrowed slightly. There was a long silence before he spoke. "This is a private conversation, Major," he finally said, coldly and with considerable restraint.

"In my opinion, the army needs more discipline—not less," the man continued, ignoring Wilder. "Damn shame some officers are going soft on discipline," he said pointedly, looking straight at Wilder. "First thing you know, the troops will be taking a vote on what they want to do."

"Pardon us, Major Zimmer, but we were just on our way to supper." Wilder turned and pulled out some bills to pay for his purchases. He accepted his change and then led us through a door into the adjoining restaurant, where the sutler also had a reputation of setting a pretty good table.

"Looked like he knocked a few sparks off you," I remarked when we were seated.

"I'm sure I'm prejudiced, but his type of officer perpetuates the kind of horseshit I was just telling you about. He's ambitious. Would walk over anybody for higher rank and command. Like Miles. Probably overheard my remark about Custer and resented it. Two of a kind, in my opinion. Colonel Wellsey must have the patience of a saint to put up with his arrogance. Wellsey isn't the type to pull rank unless he's forced to, but even he has had to call Zimmer down once or twice—most recently for that little episode in Cheyenne."

"It sounded like he was actually trying to goad you into a fight."

"Not a fight. He was trying to get me to do something like slug him so he could bring charges against me for insubordination."

"I think he'd had a few."

"Yeh. He hits it pretty heavy when he's off duty. Probably helps bolster his opinion of himself. He probably started drinking as soon as we hit the fort. And I imagine he's nursing a grudge because of the reprimand Wellsey gave him on my account."

CHAPTER
Five

THE warning from Crazy Horse had just the opposite of the desired effect on General Buck. He was so eager for action that he hardly gave us time to get our clothes washed and dried before he started us north up the old Bozeman Trail at noon on May 29. As the columns filed past Hog Ranch, dance-hall girls with waving handkerchiefs and bartenders in their white aprons came out to wave good-bye to the troopers.

Five companies of the 5th and 9th Infantry had been added to our expedition as escort for the slower wagon train. Not only were our numbers multiplying, but so were the commanding officers. And all the officers had aides and adjutants, who all had orderlies. I even had a soldier—a Corporal Schmidt—to take care of my horse and wait on me as if I were an officer. In fact, I found this treatment a little embarrassing at first since I had not asked for it and wasn't used to having what amounted to a servant. I didn't know if he had volunteered for this personal service or if Wilder, Lieutenant Shanahan, or one of the officers appointed him. But he certainly went about it cheerfully. When I told him it wasn't necessary for him to do all this, he just grinned. "Don't mind at all, Mr. Tierney. Besides, you're no raw recruit. You've seen action during the war. And any friend of Captain Wilder's is a friend of mine. And, if I wasn't doing it for you, I'd be doing it for one of the officers." Schmidt said this with a finality that demolished any and all of my arguments to the contrary. He told me he was a native-born German but spoke English with no trace of an accent since his parents had immigrated when he was only a child.

"Well, I'm afraid all this is going to spoil me," I told him the first night when we were camped about fourteen miles north of Fetterman at Sage Creek. "Except for all the riding, this has been like a big summer picnic so far."

Corporal Schmidt became serious immediately, as he paused in currying my horse. "Don't let this peace and quiet fool you, sir. Those Indians are out there, all right. I've been on a couple of these campaigns before. When they want us to know where they are, we'll know. Until then, you'd swear there wasn't a redskin in the whole territory." He shrugged and went back to his currying.

I went back toward the fire and a supper of steak, potatoes, corn, biscuits, and stewed apples.

"Damn you to everlasting hell, you son of a . . ."
I was jarred out of a sound sleep by an enthusiastic packer the next morning. I came awake to the sounds of braying mules, shouts, curses, the general din of creaking wagons and harnesses, the rattling of gear, all of which was only slightly muffled by the white canvas of the tent. It was full daylight. I fumbled for my watch in my jacket pocket. It was six-ten.

When Colonel Peterman had charge of our column, he had us up and on the trail by five-thirty or six. Now that General Buck was in command, he had the infantry and wagons move out at six and the faster moving cavalry at seven-thirty. This, Wilder explained, was to give the horses more rest for when they were really needed and would have to be pushed hard. The bugler must have been farther away than usual, or else I was extra-tired, I decided, as I pulled on my pants. I had slept through reveille and my tentmates, including McPherson, were already up and out.

I went outside and took some hot bacon from Lieutenant Shanahan, whose turn it was to cook for our mess, put the meat on some hardtack, and poured myself a tin cupful of coffee. Since we had plenty of time before we marched, I walked down the line, eating my breakfast, toward the mule packers who had awakened me.

There were so many of them milling around that I couldn't pick out Wiley Jenkins for about ten minutes. But I finally spotted him. He and another man were on either side of a mule. Each packer had one foot braced against the animal's sides, cinching up a huge pack. The mule was braying his protest at being nearly squeezed in two. In fact, the whole camp echoed to the racket of braying, swearing, whips cracking, and mules kicking and jumping as this scene was repeated nearly a thousand times, since that was the approximate number of pack mules we now had in the command, in addition to the six-mule teams pulling each of the wagons.

To my eyes, there appeared to be enough wagons and pack animals to carry ammunition and supplies for half the city of Chicago. Since Jenkins had his hands full and then some, I didn't attempt to get his attention.

We marched that day to our next bivouac on the South Fork of the Cheyenne River. Because we were getting deeper into Indian country, the command was kept well closed up on the march, or as well closed up as possible for a command that stretched out four miles.

The terrain looked a little better than what we'd seen before, but the whole country generally had a half-starved look about it, even in spring. There was a little green here and there and usually some decent grass and trees along the watercourses. But I hadn't seen twenty acres in more than three-hundred miles of marching that could compare with any land in Iowa or Illinois.

The Wyoming Territory was certainly rich, though, in rocks, hills, ants, snakes, weeds, and alkali. It was also full of coal, or lignite, which lay in seams near the surface and, where the soil was worn away, accounted for a lot of fine, black dust. The seams were exposed in giant layers where streams had sliced down through the bluffs. In fact, there was such a seam exposed in the face of the bluff across from our camp that night. It was apparently due to this lignite, alkali, or some deposits, that the water was so bad in this muddy rivulet called the South Fork of the Cheyenne.

Just after supper, I went down to this poor excuse for a stream to fill my canteen. As I passed the surgeon's tent, I saw a group of men standing around outside. From snatches of conversation I gleaned as I went by, they were all suffering from stomach cramps brought on by drinking the water. Our side of the stream bank was thickly covered with undergrowth beneath some large cottonwood trees. I filled my two-quart canteen from the clearest of the milky-colored water. When I got back to our camp fire I strained the water through a clean handkerchief into a pot and boiled it over a fire.

"That's not going to help a whole lot," Wilder said, coming up as I was pouring the cooled water back into my canteen. "This stuff is full of alkali, just like the soil around here. Best thing you can do until we get to good water is drink as little as possible." He pulled off his gauntlets and sat down cross-legged on a blanket by the fire. "Might try putting a little vinegar in it. Not only improves the taste, but it's also easier on your stomach. Balances some of that alkali with a little acid." He grinned. "You'll notice the coffee tasting a little peculiar for a while, though."

I dug into the stores we had bought for our mess, pulled out the vinegar, and followed his suggestion. "Curt, General Buck told me in Omaha that he was going to recruit some Crows and Shoshones to go with us as scouts and allies. What's the latest on them?" I knew he had just returned from a briefing in the headquarters tent.

"General's sending out a detachment under Major Zimmer tomorrow to see if they can intercept the friendlies somewhere north of here. They're supposed to meet us somewhere in the general area of old, ruined Fort Reno. He's eager to get them in camp before we strike the hostiles."

"Are they really that indispensable to this campaign?"

"Sure are," Lieutenant Shanahan interrupted, coming up and dropping the cleaned cooking utensils with a crash. When it was his turn to cook, he also did all the washing of the pots and pans, rather than delegating this to some orderly. I had found him to be a quiet, somewhat stuffy, compulsively neat man, devoted to literature, who was incidentally a good cook.

"What makes them so valuable?" I urged when he didn't continue immediately.

"General Buck is convinced that one Indian can smell out another better than any white man. Why do you think we have these half-breed scouts?"

"For interpreters?" I suggested.

"That's only part of it. Most of them are at least half-Indian and even if they weren't brought up in the savage's lore, they've inherited that way of thinking, the instincts, if you will, and can anticipate for us what the savage mind is liable to conjure up. Poor bastards don't really belong anywhere. Whites who don't know them, don't trust them. And, to the Indians, they're only second-class tribal members, at best.

"But, getting back to the friendlies, the Crows are the traditional enemy of the Sioux. So they were glad to have the whites to help them even up an old score with their stronger enemies. They've been killing each other off in raids for centuries. The Crow figure if they can't whip the Sioux, they have no chance of standing against the white, who are, as they say, 'as many as leaves on the trees.' The Snakes, or Shoshones, and the Crows are pretty rough customers themselves, but General Buck believes in fighting fire with fire. Claims to have worked this strategy to perfection against the Apaches in Arizona."

"Says using an Indian against one of his own race demoralizes the enemy as well," Wilder added. "It's even better if you can get some from the same tribe."

Lieutenant Von Bramer and McPherson had joined the group during this exchange. Von Bramer sat down on a log that had been dragged up near the fire in front of our tent and began packing the ever-present curved pipe. Wilder apparently took the cue and pulled out his own stubby briar for a smoke.

The blue sky was streaking with a rosy hue over the cottonwoods and dusk was settling into darkness in the shallow valley. During a lull in the conversation, I became aware of the quiet background noises of a large camp settling in for the night—a murmuring of voices, a faint explosion of laughter, the tinkling of a bell mare among the mules, and an occasional braying, the stamping and snorting of horses being put on the picket line, the thunking of an ax into wood, the lowing of some of our beef cattle grazing just south of camp, the nostalgic strains of "Shenandoah" drifting to us from a mouth organ. The smell of wood smoke permeated and hung like a flat, bluish cloud at treetop level in the still air.

"As I understand it," McPherson broke the silence, "the purpose of this expedition is to catch the hostile Sioux and Cheyenne between us and General Gibbon's command coming down the Yellowstone from the north and General Terry's column coming from Fort Abe Lincoln to the east. Is that about right?"

"You've got it," Wilder replied.

"Is the army supposed to try to kill as many of them as possible, per General Sherman's extermination policy, or just herd them all back onto the reservation?" McPherson inquired.

"A state of war exists," Shanahan replied patiently and, I thought, a little condescendingly. "They've ignored persuasion, deadlines, and ultimatums to return to their reservations peacefully. They've as much as said, 'come and get us, if you want us.' They're thumbing their noses at us. That's why the Indian Bureau has finally come to its senses and turned this whole problem over to the army, where it should have been all along.

"Crazy Horse is probably their most able leader and warrior. He'll never surrender to white domination. And there are many other chiefs who feel the same— Sitting Bull, Gall, Dull Knife of the Cheyenne, American Horse and others. The Indian agents report that hundreds of young bucks are slipping away from the agencies to join them. They're well armed, well fed, and rested from a winter on the reservations at taxpayer expense. The Indian Bureau has supplied them with Lancaster rifles and .50 caliber Springfields for hunting. And the Indians have also stolen or traded for many repeating rifles—better than the ones we're supplied with. Our scouts report them massing in unusually large numbers somewhere south of the Yellowstone, north of the Tongue and west of the Black Hills.

"We'll entrap them between our three forces and we'll drive them back onto the reservations. If they resist, well . . . we'll have no choice but to kill as many of them as we have to. If it happens, they'll be the ones who'll start it."

It was the longest speech I'd heard Shanahan deliver at one time since I'd known him. He'd started quietly enough, but the longer he talked, the more emotional his voice grew, and I could tell, without even seeing his eyes in the darkness, that this was a subject about which he had formed a strong opinion. I couldn't believe I was hearing the normally quiet, intelligent Shanahan oversimplifying such a complex problem as this. But I kept quiet, thinking it was maybe for McPherson's benefit. In fact, I was grateful to Mac for voicing some of the questions that were in my mind.

"Do you actually think a force this large, bogged down with all these wagons, can really do battle with the natives on their own ground?" Mac persisted, poking at the embers of the dying fire and not looking up. "Sorta reminds me of the Redcoats against the Colonists a hundred years ago, except in reverse."

In the darkness, all eyes shifted to Shanahan for his reply. But I knew the discussion was over when Shanahan begged the question by replying, "Apparently you don't know much about Indian warfare and tactics."

"Apparently not," Mac replied a little sharply, as he rose from a squatting position and slapped a mosquito. Either the smoke or his lung ailment brought on a sudden fit of coughing. "Bugs are getting to me, gentlemen," he said when he had recovered his breath. "Good night." With that he stepped over me, ducked under the tent flap and disappeared inside.

A somewhat strained silence fell over the rest of us for a few minutes. Finally, Von Bramer yawned mightily, stood up and stretched. "Vell, I tink I'll turn in. Ve have to roust out too early to suit me." He struck a match to relight his pipe for his customary last-minute smoke.

The crash of gunfire and the most inhuman screeches I've ever heard shattered the quiet.

The match went out, and we all dove for cover and our guns at the same time. As I scrambled in the dark toward the gun belt I'd left on our canvas mess cover, I could hear the bullets thudding into the trees and popping through the tent. The camp was in an uproar instantly. I finally found my pistol and crouched, waiting. But I suddenly realized that I had only the vaguest idea where the firing was coming from. The shots slackened up for a few seconds and then started again, along with those unearthly yells that made chills run up my back.

Without a word, Wilder had sprung away in the dark and I could hear his voice, among others, calling the men of his company together.

"Matt?"

"Over here, Mac."

"Sounds like the Indians didn't wait 'til we crossed the Tongue." His voice sounded matter-of-fact. The attack was so totally unexpected and sudden, it didn't seem quite real to me. But my pounding heart was real enough.

"Can you see any muzzle flashes?"

"No. Must be coming from the bluffs on the other side of these trees."

In the darkness to our left I could hear the commands and the sounds of the well-drilled troops falling into ranks. The shots and the yelling tapered off and ceased quickly as some of the infantry swarmed across the tiny stream and another mounted company rode out toward our beef herd.

There were scattered shouts from our own men and some firing.

I moved toward Mac's voice around the dull glow of a few remaining embers. And suddenly I tripped over a prone figure. Tense as I was, I must have jumped about six feet and collided with McPherson, and we both went down.

"What the hell's wrong with you, Matt?"

"Fell over somebody on the ground. Strike a match."

"Liable to get our heads blown off if we show a light."

"Hell, they're gone now. Strike a match."

Instead, he leaned down, blew on the fire and lifted out a stick that flared up.

"Hold it over here."

"Oh, God!" McPherson groaned.

The flickering glare showed Lieutenant Von Bramer flat on his back, arms outspread and stone dead. A trickle of blood oozed from a bluish hole in the center of his forehead.

"He must have caught a chance bullet from that first volley."

His jaw was slack under the bushy blond mustache, and the curved pipe he had been in the act of lighting lay beside his head on the ground. His eyes were closed as if in peaceful slumber.

"Poor guy never knew what hit him," I managed to say through a tight throat, as the fire on the stick flickered out, plunging us into darkness again.

"A fate most of us will not be able to share, I'm afraid," Mac said, coughing with the deadly consumption we both knew would eventually claim him.

I felt clammy and shaky and half-sick as I holstered my Colt. It wasn't as if I'd never seen violent death before. I had served through the last year of the war. But this was different. We had thought ourselves secure—had no idea there was an Indian within miles. To be talking calmly to a man one second and to have him hurled into eternity the next . . . It was evident my thinking would have to undergo an abrupt change to cope with Indian warfare.

We threw some wood on the fire, covered the corpse, and sat down to await the return of the soldiers.

CHAPTER
Six

" 'MAN does not know his hour; like fish caught in the treacherous net, like birds taken in the snare, so is man overtaken by misfortune suddenly falling on him.' "

As General Buck's deep voice paused in his reading and he sought another passage, the cold wind fluttered the pages as if to rip the leather-bound book from his hands. It tore at the hair and forked beard of his Moses-like figure, bringing tears to his eyes. He blinked a couple of times and went on.

" 'There is an appointed time for everything, and a time for every affair under the heavens. A time to be born and a time to die; a time to plant and a time to uproot the plant. A time to kill and a time to heal. A time to tear down and a time to build. A time to weep and a time to laugh; a time to mourn and a time . . .' "

I ceased to hear the familiar words as I glanced around at the grim faces of the command, who stood, bareheaded, company by company, around the two freshly dug graves. The bodies of the men killed in the attack, Lieutenant Von Bramer and Oswald Sprague, a herder, lay wrapped in blankets beside each opening in the earth. We stood in calf-deep grass on the flat bench land just above last night's camp on the floodplain of the river. The weather had turned appropriately cold and windy for the somber occasion. In fact, if felt as if

51

we had been plunged back into the month of March in the space of a few hours. The temperature had dropped to below freezing and a vicious north wind was swirling around us, raising clouds of alkali dust out of the valley to sear our eyes and to make everything at a distance look hazy.

" 'Do not grieve as those who have no hope. . . .' " General Walsh was intoning.

I shivered in spite of the army overcoat I had borrowed. Mac, standing beside me, was huddled down in his coat collar, coughing softly and looking as gray as the low morning overcast.

The commander snapped the Bible shut. "We commit the bodies of our comrades to the earth in the hopes of their rising again on the last day. They were both good men. May the Lord have mercy on them. May they rest in peace."

He signaled and the four soldiers by each body lifted it by ropes and lowered the corpses into the graves. A bugler blew taps. It was the most mournful sound I'd ever heard, the notes rising and falling on the wind. The last, lingering note died away and the troops were dismissed.

"Helluva start for this campaign," Curt Wilder remarked, tight-lipped, as he fell in beside me on the way back to camp. "We really got caught with our pants down. Lollygagging around camp as though we're on a summer outing while a flying war party infiltrates the sentries, shoots up the camp, kills two men, wounds another, and kills a couple of horses besides running off all our cattle."

"Any chance of getting the herd back?" I asked.

"None. The scouts who went out with Company H at daybreak reported the trail of the herd leading back toward Fetterman. But it's my guess they'll never get there. The Indians have probably already rounded 'em up and herded 'em toward the nearest village. The horses would've been stampeded too, if they hadn't been picketed. The Indians were just trying to hit us quick, create some confusion, and run off all our stock they could get. Probably just happened on our camp by accident."

"I guess that's the end of the steaks, roasts, and beef tongue."

"Sure is. Mostly bacon and beans from here on, with possibly a little embalmed beef thrown in for variety. Hopefully, we'll get some fresh game."

We walked into camp, where some orderlies were striking our tent and preparing for the trail. Lieutenant Shanahan was packing some personal gear into his saddlebags. Apparently, he was in the middle of a bitter discourse with himself, because he turned to us and, with no preliminaries whatever, said, "I just wish some of those almighty, pious, Indian-loving members of the Peace Commission could've been here for this. Do you reckon those Quakers in the Indian Bureau would've been so damn quick to turn the other cheek to those savages? Huh!" He went back to his packing as though he had vomited and rid himself of some bile.

Shortly, we were on the march again. We didn't look as motley now since the men were all wearing overcoats and appeared a little more uniform. The whole command marched in gloomy silence all morning.

About noon, we topped a divide. The clouds tore apart for a few minutes—long enough for a fitful sun to give us a few of its last rays for the month. From this high swell in the prairie, we could make out the snow-capped Big Horn Mountains to the north and west of us, probably a hundred miles away. With field glasses we could see the edge of the Black Hills of Dakota to the east. And to the northeast in front were Pumpkin Buttes—four long, irregular bulges of mountain aligned north and south that jumped up abruptly from the prairie to a height of several hundred feet.

Then the sun went out and the norther blasted us again. We marched only twenty miles that day before going into camp at a place that went by the appropriate name of Wind Creek. The wood was scarce, the water terrible, and the ground covered with various kinds of spiny cacti. The storm increased in fury as the night wore on. By order of General Buck, our stoves had been left at Fort Fetterman to reduce weight, and I'd never spent a more miserable night trying to get warm enough to get to sleep. Several tents were blown down, and toward morning it actually began to snow heavily. June 1 dawned looking like January 1 in Chicago. But, as we hit the trail, the sun relented and came out to begin melting the white stuff that covered the ground.

While the sun dried things out and warmed us a little, we marched only about twenty miles (due to the pace of the infantry) and bivouacked on the Dry Fork of the Powder River. The next morning we rode a little less than twenty miles to the ruins of old Fort Reno, one of the three forts on the Bozeman Trail abandoned under a treaty with the Sioux in 1869. For about twelve miles, we followed the bottom of Dry Fork Canyon through some dense stands of cottonwoods and saw the remains of several Indian villages.

Coming out of the canyon, we drew up our horses on a low bluff and caught sight of white tents and grazing horses on the grassy banks of the Powder River in the distance. I was riding far out front with Captain Wilder and head scout, Frank Grouard.

"Major Zimmer and his company back from scouting for the Crows," Wilder said, lowering his field glasses.

The tone of his voice made me look across at him. "Something wrong, Captain?"

"No. Nothing," he replied quickly. Jamming the glasses into a leather case, he spurred his horse suddenly and the startled animal leapt forward into a trot.

I followed at a discreet distance, respecting his wish to be alone. Whatever was bothering Wilder had started several days before and had just gotten worse with the death of Von Bramer. The loss of this popular officer had cast a pall over our mess, and I made a mental resolution to get Wilder away from his usual routine this evening in camp—to think of some diversion that would bring him out of his depression.

I rode into camp just in time to see Wilder dismount

and go with Grouard into what I took to be the head-quarters tent. A couple of minutes later Grouard emerged, and I heard a voice raised in anger from inside the tent wall. As I watched curiously, Wilder emerged, red-faced, and remounted. As he rode away, a heavy, florid officer sporting muttonchop whiskers emerged from the tent and stared in my general direction, hands on hips. It was Major Zimmer.

While waiting for the command to catch up, I rode across the shallow Powder River to poke around the ruins of the old fort that was nothing but a few bare walls and piles of scrap iron—rusty gun carriages, wagon wheels, and old stoves. The fort had hardly been vacated before the Indians had moved in to demolish everything that could be demolished, including the breaking of gravestones and the splintering of head-boards in the post cemetery. A few words and names could still be distinguished on these markers—Holt, Slagle, Murphy, and others who had been killed in 1867.

A half-hour later I splashed back across the river, noticing the muddy water that looked as if it contained dissolved gunpowder—the trait that had given the stream its name.

"Curt, I don't know about you, but I sure could use a shot or two of good Kentucky bourbon," I remarked off handedly to Wilder after an early supper that afternoon. He looked up sharply at me from the tiny mirror he was using to shave by. I glanced around to be sure we were out of earshot of Shanahan and McPherson. Wilder had gone back to his shaving, leaving his question unspoken. "Yeh," I continued, "I need a little something to settle my nerves and dispel some o' the gloom that's settled in around here."

"Well, I've got a bottle of rye in my saddlebags if you're hinting for a drink," Wilder said, "but I keep it mostly for snakebite, wounds, and upset stomach on the trail. Too many drinking officers in this man's army already."

"That's not really what I had in mind."

"Oh?" He flung the soap off the razor and rubbed a speck of blood on his neck.

"I know where you can get a drink or two of the finest Kentucky bourbon bottled."

"So do I. But we're a long way from Louisville."

"Less than two hunderd yards from here."

He turned toward me, his interest finally piqued, and blotted his face on a towel. He wiped off the steel blade of his razor, folded and replaced it in its case. Then he adjusted his shirt collar. "Well, don't just stand there. I'm not asking any questions. Let's go."

Twenty minutes later, Wilder and I were seated on folding stools around a camp fire with Wiley Jenkins, basking in the genial glow of sour mash and the long, slanting rays of the late afternoon sun.

Even after I had made the introductions, Jenkins and Wilder did not recognize each other from the Cheyenne saloon. And I was just as happy to leave it that way. "Too bad about Lieutenant Von Bramer," Jenkins was saying. "I didn't know the man personally, but it seems a real waste of human life."

"Well, I knew him," Wilder said. "We've served together for some time now. I'm sorry you never got a chance to know him better, Matt. Great sense of humor, in spite of his Teutonic background."

"You know," Jenkins said, "it's pretty ironic that a mercenary like that, who's fought with Garibaldi, and in his own Prussian Army, and even in our own War Between the States, without getting a scratch, should meet his end by some stray bullet fired by some chance war party trying to scare off some livestock."

"His luck just ran out," Wilder said.

"I guess he who lives by the sword, usually dies in the same way," Jenkins observed.

I tensed slightly, waiting for Wilder to take offense, or at the very least, to defend this slap at his way of life. But, surprisingly, he said nothing—just tilted back in his chair and seemed lost in thought as he studied the shafts of sunlight making the bourbon glow like amber in his hand. When he brought his head up, it was to change the subject without further comment.

"On the march today, Frank Grouard picked up the trail of several dozen shod horses. We figured it was a party of whites headed for the Black Hills. And it wasn't two hours later, we found a message written on a board that confirms it."

"I didn't know about that," I said.

"Forgot to mention it, after my little set-to with Major Zimmer. Let me get it out of the tent and I'll show you." He was back in a few minutes and held out a rough piece of board on which was written the following:

Dry Fork of Powder River, May 27, 1876.
Captain St. John's party of Montana miners, sixty-five strong, leave here this morning for Whitewood. No Indian trouble yet. Don't know exactly how far it is to water. Filled nose bags and gum boots with liquid and rode off singing "There's Room Enough in Paradise."

This strange document was signed by men named Sullivan, Daniels, Barrett, Morrill, Woods, Wyman, Bussee, A. Daley, E. Jackson, J. Clark, Buchanan, and others.

"Optimistic bunch, whoever they are," I remarked.

"Or foolhardy." Wilder frowned.

"Is this expedition going to fight to make the Black Hills safe for poachers like these?" Jenkins asked in disgust.

I was convinced Wiley didn't intentionally try to bait his listeners, but he had an uncomfortable knack of cutting through any pretext to expose the raw nerves of a question.

But, again, Wilder surprised me with his reply to this rhetorical question. "I'm afraid so. It's a damn shame. Lot of good men, both red and white, will be shot up for the sake of a few men's greed."

Jenkins gave him a long look, propping his booted

feet against a tree trunk. "Then let me ask you something. As a career soldier, do you really believe that we need to destroy old cultures to make way for the white civilization?"

"No," Wilder answered flatly. "Even though I think it will eventually happen, I don't think it has to be done by force. God knows why things happen as they do." He shook his head and sipped his drink.

"Seems like violence is usually the cutting edge of change," Jenkins added.

"Speaking of cutting edges," I broke in, "what did your old friend, Major Zimmer, have to say?"

Wilder's face clouded, and he glanced uncertainly at Jenkins. "Not much."

"Why does someone with the rank of major get sent out on a scouting expedition?" I asked, trying to get him off the hook.

"He volunteered. Anything to keep himself at the center of the general's attention. He who gets noticed often gets the promotions. And promotions are hard to come by in the Regular Army since the war, regardless of any brevets."

"Could that have anything to do with all this ruckus that's been kicked up on the frontier?" Jenkins asked. "The Canadians don't seem to be having much trouble with their Indians."

"Possibly."

"A good war never hurt an army's appropriations."

"Apparently Zimmer didn't find the Crows," I remarked, trying to steer the conversation to safer ground.

"You know, I made that same observation myself when we rode in." Wilder grinned at me. "He nearly had apoplexy. Hates to look like a failure, especially to a subordinate."

A low rumble of galloping horses interrupted our conversation, and we saw the outlines of several dozen mounted riders rein up in the twilight near the headquarters tent.

"Who in the hell could that be?" Wilder wondered aloud.

Some of the men dismounted in the swirling dust, and we could see them talking to General Buck and several officers. From some two hunderd yards away in the gathering dusk, the men appeared to be well armed and leading a string of pack animals. A few minutes later a young orderly rode past us at a trot.

"Hey, soldier, who are those men?" Wilder called.

"Miners, sir. From Montana. Sixty or seventy of them. On their way to the Black Hills. They're asking for the general's permission to join up with us for protection." The orderly rode on.

"They've got a lot of brass," Wilder remarked.

"Reckon it's the same group who left this note on the board?" I asked.

"Sounds like it. And from the fresh rifle pits we saw dug the past day or so, I'd say they've had some experience traveling in hostile territory."

While we were still discussing the new arrivals, the miners remounted and came riding slowly toward us, apparently to a level camping area on the edge of the command.

"Pretty scruffy-looking bunch," I remarked as the riders filed past, their tired horses hanging their heads.

"You don't look like you've just stepped out of a haberdasher's shop yourself." Wilder grinned.

"My God!"

There was a crash behind me as Jenkins's tilted campstool fell over backward, with him in it. He jumped to his feet, his wide eyes riveted on the riders.

"What's wrong?" I was suddenly alarmed.

He swallowed hard before he answered. And when the words finally came, they were low and hoarse. "There . . . there goes my dad and my sister!"

CHAPTER
Seven

SUNDAY morning, June third, dawned as the most beautiful of the trip. The cavalry, riding in columns of two, the "walk-a-heaps", as the Indians called our infantry; our high-wheeled wagons, white tops shaking, pack train on the flanks, with Wiley Jenkins somewhere among the packers and the ambulances—all rode, marched and rolled like a four-mile long snake across the prairie swells that were covered with sparkling frost.

It was a thirty-mile march due northwest to Crazy Woman's Fork. The mighty wall of the Big Horn Mountains rose directly in front of us, about fifty miles away, dominated by snowcapped Cloud Peak.

Crazy Woman's Fork was one of those clear, melted-snow streams flowing down from the Big Horns. The pure, ice-cold water was a real pleasure to drink and wash in after the silty alkali of the Powder River.

General Buck was far out front of the command with a couple of orderlies and an aide-de-camp. He forbade any more bugle calls. I couldn't figure out why. Any Indian scout within twenty miles who wasn't blind could see our column on this treeless plain, or at least could spot the dust cloud we were raising.

The night before I had made some quick excuse,

thanked Jenkins and hustled Wilder away. Jenkins was so stunned I don't think he was even aware we had left. On the way back to our tent, I briefed Curt on the situation. He seemed liquor-relaxed and only mildly interested in Jenkin's problem. In fact, his only interest stemmed from the fact that there was a young woman in camp. But I swore him to secrecy on this point until I could check out developments. I was eaten up with curiosity, but I stayed away from Jenkins for the next few days, hoping to give him some time to straighten up some of his private family affairs.

We marched the next day to Clear Fork, about eighteen miles from Crazy Woman. The water here was like icy crystal and was also alive with trout. In fact, it was no trick for even a nonfisherman like me to land three of the sleekest, juiciest fish I'd ever seen—or tasted. Fried up with potatoes and onions, they made a great break in our usual fare that night.

The next day was one of our shortest marches, about sixteen miles. We arrived at Fort Phil Kearney about noon and went into camp in a beautiful, grassy valley near the foot of the Big Horns. This was the site of the famous massacre of Captain Fetterman and eighty-three soldiers ten years ago.

General Buck wanted to establish his base camp at a place called Goose Creek, which our Indian guides indicated was only about eight miles farther. But their conception of distance in miles was a lot different from a white man's, since we marched a good twenty-five miles the next day without reaching it. One reason we probably didn't get there was that General Buck changed directions. After several hours of riding through beautiful ravines filled with fragrant flowers, he veered the column northeast, away from the Bozeman Trail, and began following the course of a stream called Beaver Creek. On the way we struck a buffalo herd, and some of the hunters killed six of them for meat.

The next day, the seventh, we marched about eighteen miles, following Little Goose Creek, crossing and recrossing it several times, having to put our feet up on our saddles and hold our guns over our heads to keep them dry.

"Are you familiar with this country?" I asked Wilder as our horses lunged up, dripping, from the creek for about the fourth time.

"Only vaguely," he replied. "Looks a lot different than it did last March when it was covered with snow."

"Well, I guess the guides know where we're going."

"The best ones aren't even with us now."

"Where are they?"

"Frank Grouard, Louis Richaud and Baptiste Pourier left this morning. General Buck sent them toward the Crow reservation to see if they could have any better luck than Major Zimmer did at finding the warriors they promised."

"Pretty dangerous."

"Sure is. That's why General Buck hasn't let any couriers go out lately with your news dispatches to Fort Fetterman. But if anyone can travel through hostile territory and make it, those three are the ones to do it. Grouard is the best tracker and scout I've ever seen. And I'm not the only one with that opinion. General Buck once remarked to me that he'd rather lose his whole command than to lose Grouard. He may be half-French and half-Negro, but he's more Indian than the genuine article."

He spurred his bay forward. "He was captured by the Sioux a few years ago when he was working as a mail courier for the government. They didn't kill him. For some reason, Crazy Horse himself took a liking to him, so the story goes. Maybe because he wasn't completely white. Dubbed him 'The Grabber' because they captured him in the winter, and when he stood up to fight them in that furry buffalo robe, he looked like a big, standing bear. After a few years he escaped."

The wagons had a tough time keeping up that day and finally straggled into camp after dark where we had camped at the junction of Prairie Dog Creek and Tongue River. It was only after we had arrived at the Tongue that General Buck realized we had taken a wrong turn and had been following Prairie Dog Creek instead of Little Goose Creek.

I decided to connect with Jenkins and went over to his tent after I'd worked over my notes for the day. "Well, have you let 'em know you're with the command yet?" I asked that evening as I lounged in his tent, munching a tortilla full of hot beans, provided by one of the Mexican packers who was doing the cooking nearby. Three other men were in the tent, conversing softly in Spanish.

"Yes, but it took me a day or so to decide," Jenkins replied, lighting up a long, slim Mexican cigar.

"Whew! That thing's rank. Where'd you get it?"

He jerked his head in the direction of the cook. "Alfredo Gomez. Makes great food, and what he doesn't know about mule-packing hasn't been thought of yet. But these cigars of his *are* pretty strong. I'm saving my few good Cuban stogies for some special occasion later. Let's take it outside." He motioned for me to bring my food, and when I was finished, began to stroll toward the miner's camp. Once there he threw back the flap of one of the wall tents on the end of a short row of variously shaped tents. Over his shoulder I could see a tall, lean, clean-shaven man of middle age with a full head of silver-white hair swept back in wavy splendor.

"Dad, I'd like you to meet a friend of mine. This is Matt Tierney. My father . . ."

He gripped my hand briefly without smiling.

"Mr. Jenkins."

"What's your connection with this outfit?" he asked abruptly. "You a mule packer, too?"

From the tone of his voice, I gathered he considered the work menial. "No. I'm a newspaper reporter."

"Huh!" he grunted, looking down at me from his impressive height as if trying to decide whether my occupation was a cut or two below that of a mule packer.

"Where's Cathy?" Wiley asked.

"Back there." He jerked his head toward the back half of the tent that was partitioned off with a wall of white canvas.

"Wiley? Thought I heard your voice."

The partition was pulled aside and Cathy Jenkins appeared, wearing Levi's and a short, buckskin jacket. She had thick, brown hair, almost blond, that just touched the collar of her jacket, a slightly aquiline nose, and delicate features that looked unusually fragile in these rough surroundings—or was it just that I hadn't seen a woman for almost a month? She also had a surprisingly strong grip, I noticed, for a girl about five feet five and slim of build. As I mumbled a greeting and took her hand at Wiley's introduction, she favored me with a quick, friendly smile, showing the most even and amazingly white teeth I had ever seen. They looked even more dazzling against the tan of her face.

I felt as awkward as a boy on his first date.

Her regular features were not quite beautiful, but they seemed somehow to go together, and her face had an animated quality about it that kept my eyes riveted on her. "Nice to know you, Mr. Tierney. If Wiley recommends you as a friend, that's good enough for me— unlike some of his girl friends I've met." And she shot a mischievous glance at her brother.

As she talked, she tossed her head unconsciously every few minutes, a habit I guessed she had acquired from wearing longer hair recently. "Let's take a walk so we can talk," she suggested after the introduction.

"Don't go outside the miners' camp," her father ordered her, as the three of us ducked out through the canvas.

"Okay, Daddy."

"Is he afraid some of the soldiers are going to rape you if you set foot in our bivouac area?" Wiley asked.

"I guess so," she sighed resignedly. "I've been around men all my life, in all kinds of boom towns and rough mining camps. I don't know why he's suddenly getting so protective. The soldiers are under a lot more discipline than most of these miners."

"Maybe he thinks that by keeping you over here, no one will know there's a woman in camp."

"Not much chance of keeping a secret like that," I observed.

"Well, there's safety in numbers, anyway," she laughed, tossing her head in that very fetching way. Even with her short hair under a hat I knew there was no mistaking her figure or walk for that of a man—even at a distance.

"Who is this bunch you and Dad are traveling with? I thought somebody said they came from Montana."

"They did. But, because of the Indian scare, they came down to Cheyenne to wait and see if things settled down before trying to get into the Black Hills. Daddy and I were also in Cheyenne waiting for the same chance. The New Hope Company wanted him to get in on the ground floor of any good prospects. Custer's report of gold at the grass roots was a little hard to believe, but the company directors decided they couldn't overlook the possibility of some good, mineral-bearing ore there."

"Greed has invaded more land than anything else in history," Wiley mused aloud.

"Well, anyway," she continued, "we joined up with them for protection. But they were so anxious to get started they couldn't wait for the army to clear the way. Afraid someone would beat them to the best claims, I guess, so they voted to start ahead of this expedition. But we've seen so much fresh Indian sign in the past few days, we finally started walking between columns of our horses for fear of an ambush." Her eyes sparkled as she spoke. "But they finally got so nervous they decided to slow down and wait for the soldiers. And, here we are."

"You'd have been a lot safer staying home in Kentucky, or even in Cheyenne," her brother grumbled.

"Huh! And a lot more bored," she shot back.

We walked along among the tents in silence for a few moments.

"Anyway, you never did tell me why you, of all people, joined an expedition like this," she said to Wiley.

"Well . . ." He seemed uncomfortable, searching for some way to answer. "I don't really know. Maybe I was bored, too. Just because I'm here doesn't mean I approve of everything that goes on around me," he replied rather lamely.

"Are you and Dad any closer to a reconciliation?" she asked, changing the subject.

"Well, I haven't talked to him too much since he got here. But I'm afraid the best we can hope for is a compromise—a truce, if you will. We just don't have the same values or the same goals."

"You always did take after mother's side of the family—in looks as well as temperament."

I drifted slightly off to one side and pretended to be interested in the details of the camp. Although they took no notice of me, I felt a little embarrassed to be overhearing their family conversation. Out of the corner of my eye, I noted that the two of them, except for similar hair and coloring, looked no more like brother and sister than two unrelated strangers.

CHAPTER
Eight

"WELL, I had about given up ever seeing our scouts again, but, by God, here they are."

I stuck my head out of the tent at Wilder's exclamation and saw Frank Grouard, Louie Richaud, Big Bat Pourier and a gigiantic Crow riding into camp. It was about noon of the fourteenth, and we had finally gotten into our base campsite at the correct location at the junction of Big and Little Goose creeks. It was a beautiful, green area with plenty of trees and grass and clear water. In fact, our men had dubbed the place "Camp Cloud Peak" after the snowcapped peak of that name that dominated the Big Horns to the west of us. From looking at this peaceful, pastoral setting. I wouldn't have guessed there was an Indian within a thousand miles. The scouts rode straight toward General Buck's tent, and we followed. As they dismounted, several officers and men crowded around them, everyone talking at once.

General Buck stepped outside and waved his hand for silence. "Where have you been, Frank? And why are you just bringing in one old Crow?"

"I tell ya, General, a war party of Sioux almost got us. Chased us into the mountains. Took us four days to shake them. We finally found a big village of Crows on the Big Horn River, but they saw the smoke from our camp. They came across the river and attacked and almost killed us before they discovered we were friendly. Big Bat finally yelled to them in the Crow tongue and they recognized him."

"Well, where are they?" General Buck demanded, impatiently.

"We had a tough time trying to talk them into coming with us. They wanted to go after the Sioux, all right, but they were afraid you might stay out all summer, and they didn't want to miss the good buffalo hunting. We did some powerful palavering, but we finally talked about a hundred and seventy-five of their warriors into joining us."

"Great. Where are they?" General Buck urged, even more impatiently.

"They were afraid of a plot, or a trap," the big head scout continued, unhurriedly. "When we came into this camp about a week ago with about a dozen warriors and no one was here, they really began to suspect a trap. You know how suspicious they are. Some of them told Big Bat they thought you had given up the campaign. They're back a few miles waiting for some assurance that they're not riding into an ambush."

"Major Zimmer, take Louie Richaud and this chief and ride back to those Indians and see if you can convince them that everything is okay," General Buck ordered.

I had not noticed Major Zimmer in the group, but I saw his eyes glint with pride at being selected for this delicate diplomatic chore. "Yessir." He saluted and the three of them moved out immediately.

"I don't see how even Zimmer could make a mess of it this time," Wilder remarked to me as we walked away. "Looks like we're finally going to get our Crow allies."

And we did. About six o'clock that evening. General Buck had the troops drawn up on a flat just north of camp to receive our allies. The regiment, mounted at close order, company by company, stirrups just touching, took up about four-thousand feet; the infantry, in double line, another three-hundred or so. The soldiers formed an impressive array, nearly a mile long. Most of the civilians walked down to the creek to see them.

The Indians broke into a fierce yelling as they rode in, each man leading an extra pony, and rode past our troops in a column of twos—as orderly as any cavalry company. The Indians continued howling an unintelligible savage greeting and waving their lances and bows as they circled past our regimental formation. The cavalry horses and the Indian ponies were snorting and plunging at the sight and smell of each other. All the reporters, packers, and teamsters stood back and watched the spectacle. I think General Buck's idea was to impress the Crows with the strength of the command, to make sure they didn't decide to leave us after all.

After they had dismounted and set their horses to grazing alongside ours, they began building their lodges of saplings covered with blankets and strips of canvas. The officers and men mingled with them and attempted to make conversation. Some of the men knew a few words of Crow, and some of the Crows knew a few words of English. This, along with a lot of sign language allowed some communication, along with a lot of laughter.

"Not a bad-looking bunch," McPherson said as we watched them make short work of erecting their shelters.

"As fighters or physical specimens?"

"Physical specimens. Don't know about the fighting part yet."

"They *are* a handsome race. I'd say at least a third of them are over six feet tall. Lighter skin than most Indians I've seen, and regular features."

"Be interesting if a man had some means of tracing their ancestry to see what kind of stock they came from hundreds of years ago."

I laughed. "I'd like to be able to do that with my own ancestors."

Most of them wore flannel, cotton, or buckskin shirts; breechclouts; leggings of blanket; moccasins of deer, elk, or buffalo hide; coats of brightly colored blanket. Many of their headdresses were made of old black army hats with the top cut out and the bands decorated with eagle feathers, fur, or red cloth strips. I noticed that their arms were all breech loaders with metallic cartridges, most of them .50 caliber. "God, Mac, how'd you like to get hit with one o' those tomahawks?"

"Murderous-looking things. Makes my skin crawl just to think about it."

The weapons were made by inserting long knives in handles or shafts of wood or horn, and virtually every warrior carried one. The only ones who didn't were the four women, wives of chiefs Old Crow, Medicine Crow, Feather Head, and Good Heart. There were also about a dozen boys in their early teens, who were brought along as horse holders who were not armed, except with small bows and arrows. The Indians quickly got their tepees up, cook fires going, and were into their suppers of dried deer and bear meat, supplemented by sugar, hardtack and coffee—luxuries furnished from our commissary wagons.

Few of the troops seemed in a mood to disperse to their own tents. Everyone seemed to be milling around the center of the bivouac area. As darkness began to come on, a big bonfire was built and lighted. Wilder joined McPherson and me at the general soldiers' mess. I even noticed General Buck get in line for a cup of coffee like any private. He was in a shapeless felt hat, run-down boots, and out of uniform as usual. No stranger could have picked him out as the commander of this entire expedition. But his mind seemed to be constantly on things other than his personal appearance.

"Look at that, Curt," I said, nudging Wilder and indicating the general. "Quite a contrast to Brad Shanahan, isn't he?"

Wilder grinned. "Brad's probably had a bath, shave,

had his boots shined, and waxed his mustache today. Wonder when General Buck last had all that done?"

I laughed. "Well, they're damn good soldiers in their own way."

As we carried our tin plates of food off to one side and sat down to eat crosslegged, I noticed several of the warriors raise their heads. "Ugh! Ugh! Shoshone." They pointed south and spoke rapidly among themselves. We looked up to see a column of Indians riding down the bluffs toward us.

General Buck immediately directed a scout to go out to meet them. But before Big Bat could even get mounted, the Shoshones splashed across the creek and rode into camp, the leading riders carrying two big American flags. Most of them wore large headdresses and red shirts and blankets. They were not as large or handsome as the Crows, but they looked tough and sinewy. As they galloped past us and the Crows, yelling and shouting a greeting, Wilder and I roughly estimated their number at about eighty-five.

Tom Cosgrove, chief of scouts in the Wind River Valley, was with them, along with a white assistant and a half-breed interpreter. While these last three, along with the two sons of Old Chief Washakie, were presented to General Buck, the rest of the Snakes were quickly bivouacking and getting to their supper.

"Now comes the 'big talk'," Wilder said to me and McPherson as we sat, smoking our pipes about an hour later. Some soldiers had piled more dry wood on the huge bonfire near General Buck's tent, and the flames roared and crackled, pouring an unseen column of smoke into the blackness above. We watched the Indians of the two tribes gather around the fire in a circle with General Buck and several of his senior staff, including Colonel Wellsey and Major Zimmer of the 3rd Cavalry, in the center with the chiefs. Louis Richaud acted as interpreter. Each tribe selected a spokesman, and about ten minutes elapsed between each sentence spoken, since Richaud had to interpret in three or four languages.

I had my pad and pencil out to record as much as I could of all this scene. In the picnic atmosphere of the campaign so far, I had almost forgotten I was here to report what I saw and heard to a reading public who were, for the most part, sitting in their homes and offices in the Midwest, safe and comfortable.

A slight breeze was blowing the flames and smoke around. The flickering flames were pushing back the intense blackness. At the wavering edge of this circle of light stood and squatted the stolid Indians, black eyes glittering in their bronzed faces. Some of those squatting on their heels were passing around a long pipe. The red-, white-, yellow-, and black-banded blankets of the Indians contrasted with the blue coats of the soldiers and the white tents and wagon tops. General Buck, his aides and interpreters, and the chiefs stood in the center of this circle as near the fire as the intense heat would let them. General Buck stood with his hands in his pockets through most of the council, looking half-bored and half-happy with the whole thing. The gist of the speeches made by the chiefs of the Crows and the Shoshones, as relayed laboriously through the interpreters, was that they welcomed the chance to take part in this campaign. They were eager to break the spirit of their cruel, hereditary enemies, the Sioux. They asked, however, the privilege of scouting in their own way. General Buck readily granted this, apparently knowing their dislike for military discipline and procedures.

While the slow process of welcome and pledging of support went on, I glanced around and saw Wiley Jenkins and Cathy standing a few yards behind us in the crowded semidarkness. I motioned for them to come up and sit down.

"Quite a sight," Cathy whispered as the pair sat down beside us, cross-legged. "With all that paint, they look as scary as any Indians the soldiers may be looking for."

I nodded my agreement. "Cathy, this is Captain Curtis Wilder. Cathy Jenkins, Wiley's sister. She came in with the Montana miners."

"Hello, Captain." She gave him a pleasant smile, showing her magnificent teeth, and offered her hand.

I could see the suppressed excitement in Wilder's face as he acknowledged the introduction. "Miss Jenkins."

"Miss Jenkins?" she repeated, making a face in mock irritation. "That makes me sound like an old maid. Call me Cathy."

"Okay, Cathy. And I'm Curt."

They struck up an animated conversation about the Indians, the campaign, the Black Hills, and left Wiley, McPherson, and me to ourselves. "Where's your Dad, Wiley?"

"Oh, he was standing back there awhile with us, but he lost interest in a hurry and went back to his tent. When he saw there was nothing in this for him, he got bored and left."

I looked sideways at Jenkins. "C'mon, now, that's not quite fair, is it? This is really none of my affair, but you seem to be judging his every action."

"Yeh, I suppose you're right. Well, anyway . . ." He shrugged.

Our low-toned conversation flagged, and I looked up to the central drama before us as Louis Richaud was delivering a few sentences in guttural Crow. Behind him, Major Zimmer was looking in our direction. It took me a few moments to realize that he was actually staring at Cathy Jenkins and Wilder, who were still deep in a whispered conversation beside me. Zimmer was bareheaded and the bushy sideburns framed his somewhat fleshy, but handsome, face. His ruddy complexion appeared even redder in the firelight, and the brass buttons on his blue uniform coat caught the light and shone like gold. Since the formal talk with the Indians didn't concern him directly, he continued to stare in our direction with only a glance now and then at the interpreter to make it appear he was following the "big talk".

The Snakes retired from the council first, having said very little. Then General Buck and the Crow chiefs shook hands amid many "Ughs" and shouts of fierce satisfaction, and the Indians headed for their tepees.

"There won't be any peace around here tonight," Wilder remarked to Cathy as we all got up and stretched our legs.

"What do you mean?" she asked.

"They'll be putting on more paint and chanting and dancing most of the night."

"Really? They must have ridden fifty or sixty miles today. I would think they'd want to rest."

"Most Indians have tremendous endurance. They'll be getting themselves worked up for battle, as well as asking their gods for help and all that."

He had hardly finished talking when we heard the first of the rhythmic chants begin in the distance. First one and then another of the small groups of warriors started up their own individual war dances and chants, accompanying themselves on small buffalo-skin drums.

"What a god-awful racket!" Wiley grimaced. "Are we gonna have to listen to that very long?"

"Probably not more than six or seven hours," Wilder grinned.

We walked down among the tepees, mingling with many of the curious troops, and stooped down to look in the low doorways of some of the tepees. A fire hardly bigger than two candles cast a dim light on some scenes that could have come right out of Dante's *Inferno*. The painted, half-naked savages, their long, black hair hanging down or done up in braids or loops, gyrated wildly, the light casting weird shadows on the walls of the confined space. They chanted mostly in a monotone, broken by sudden screeches, grunts, whistles, howls, as if trying to imitate every bird, wolf, coyote, and animal in North America.

"Not much competition for the New York opera companies," Wiley observed. "But, I'll have to say, it's pretty original—or aboriginal," he laughed.

"Some of it's traditional, some impromptu," Wilder said.

"All of it bad," Cathy added.

"At least to our ears it is."

"If you'd like, I can give you a detailed history of their culture," a voice behind us said.

I looked around to see the smiling face of Major Zimmer. The man seemed to have the oily facility of sliding, unseen and unheard, into the most private conversations. Cathy returned his smile politely, but glanced curiously at Wilder. His expression had clouded at seeing his superior officer. But, unable to avoid the situation, he replied, "Cathy Jenkins, this is Major George Zimmer."

"Hello, Major."

"Miss Jenkins. It's a pleasure and an honor to have you with us."

Wilder's face had set in a mask.

"May I show you around? Perhaps tell you something of these rituals and these Indians who will be our allies?"

"Well . . ." she glanced around uncertainly. "Captain Wilder was taking care of that just now. Thank you, anyway."

"Maybe later?" he persisted, smiling again.

"That would be nice," she replied, obviously sensing the tension between the two men, but not wanting to appear impolite.

"Pardon me, sir," an orderly approached and saluted Major Zimmer.

"Yes. What is it?" Zimmer snapped, apparently irritated at being interrupted.

"General Buck would like to see you in his tent right away. Captain Wilder, you are to come, too." The orderly saluted again and walked away.

Cathy and Wiley excused themselves and left, and then Major Zimmer hurried away toward the headquarters tent. Wilder started to say something to Cathy before she left, but held up since Zimmer was still standing there. "C'mon, Matt," he said when we were alone again, "You and McPherson should probably sit in on this."

"What's it all about?" I asked as we fell in beside him.

"Probably a council of war. Normally, General Buck isn't too eager to include reporters in his briefings, since he's seen himself misquoted so many times in print, but I think he'd want you to know what's going on now. Besides, he seems to like and trust you two."

"What do you think of Cathy Jenkins?"

"Beautiful girl. Seems to be intelligent and charming. And the fact that she's out here proves she's no parlor flower. Still, I'm surprised her father let her come—he must know how dangerous it is in these hills: this is hostile territory."

"From what I can gather, the young lady does pretty much what she wants to do. With the encouragement of Mr. Jenkins. According to Wiley, she rides and shoots as well as any man and has always gone everywhere with her father."

"He's a damn fool to bring her here, regardless," Curt responded shortly. "This is supposed to be a military campaign—not a fandango with every officer dancing attendance on her!"

McPherson and I exchanged glances and kept our mouths shut. It was obvious Captain Wilder and Major Zimmer had found a new, and potent, bone of contention.

CHAPTER
Nine

"MEN, tomorrow actually marks the beginning of this campaign," General Buck began in his usual abrupt way. "We've been seeing smoke signals every day since the Dry Fork of the Powder, so there's no chance of anything like a complete surprise. That small war party that jumped us probably spread the alarm anyway. We haven't been able to get a courier through to the north, but I just found out from the Crows that Colonel Gibbon's column is on the banks of the Rosebud near the Yellowstone, but unable to cross because of the Sioux holding him at bay. The Crows tell me the main body of the Sioux are encamped on the Tongue River at the mouth of Otter Creek. And they think the village of Crazy Horse is located on the Tongue River as well." He paused to let this information sink in to the officer corps in the crowded tent. A lantern suspended from the ridgepole provided the only light, keeping most of the faces in shadow, so I couldn't judge their reaction, if any.

"In the morning, our wagons will be repacked so they can be easily defended by the teamsters and civilians attached to the Quartermaster Corps. They'll be parked on the island in the middle of Goose Creek here and left behind. For mobility, the infantry will be mounted on mules. Each man will carry only the bare necessities—hard bread, sugar, coffee, bacon, and some beans. Each man, besides the clothes on his back, will carry one overcoat and one blanket. There will be no tents. Each man will carry at least a hundred rounds of ammunition—more if he can manage it. Spare ammunition and some food will be loaded on pack mules. We have a strong force. I want to be mobile so we can strike fast and strike hard. Most of you were with me on the Powder River campaign last March. We had all the advantage of surprise, but we were less than completely successful. This time we will get the village of Crazy Horse. I want his hide! That's all."

The officers filed out of the big tent and headed for bed. "Brief and blunt as usual," I commented to Wilder as the three of us stretched out on our buffalo robes in our tent. Lieutenant Shanahan was already snoring quietly nearby.

"General Buck doesn't show much emotion, but you can bet he wants Crazy Horse badly. He's really spoiling for a fight so he can put to rest all that public criticism about his so-called failure in the winter campaign." He pulled off his boots and shrugged out of his galluses. "At least Cathy will be relatively safe with the wagons and the miners. 'Night, Matt." He turned the lantern down and blew it out.

It was past midnight. I stretched my grateful muscles on the soft buffalo robe, wondering how long it would be before I would have a bed this soft again. I especially wondered about the rigors of the trail taking their toll on the fifty-year-old consumptive beside me. I had come to admire McPherson for his wit, his quiet acceptance of things, but most of all for his toughness; he never asked for any special treatment, even though all of us would have accorded it to him.

The last thing I remember was the muffled drumming and chanting that blended into the noises of the night.

*   *   *

The men on watch told me the racket had kept up all night, but the Indians were up early in the morning to receive rations, ammunition, and, for those who needed them, new government guns. They sat in a huge semi-circle around the quartermaster's wagons and tents and received the handouts with no emotion other than an occasional grunt of satisfaction.

The morning was spent overhauling gear in preparation for the next day's start. Arms were cleaned, horses reshod, saddlebags packed, and ammunition stowed wherever it could be carried. Since General Buck was determined to have the infantry mounted so they could keep up, about two hundred mules were brought to a flat grassy area a few hundred yards from camp just after lunch. McPherson and I were among the crowd of cavalry and Indians who gathered to watch the fun. "From the looks on some o' those poor bastards, I don't know whether to laugh or cry," Mac remarked to me as the mules were being caught and saddled.

"The mules or the infantry?"

Mac laughed.

The braying, bucking, and squealing of the unbroken mules made it hard to carry on a conversation even though we were standing next to each other. The regulation cavalry bridle was first put on each animal, then the McClellan saddle cinched tight. As each mule was saddled, he was released to vent his indignation by running and bucking and rolling on the ground. They gradually quieted down and the infantry soldiers were brought up to mount them.

"Yeeeooouuu!!"

Several bodies shot straight up over the steel-shod hooves, as all hell broke loose when the heads of the mules were let go.

"Oh, God, I can't look," Mac laughed, as the thudding of bodies and hooves mingled with braying squeals, curses, and yells. Even the normally stoical Indians were slapping each other on the back and howling with laughter at the sight. Now and then, an Indian would grab a runaway mule, leap on its back and demonstrate to the command what truly magnificent riders they were. "Now, that's the way it should be done."

"Seeing and doing are two different things," I answered, looking at some of the battered and disgusted soldiers. Some mules ran and bucked, some bucked in place, some tried falling down, some leapt and twisted. As quickly as the poor soldiers were thrown, they got back up and chased down their animals for a remount. "They're a game bunch, Mac."

"I don't think they have much choice." He nodded at the officers who were standing by to supervise. "This is what you might call a 'crash course in riding.'" The course continued for the better part of two hours until the men and animals just about wore each other out and eventually came to a truce. "Gonna be some sore muscles in the morning," Mac said as we walked back to camp to get our own gear together for the start. "That deep grass is probably the only thing that saved some broken bones."

In the afternoon, the wagons were brought across to the wide, flat island in the middle of the stream and formed into a large oval. About a hundred men, both military and civilian, were detailed to stay behind and guard them. Some were relieved at the news, other irritated that they would miss out on any action.

I knew Wiley Jenkins would accompany the column, since he was one of the mule packers who had to handle the supply train, but he had disturbing news for me. "All the Montana miners are going, including Cathy," Wiley told me that evening when I sought him out after supper. "God knows we tried to talk the stubborn little so-and-so out of it, but she insisted. And she *is* twenty-one. Just had a birthday." He shrugged disgustedly as he handed me a cup of hot chocolate. We sat down on two campstools.

"Doesn't she realize what we may be riding into?"

"I'd say she knows it, just like I know it, but she doesn't realize it. She's never experienced a war any more than I have."

"What did your father have to say about it?"

"Not much—as usual. He left it to Cathy, as he always has."

"What about the military?"

"She didn't exactly broadcast the fact that she was going, but in any case their position seems to be that she can come along at her own risk just like any other civilian. She and the chiefs' squaws will be the only women there. She's looking forward to it, like some big lark, if you can imagine that."

"Aren't we all?"

He looked at me steadily and thoughtfully for a moment. "I see what you mean, Matt. To a lot of these men, this is just a big adventure. Something exciting to stave off boredom."

Later, when I mentioned Cathy's decision to Wilder, his face tightened perceptibly but he said nothing. There was, after all, nothing he could do.

Mac and I spent the rest of the evening writing up our dispatches in final form and getting them ready for the courier. A tough, thirty-year-old frontiersman named Jed Moreau was going to make a round-trip ride to the nearest telegraph point—Fort Fetterman. All the correspondents pitched in to come up with his fee— $300. It was high, but so were his chances of not living to spend it. It was a fairly common occurrence for someone to come across the dismembered body of a mail courier on some remote trail in this region.

The bugles were silent the next morning, but the whole command was up two hours before dawn. Even so, the soldiers didn't beat the Indians out of their blankets. The chiefs of the Snakes and Crows were haranguing their warriors in their native tongues for at least an hour before we had breakfast. The exhortations finally ended and they all gathered around their cooking fires to feast to satiety on the rations that had been issued the day before. It was common practice, Wilder told me, for Indians on the warpath to feast at every opportunity. Apparently, the thought of battle didn't affect their appetites.

As for the rest of us, it was black coffee and hard-tack before we were in the saddle and moving out. There were fifteen companies of the 2nd and 3rd Cavalry, followed by the mule pack train. Bringing up the rear were about two hundred of the sore, but game, infantrymen mounted on the mules. The Indians, head-dresses nodding, eagle feathers blowing, steel lance heads flashing in the rising sun, rode strung out along our flanks. Counting the miners and packers, we totaled just over thirteen hundred—enough, as Lieutenant Shanahan put it, to "rout any damn bunch of rene-gade Sioux or Cheyenne."

"I can see why the Sioux want to protect this region," I remarked to Mac, as the morning sun sparkled on the dew of the greenest grazing land I had seen since we left Cheyenne. We rode along the top of a broad ridge in a northeast direction, bearing slightly away from the Big Horn range on our left.

About noon we rode up to the top of a grassy ridge and the sight that greeted us was breathtaking. A herd of several thousand buffalo was grazing in the shallow valley below us. They looked like a black, furry mat covering several square miles.

"Easy, men. Hold your ranks," came back the order from the officers as several troopers reached for their carbines and their horses began prancing and edging out of column.

A hideous yelling split the air as the Indians, who were under no restiction, tore down the slope after the buffalo. The startled herd lumbered away into a gallop as the Indian ponies ran quickly alongside. The yelling continued as the heavy caliber guns boomed, and the brown, shaggy bodies, one by one, began to stumble and fall. The thundering herd shook the ground beneath us, and several of the younger men looked plead-ingly at the officers, silently begging for permission to join the chase. But the word was not given and their sparkling eyes and nervous grip on their horses were the only signs to betray their frustration.

Then I saw General Buck riding back toward us on his black horse. And if looks could kill, there would have been a lot of dead Indians below us at that moment. Whatever chance remained of us surprising the camp of Crazy Horse on the Rosebud, was now gone.

"Colonel Wellsey!"

"Sir?"

"Take some men and . . ." The general reined up his horse with a vicious jerk on the reins that made me wince at the pain the bit must have caused the black's mouth. The general sat, gritting his teeth without finishing the command. Apparently he was remembering his promise at the council fire to let the Indian allies regulate themselves and set their own pace. "Never mind," he snapped at Colonel Guy Wellsey and spurred his charger back toward the head of the column.

I looked out over the valley and watched the herd fading away from us in a thin veil of dust. Most of the Indians were dropping away from the flanks of the herd to go back to the brown lumps that lay scattered here and there on the prairie. But some Indians continued the chase, and I could see the sun flash on the steel arrowheads once or twice.

"Forward!" The command was given and we moved off at a walk, leaving the Indians to the slaughter.

"Damned if I don't think this is probably the closest I'll come to paradise," Mac proclaimed to me as we rode along, side by side. He took a deep breath of the fresh air, made even more fragrant by the smell of the thousands of prairie flowers being crushed underhoof. "Look at this grass, and these clear little streams running down through here everywhere. And these clumps of trees." He swept his arm at the scene around us, and I followed his glance as he looked up at the blue sky arching overhead. A hawk or a golden eagle soared high above us on the silent thermal currents.

The column wound over hills and through small valleys at a quiet, easy pace. Once, the scouts, riding a couple of miles in advance, reported that they had sighted, and been seen by, a hunting party just over the divide between the Tongue and Rosebud rivers. Since we had already lost the element of surprise, the sighting did little harm. We rode a total of thirty-five miles that day and finally came to a swampy lake about five hundred yards across that formed the headwaters of the Rosebud. We bivouacked in a huge circle near this lake, with the horses and mules in the middle as a precaution against surprise attack. Pickets were thrown out on the low bluffs surrounding the lake. General Buck passed the order that no camp fires were to be lighted. But while the soldiers ate cold suppers, the Indians started what fires they wanted and gorged themselves on fresh buffalo tongue and hump.

When Lieutenant Shanahan remarked to one of the Indians about the waste of all those buffalo, the Indian answered back, through an interpreter, "better kill buffalo than have him feed the Sioux." This sounded strangely like the reasoning I had heard from some of the whites.

I had no time or opportunity to look for Wiley or Cathy that night. With no fires or lanterns allowed, and after a long day in the saddle, Wilder, McPherson, Shanahan, and I stretched out under our single blankets shortly after dark.

"Damn, it gets cold at night in these high plains," Mac shivered, "even in June."

"Think what it's like in January."

"Oh, don't even talk about it." He wrapped the blanket tighter around his fully dressed body and drew his legs up.

Wilder stretched out, with a weary sigh, under his blanket on the other side of me. He settled his head on the saddle he was using for a hard pillow. The indefatigable Crows and Shoshones were intoning their weird war chants again farther down the campsite, as usual. "Matt," Wilder remarked in a low voice, "we'll have a fight tomorrow. Mark my words. I feel it in the air."

That was the last thing I remember before sleep took me.

CHAPTER
Ten

FALSE dawn had not even begun to lighten the eastern sky when we rolled out the next morning, stiff and cold from sleeping on the hard ground. No bugle sounded, and no one had awakened us; the whole command seemed to come awake on its own. Up and down the line small cooking fires were lighted, and we had our usual scalding black coffee, bacon, and hardtack.

The general ordered his half-breed scouts to instruct the Indians to send out some of their braves as scouts. But most of them were very reluctant to go. Finally, Grouard and Big Bat were able to convince the little Shoshone, Humpy, and a few of his tribesmen to go. Then, out of shame, a few of the Crows also rode out to look for the village of Crazy Horse, but they weren't happy about it.

"They'll do a lot of chest thumping and chanting, but when it comes right down to tangling with the Sioux, they get mighty sober," Wilder remarked to me as he saddled his horse. An orderly held his horse's head in the semidarkness. Some of the troops who were already mounted, leaned forward on their horses' necks, and catnapped before the word was given to move out.

The mule brigade of infantry led the way in the gray dawn, followed by the orderly columns of cavalry. We wound down the valley of the south fork of the Rose-

bud. The valley continued to be as beautiful as it had
been the day before—green pine trees on the hills,
green grass carpeting the riverbank and slopes. Clusters
of wild, pink rosebuds dotted the hillsides. We de-
scended the east bank of the stream that was as crooked
as a corkscrew. For a time we would hug the bluffs
through a narrow, winding valley where we could
hardly see fifty feet ahead, and then we would break
out into a wide glade, and I could see General Buck's
black charger picking his way along the bank several
hundred yards ahead.

Shortly, the Rosebud was joined by its north fork
and the entire, runoff-swollen stream turned east and
flowed for more than two miles. I was looking ahead
where the river started another big bend to the north,
when the head of the command reined up and began to
dismount. I looked curiously at Wilder as we both stood
down from our bays. "What's up? We've only gone
about five miles."

"Just a short rest stop. I think the general knows the
animals are still tired from that tough march yesterday."

The word was passed back to unsaddle the horses
and turn them out to graze. The valley looked very
much like the one we had bivouacked in the night before. There were low bluffs all around the wide, shallow
valley. The Rosebud flowed sluggishly down the middle, dividing it equally north and south. We were within
easy rifle shot from any of the bluffs, and pickets were
thrown out on the bluffs around us.

I pulled out my watch. It was just after eight. But the
sun was already growing uncomfortably hot in the
windless air. Wilder lifted his hat and wiped his brow
with a shirt sleeve and we both stretched out on the
inviting grass. He pulled out his short pipe and packed
a slow smoke. Without speaking, we stared around at
the beautiful green valley, drowsing in the summer
morning sun. Honeybees buzzed around a bush of
sweetbrier a few feet away. The column continued to
arrive and dismount. Ten minutes passed, then fifteen.

Some of the men were borrowing and lending chews. Others had broken out a deck of cards. On the opposite side of the river, some of the Indians were racing their ponies up and down, and the soldiers appeared to be betting on the races.

I put my head in my saddle, shaded my eyes with my hat brim, and dozed. I became faintly aware of a distant popping noise.

"Damned Crows off chasing buffalo again," Mac remarked.

I didn't open my eyes.

"Lakota! Lakota! Sioux! Heap Sioux!"

The terrified shouting brought me straight up. About ten of our scouts were plunging their ponies down a steep bluff toward us, yelling and pointing. Humpy, the little Shoshone, rode with one arm hanging limp. And several hundred yards behind them, in pursuit, came a wave of Sioux and Cheyenne in full battle array. In the few seconds I had to look, a ragged line of them topped the skyline of the bluffs and swept down toward our troops—and then more riders came over the ascending ridges farther back.

I ran toward my bay. He shied away up the slope, dragging his reins on the ground. I forced myself to walk slowly toward him, and talked slowly, reassuringly. But his wide eyes and pointed ears were fixed on the tumult behind me. When I got within three yards of him, I dove forward and grabbed the reins. He plunged and dragged me a few feet before I was up and leading him back down to where my saddle lay. Pandemonium had broken loose as men scrambled wildly for their horses and officers were shouting commands. I grabbed the saddle blanket and threw it onto the bay's back, holding his head with my left hand at the same time. Then I heaved the light McClean saddle into place. I could see flashes of what was going on farther down the valley. The soldiers were not panicked, but were totally surprised by the sudden attack. I could see Wilder just springing into the saddle and yelling for the men of Company B to form up.

Mac had tethered his horse to a nearby bush, so he was already in the saddle and rode up to hold my horse's head for me. As I took a few extra seconds to make sure my cinch straps were tight and my rifle was in its scabbard and loaded, I could see over the back of my bay that more and more Indians were pouring over the bluffs to the north and west. They came in lines and clusters and were riding singly, out of every cut and defile in the broken terrain. Most were naked, except for breechclout and paint. Some wore the full eagle-feather warbonnet that flowed out on the wind five or six feet behind the rider. Some of the Cheyenne wore the buffalo cap with the horns still attached, as a charm against death. Others wore half-masks of wolf skins with the pointed ears. Their dark bodies were streaked with yellow and red and black paint. Above the hideous yells, gunfire, and rumbling hooves, I thought I could just make out the shrill squeal of the eagle-wing whistles Wilder had told me the Cheyenne blow as a charm against death when they ride into battle.

The sweat on my back went cold at the sight. It was like hell had split open just beyond the bluffs, and all of its devils were bursting out upon us.

"C'mon, Matt! You gonna stand there all damn day, gawkin'?" someone yelled behind me. It was McPherson.

I leapt onto my horse's back and we trotted toward Wilder, who was trying to get the men of his company into line. Only about half of them had managed to catch and saddle their frightened horses. The cavalry horses were used to gunfire, but the sudden noise had them milling, and the booted troopers were wasting precious minutes chasing them and getting ready to join battle—and, I could see, it was minutes they didn't have. It was going to be close. If the first wave of Indians reached us while most of our men were afoot, they'd ride right through and cut us to pieces.

Then Major Randall, a gray-haired veteran who was chief of scouts, came riding from the left, leading about a hundred Crows and Snakes. Up the slopes they went,

most riding bareback, to meet the hated Sioux and give
us the vital minutes to get ready. When they were about
five hundred yards away from where I sat, the charging
lines met. Even from that distance, I could see it was
mostly hand-to-hand with knives, lances, and the
deadly war clubs. Sun flashed on steel in the swirling
dust. It was impossible to make out ally from enemy,
even though our Indians wore red arm bands to distin-
guish them.

At the first sign of attack, General Buck had left
vague orders to hold the bluffs to the north where the
heaviest force seemed to be coming from. Then he had
spurred his black charger to the top of a low hill nearby
to get a better view of the size of the force coming
against him. Colonel Wellsey sat his Morgan, his cool,
gray eyes under the shade of his hat brim sizing up the
situation. Then, in spite of the uproar around him and
the whine of bullets close over our heads, he gave a
firm, clear command for the infantry to form a skirmish
line to advance on our right, leaving their mules behind.
Other cavalry companies he ordered to stay south of
the river and guard against surprise attack from the
south and east. He ordered Major Zimmer to take three
companies to the relief of the Crows and Shoshones,
who were locked in battle just to the west of us.

"Companies B, E, I, and M, right into line!"

Mac and I guided our bays alongside Captain Wilder's Company B as the troops swung into line. Colonel
Wellsey rose in his stirrups.

"Charge!"

My stomach had been churning with nervous excitement and just plain fear, but I let go the tension with a
terrific yell like everyone else as we spurred into a gallop toward the northern bluffs. The ground was rough
and steep and, out of the corner of my eye, I saw two
or three horses stumble, pitching their riders over their
heads. A group of Indians had stopped on the heights,
apparently awaiting our charge. We were going too fast
to use carbines, but several of the men on either side of
me began firing their revolvers. The Sioux let us get

within fifty yards or so before they broke and ran. A cheer went up from the troops. But the Indians had merely retreated out of range, apparently hoping to draw us after them.

As we reached the top of the rocky ridge, Colonel Wellsey ordered a halt. Every fourth man held the horses and the rest of us deployed as dismounted skirmishers to hold the ridgetop. I slipped my Winchester from its boot as I swung down from the saddle and scrambled along, crouching low. The men on either side of me opened fire on the retreating Indians who were still within carbine range. As I levered a round into the chamber, aimed and fired, I uttered a prayer of thanks for the repeater I carried. Most of the soldiers had only breech-loading single-shot Springfield carbines. The same weapon was carried by the infantry, except in the longer barreled .45-70 rifle model. Even so, the men of the "mule brigade" were deadly accurate up to nine hundred yards with their "long Toms" that carried seventy grains of powder to the cartridge.

The Sioux and Cheyenne stopped on the next ridge and rode up and down out of range, taunting us, slapping their rumps, and motioning for us to come after them. We slacked our fire and I rested on one knee, awaiting orders. I looked around at Mac a few yards away, lying flat on the ground, reloading. I wanted to shout something to him that this sure beat the hell out of a stuffy editorial office, but the noise and the distance were too great, so I just waved and grinned. He responded with a wave of his rifle barrel.

Then orders came up from General Buck to drive the hostiles back from the next ridge. We remounted and charged again. Again the Indians, after a few shots, retreated across a shallow depression to a still higher ridge.

"Stand and fight! You damned red cowards!" one of the younger privates yelled as we reined up, in possession of the second height.

"Don't get cocky, son," the lanky Sergeant Killard

said, spurting a stream of brown tobacco juice into the dust. "They ain't afraid of us."

The breeze freshened from the west, and we could hear the roar of battle plainly from a mile or more away. Suddenly the yelling increased from in front of us, and the Indians swung their ponies toward us and countercharged. Our companies braced to meet them, but the hostiles' ragged line divided and swept off wide and down the gulches on each side of our line of bluffs.

"They're flanking us!"

Some of the newer men stood, hesitant. When they saw the Indians were intent on something farther down the valley, the men looked around for orders. These weren't long in coming.

"Prepare to mount! Mount!"

General Buck was too far away to command us effectively by messenger, so Colonel Wellsey ordered a withdrawal. As we swung into our saddles and started back down, we could see from the crest about a half-dozen running fights developing up and down the broken ravines and ridges along a two- or three-mile stretch of the open Rosebud valley. Some infantry companies were coolly defending the flank of a grassy hill a half-mile to the east, holding the raiders at long range with their accurate rifle fire.

About half of the Indians we had been chasing a few minutes before were now riding in behind Zimmer's cavalry, catching them in a cross fire. The other half of the group of Indians were apparently after some of our horses that were being held in an isolated grove of trees at the bottom of a ravine some six hundred yards below on our left. But Lieutenant Hogan's gray-horse troop had seen them coming and used one of Crazy Horse's own tricks by hiding in the trees until the Indians were abreast of them. Instead of riding in among a few defenseless horse holders, the warriors were surprised by a terrific crash of rifle fire. Several of them pitched off their ponies, and the riderless mounts went running loose in all directions. The rest of the Indians swung back toward us and rode hard for the safety of the hills.

As a reporter, I was getting so interested in watching the progress of the battle that for a few seconds I forgot I was in it. Then I saw Colonel Wellsey signaling with his arm, and our Company B swung left with the others to try to cut off the fleeing hostiles. My big bay lunged forward with my heels in his flanks as we charged again. We were at an angle to them as they came uphill toward us, but the distance across the wide ravine was great. What at first looked like a long-range fight gradually changed as we began to close with them. Some of the agile brown bodies were hanging on the off sides of their horses for protection, firing at us under the ponies' necks. It was an amazing demonstration of horsemanship.

As the ravine grew steeper, their tiring horses began to slow, and we were closing with the enemy. I could see the wild eyes and flaring nostrils of the straining Indian ponies. Since I couldn't sight a rifle from the heaving back of my horse, I was firing my Colt on the chance that I might hit something. The wind was whistling in my ears and I could hear the drumming of hooves. The puffs of smoke from the guns told me there was a lot of firing going on, but the muzzle blasts blended into the general roar of sound around me.

As I came within a few yards of one savage, I holstered my Colt and jerked my rifle from its scabbard. I could only see one arm and one leg of the Indian who was hanging off the opposite side of his horse. But I thought I could at least hit his pony by shooting from the hip at close range. Crouching in the saddle, I gripped the stock under my left arm and let go of the reins to steady the bouncing barrel with my right hand.

Just as I squeezed the trigger I felt my horse's head go down. The next instant I was being catapulted from the saddle. For what seemed like a minute, I could feel myself turning a slow somersault in the air. I lost all sense of direction before something slammed into my back and shoulders with stunning concussion, and I felt my arms and legs go limp as I slipped into the black hole of unconsciousness.

What must have been only a few seconds later, my eyes popped open and I was staring at the deep blue sky with some high wispy clouds that seemed to reel in my vision. I moved slightly. Nothing seemed to be broken. I had landed flat on my back and shoulders. My head must have snapped back and hit the ground. Dark forms were going by on both sides of me in a thin veil of dust. I rolled over and tried to rise, but my head was still spinning, and the earth rushed up to meet me. I tried again. This time I got to one knee. As my senses began to clear, I saw riders, both Indians and soldiers, pounding up the ravine past me. Whether my horse had been shot or stepped into a hole, I didn't know, but he was nowhere to be seen. I had to get to shelter.

Suddenly, I was aware of a horse coming at me. A savage face leaned down and I caught a quick glimpse of a tomahawk at the end of a brawny arm. I dodged back and down. The stone ax whistled past my face. The Indian wheeled his dun pony in a tight left circle, and I glanced quickly around for my rifle. The running battle had almost passed us by up the gulch. The Winchester lay a few yards away, but I could see there was no way for me to reach it before the savage bore down on me again. He raised the tomahawk, and I knew he was already counting coup on me and would brag in his lodge tonight of my fresh scalp lock hanging at his belt. I feinted to my left as if to dodge again, but at the last possible instant, leapt to the right in front of his running pony. One flying forefoot caught me in the thigh and spun me down in excruciating pain.

But the Indian had gone by me leaning to the other side. I rolled to my feet, ignoring the pain. As he wheeled his pony for yet another try, I half ran, half crawled to my rifle. I dove for it and rolled over, levering a fresh cartridge into the chamber just as he charged down on me for the third time. From a sitting position, I only had time to raise the rifle and jerk the trigger. The rifle jumped and crashed and I flinched, waiting for the impact of the ax as the painted, glistening body came hurtling off his mount to land on me.

But the Sioux was dead before he hit the ground.

Breathing hard, I weakly rolled the lolling arms and legs off me. My .44 bullet had shattered a horn-shell necklace and penetrated just above the breastbone. He lay as if asleep, his black pigtails splayed out, the yellow and black parallel lines of paint forming a pattern on either side of the beaked nose. The heavy torso, streaked with sweat and dust, throbbing with life a few seconds before, was still, its spirit winging toward some unseen, happier land to join its ancestors.

But these thoughts were only fleeting, as I rolled to my knees, favoring my bruised thigh and gasping for breath. I had to get back to the shelter of my friends, or at least out of the open. The throbbing pain in my thigh subsided to a dull ache as I struggled to my feet. A slight tightness told me it was already beginning to swell. I tried to get my bearings. I was temporarily alone. What troopers I could see were scattered in a ragged blue line up the ravine. Up to my right, about a half-mile away on a hilltop, I could just make out what looked like a group of white civilians clustered behind a natural breastwork of rocks and firing to the east and north, away from me, at some unseen targets beyond the hill.

Gripping my rifle, I ran toward them. Or rather, I started jogging toward them on what was beginning to feel like a wooden leg. The terrain was steepening and over my labored breathing I could hear my heart pounding in my temples. I ran only about two hundred yards. In spite of the danger, I knew I had to rest. I sank to one knee, head down, sweat dripping off my nose into the bunch grass. My pale blue shirt was plastered to me in dark, wet splotches. The light brown corduroy pants I wore were gray with dust. My hat was gone. I cursed the hot boots that felt like iron, wishing I could trade ten pairs of them for one set of moccasins or infantry shoes.

Approaching hoofbeats brought me around to face some new danger.

"Hey, Matt!" I recognized Wilder's form on the bay as he galloped up to me. "Here, jump on."

He leaned down with one arm and I clumsily threw myself up behind him. The horse plunged away, nearly throwing me. I gripped his coat, still too winded to talk. "I didn't see you go down," he shouted over his shoulder. "When I was finally able to look back, you were having it out with that Indian, and I was too far away to do anything about it. Turned the troop over to Shanahan and tried to get back for you. Where's your horse?"

"Don't know," I yelled into his ear. "If he was shot, he didn't fall anywhere around me."

"You hurt?"

"Leg's bruised up. Nothing serious." I glanced to my right. We were now close enough for me to recognize the civilians as a group of our mule packers and miners behind the rocks. "Drop me with that bunch of packers. You can't carry double. I may not be mobile, but I can still shoot."

He nodded and turned his horse. I half slid from my perch, and Wilder spurred his mount away.

"Matt! What happened to your leg?"

I tried to pick out the familiar voice in the group of twenty or so, as I crawled painfully into the partial shelter of the jutting boulders. "Wiley Jenkins!" I almost dropped my rifle in astonishment, as I looked up at the familiar youthful face. "By God, you never cease to amaze me." I hitched myself into position behind a cleft in the rocks. "Apparently what you say and what you do aren't necessarily the same. Who's minding the mules?"

He looked away from me. "Well, I thought since I had come this far, I might as well get a closer view at what it was all about."

I acknowledged the nods of greeting from some of the men, as I crawled into a more comfortable position and checked my rifle for dirt. "Looks like some of the miners and packers made this their fight," I remarked to Jenkins.

"They volunteered as sharpshooters."

"And you? Oh, that's right, you came along for the show."

Then I noticed he was carrying a Spencer repeater he had borrowed somewhere, but it looked like a broom-stick in his hands. I took a snap shot at a mounted In-dian who was nearly out of range. Wiley crouched be-hind me, peering over the rocks. I laid my hand on the rifle barrel. It was cold. "Got any cartridges for that thing?" I asked, without looking at him. I busied myself squeezing off another shot.

"Yeh, it's loaded. And I've got some more in this ammunition box one of the soldiers gave me."

None of our conversation was overheard by the other men around us in the semicircle as they kept up a spo-radic fire, the flat crack of the .44 Winchesters min-gling with the heavy boom of the .50 caliber Sharps. Now and then one of them would yell as an Indian top-pled from his horse.

"My Dad's up here, too," Jenkins said.

I turned in surprise as he pointed to a tall, lean back a few yards from us. He was facing the other way and firing from one knee.

"He has nothing to win or lose up here, does he? And don't tell me he's protecting his interests in the Black Hills," I said. "The army can do that for him."

"Sailors aren't the only ones who bail when the ship is sinking," was his retort.

"Don't tell me you actually think this command is in danger of sinking!"

He brushed the wavy brown hair back from his fore-head. "Have you taken a good look at how many sav-ages are out there?" he asked. "I may not be experi-enced in battle, but I am good at estimating numbers, whether it be mules or buffaloes or Indians."

"I'd say about eighteen hundred to two thousand."

"More like twenty-five hundred or better. And they're not just armed with bows and arrows."

I took a more careful look at all the scattered skir-mishes I could see and thought of the waves of warriors

I had first seen. "Yeah, I guess you're right. Outnumbered more than two to one. Must be a helluva big village that . . ."

Zing!

Bullets striking the rock about two feet from our heads sent chips flying. We flattened out behind our meager cover.

"By the way, what brings you up from the river? Reporters aren't supposed to be combatants."

"Patriotism, maybe?" I grinned.

He snorted derisively.

The intermittent sniping dragged on for another twenty minutes or so. At the end of that time, I noticed the battalion that included Wilder's Company B was apparently being withdrawn from the fight down toward the Rosebud River. Here, they turned and rode east, disappearing below the hills. Even though we were on a high ridge, some of the other scattered action was cut off from our view by the intervening knobs and hills.

It was after eleven by my watch. The sun was getting higher and hotter, and I was getting dehydrated. My lips felt glued together, my mouth cottony. I wasted less and less effort on conversation. My leg felt swollen, but no longer sore.

"Whew! Wish I had an ice-cold beer right about now," Wiley grunted, leaning his head on his arms. "In fact," he lifted a red face toward me and attempted a grin, "I'd take that one last beer that constituted one too many back in Cheyenne. Too bad a man can't even out the good things of life."

Apparently no one had anticipated being here very long, since there wasn't one canteen among the score of packers and miners who hugged the jagged teeth of rock that afforded only scanty protection from bullets and none at all from the sun. Some of the other men were still firing, but I had stopped to save ammunition because I only had long-range, moving targets to shoot. Since I had lost my horse, all the cartridges I had were what I carried in my belt. I had lost my Colt.

"Where'd all those soldiers go?" Wiley asked me, about thirty minutes after the battalion had disappeared.

"Beats me. Not much telling what General Buck's got up his sleeve."

Wiley was eyeing the same thing I was—the ominous massing of hundreds of Sioux and Cheyenne near the positions recently abandoned by the withdrawing troops. I borrowed a pair of field glasses from one of the miners and studied the Indians. I was impressed not only by their numbers, but also by how many of them seemed to be armed with the 1866-model Winchester carbines. The sun glinted off the brass receivers of the "yellow boys" as they waved them in the air. "How far away are those mules?" I asked, lowering the glasses. "We may need to get out of here in a hurry."

"Too far."

The metallic taste of sudden fear was in my mouth again, as I saw the warriors massing like a black thunderhead on the far ridge crest for a concentrated attack. And I had been under fire before. I pitied poor Wiley who had not—who abhorred violence. I glanced sideways at his profile. His face betrayed no emotion, but I knew he must be suffering a gut-wrenching fear.

The firing of our little group had nearly stopped as the men's attention was drawn, by twos and threes, toward the spectacle. One burly miner, with salt-and-pepper hair bristling from under his broad-brimmed hat, voiced a common feeling. "By God, that's an awesome sight. No matter how many times I see it, it still gives me the quivers."

The attack started with a burst of high-pitched yipping and howling, like a shrill, wolfish barking, that no white man could duplicate. I could feel the hair stand up on the back of my neck as I watched the savage line, as orderly as any cavalry charge, sweep down the far hill against our troops in the valley below us. The thudding of thousands of hooves and the cracking of hundreds of rifles gradually rose to a thunderous roar.

The Sioux under Crazy Horse struck our column on

the right and the Cheyenne under Dull Knife struck our troops on the left, lower down toward the river. Our cavalry fell back under the shock of the furious charge. The Sioux pressed their advantage and were attempting to skirt our flank and come in behind us. All of the packers and miners were now manning the west side of the ridge that was unprotected by any rocks, and we were firing over the heads of our troops at the hostiles. Even Jenkins had begun shooting, but with what effect, I couldn't tell.

I paused to reload, slipping the brass cartridges out of my belt and sliding them into the receiver by touch as I glanced downhill to the left to see if the Cheyenne were also trying to circle our troops there. I could pick out Colonel Guy Wellsey sitting his horse to one side, directing the defensive line. Just as I looked, he reeled in his saddle, and even at this distance, I could see a dark stain begin to cover the lower part of his face. It seemed as if an icy hand clutched my heart as I watched, fascinated, for him to fall. A head wound of that dimension almost had to be fatal. He sat his horse for several more seconds before finally falling slowly forward and slipping to the ground.

The Cheyenne saw the leader fall and rushed in with greater fury. But again the Crow allies were quicker, as several of them on foot surrounded his body and disappeared into the melee of hand-to-hand fighting.

"Matt! They've gotten behind us!"

I whirled at Wiley's shout to see several Sioux struggling up the ridge on foot. The ridge face was too steep for a horse. We fired point-blank, but they came on. They were too close and too many for us. Our group now instinctively and desperately fought back to back, firing out on three sides. Wiley's father had worked his way to his son's side, while I was crouched on the other. We were firing continuously; there was no time for talk or reloading. Finally, three Indians reached the crest and rushed at us from a few yards away. Wiley's father blocked the downsweep of a war club with his empty rifle.

"Shoot!" I yelled at Wiley, and swung my own empty gun at the first brave. The stock cracked into solid bone and he fell. In a split second I shot a glance at Wiley. He seemed rigid as a statue, staring ahead. The second brave levered his carbine and fired from the hip.

Mr. Jenkins whirled and fell.

I grabbed the Spencer from Wiley, praying it was loaded, and pulled the trigger. The Spencer and the brave's carbine crashed as one. At the instant the Indian staggered back I felt as if someone had raked a live coal across the back of my hand. I yelled in surprise and pain. But before my hand could instinctively open to let go of the Spencer, a roar next to my head momentarily stunned me, and the third Indian fell dead about five feet away.

The miners and packers had turned their attention to our side of the ridge, and withering fire drove the remaining braves back down the east side of the ridge to their tribesmen who were holding their ponies. The immediate danger was past, but we were still surrounded. From what I could see with a quick look around, General Buck had thrown two cavalry companies and about three infantry companies into the fight. The steady, accurate fire of the infantry was the only thing saving us from being overrun.

I turned my attention to Wiley and Mr. Jenkins. The elder Jenkins and another wounded miner had been dragged back into the center of our tiny circle. Two men were bending over Mr. Jenkins. His eyes were closed and he was breathing heavily. The slug had taken him in the left shoulder and had possibly broken his collarbone. One of the packers had slit his blood-soaked shirt away at the shoulder with his hunting knife. Then he turned him over and found where the bullet had exited farther down near the shoulder blade. Even this slight jarring of the wound made Jenkins grimace, and sweat poured down his red face. Apparently he was still conscious enough to feel the pain. Lacking any kind of bandage, the packer then cut and tore off his own shirttail and the tail of Jenkins's shirt as well to use as a set of front and back compresses to staunch the flow of blood. No one was attending the other man. Someone had determined he was already dead.

Wiley was still standing and looking around, vacantly, as if unable to comprehend what was happening. I grabbed him by the shoulders and shook him. Only then did I notice blood dripping slowly from a streak where the brave's bullet had plowed a shallow furrow across the back of my left hand. Now that I noticed it, it began to sting like hell.

"What's wrong? What're you shaking me for?" His eyes finally focused on mine.

"You okay?"

"Yeah, sure."

But I knew he was reacting and talking automatically. He was in a state of shock. I had seen many cases just like it during the war.

He looked around at the bloody bandage on his father's shoulder, at the dead man stretched out with his hat over his face, green flies already buzzing around the drying blood at the base of the feathered shaft protruding from his chest. Wiley went deathly pale and his eyes glazed. I caught him as his knees buckled and eased him to the ground.

Just then the tempo of the battle seemed to change. Whether it was a change in the noise level or what, I wasn't sure. But something arrested my attention and I looked up sharply, forgetting Wiley and everyone else in our group for a moment. A phalanx of blue-uniformed cavalry was attacking in force from the high ridges to the north. They had somehow come in behind the foe and had caught the Indians in an enfilading fire with the infantry. The warriors were fleeing in confusion, whipping their horses toward the west, the only opening left for them. I let out a shout of pure joy and relief and was suddenly aware of several other men doing the same. The attacking troops were part of the battalion that had been withdrawn almost an hour earlier.

"By God, that old fox, General Buck, outsmarted 'em this time!" one of the packers yelled. Apparently, the Indians were going to call it a day. They were riding in large numbers over the ridge crest to the north, hotly pursued by the troopers. The field was ours.

With the sudden release of tension, my own knees began to feel a little wobbly and I sat down cross-legged and hung my head. The heat and the dust and the stench of burnt gunpowder and death and sweating horses all around me had made me a little queasy. What really made me feel sick was the sudden realization that I had twice come extremely close to meeting my Maker this day. The pain in my hand and my thigh seemed to return with a vengeance. Slowly, and with a great fatigue settling over me, I eased my gold Waltham out of the watch pocket of my pants and opened it. The slender hands, pointing at the Roman numerals, told me it was 1:47. Surely it was later than that! I held it to my ear. It was ticking as steadily and reliably as my own heart. How a delicate piece of machinery could take a pounding like I had given it today and still keep time was beyond me. Maybe the white man's culture *was* superior, after all.

CHAPTER
Eleven

"WHY don't you take a look for your horse in that rope corral," Wilder suggested about an hour later, pointing at the herd of stray animals, including some Indian ponies, that had been rounded up and were in a temporary holding pen.

"Right. Will do."

Wilder moved off, leading his unsaddled mount, whose drooping head and lathered coat told of his weariness. McPherson and I were lolling, fully clothed, in the shallow waters of the Rosebud, trying to cool off and wash some of the sweat, dust, and grime from ourselves and the smell of battle from our nostrils, all at the same time.

"Lemme see that wound, Matt."

I held out my left hand, palm down, clean and dripping. The water had washed off the caked blood and dirt but had also started it oozing blood again. He examined it critically. "Can you move your fingers all right?"

I opened and closed the hand. "Hurts some, but it still works."

"Good. No tendons were cut and, apparently, no major blood vessels. You're lucky."

103

"Don't I know it. But my leg hurts worse than my hand. And it's swollen so much I can't get my trousers off to look at it."

"You were lucky again that that horse didn't kick you in a vital spot." He grinned. "One of the surgeons will take a look at it when they get a chance."

"Mac, what the hell happened, anyway? How did the battalion get in behind those Indians?"

"Well, we were ordered off the line and made a wide detour down here by the river and started north along the bottom of a canyon about a half-mile from here. Don't know where we were going. There weren't any Indians in sight, except a handful on the tops of the bluffs. I guess we'd followed that narrow canyon about three miles, maybe four, and here comes Burke, General Buck's aide-de-camp, riding hell-bent and gives Major Zimmer some message. And then we made a sharp left and defiled out of the canyon. The canyon wasn't as steep right there, but it was pure hell getting up outta there. A lot of us had to get off and lead our horses up through those pine trees. When we finally got out on top again, we could see what was happening and were in a perfect position to come in behind them."

"And not a minute too soon, I might add."

"It still seems strange to me, though, that they took off and ran like they did, instead of regrouping for a counterattack. They still had us outnumbered at least two to one."

"I don't know, but I'm sure glad they did. I was exhausted."

"Maybe they were too."

He grabbed the base of a bush growing by the bank and pulled himself up from the water. "Whew! It's hotter now than it was at noon. These wet clothes sure feel good."

I retrieved my watch, rifle, and boots, and we started toward the holding corral Wilder had indicated about a hundred yards away. The afternoon sun was sliding gradually toward the west, but the heat waves still shimmered from the valley floor as I looked up the ravines

and ridges that had been the scene of so much turmoil
only an hour or so before. The hillsides were littered
with at least a hundred dead horses and ponies, their
bodies swelling in the heat. The sky was beginning to
fill with buzzards, wheeling silently on the afternoon
thermals, waiting their chance.

"Wonder how many thousand rounds of ammunition
were fired today?" I mused aloud.

Mac glanced sharply at me as if making sure I wasn't
beginning to come apart after the shocks of the day.
"Oh, I don't know," he replied, looking up toward the
main battlefield himself. "A lot. Maybe twenty, thirty
thousand. Takes a lot of lead to send even one Indian
to join his ancestors. Apparently, horses are a lot easier
target than men. Don't think we lost more than about
two dozen killed and probably twice that many
wounded."

"I wonder about the hostiles?"

"Sergeant Killard mentioned a little while ago that
they found only thirteen bodies on the field. The rest of
their dead and wounded must've been carried off by
their friends."

The two surgeons, aided by several volunteers, were
working feverishly on the more seriously wounded, who
were lying on folded blankets in the open, near the river's edge. There was no shade. The merciless sun was
tormenting those who had lost blood. As we walked
past, the smell of carbolic and alcohol drifted to my
nose on the stifling air, as well as the sound of some
weak voices pleading for water. There were some
groans, and a smothered cry as a probe struck an exposed nerve. My gaze swept over the pitiful sight. The
wounded Crows were bearing their pain as stoically as
they had their pleasure earlier.

"Mac, there's Colonel Wellsey! I thought he was
dead. I happened to be looking when he was hit. After
he fell, the Sioux tried to get at his body to demoralize
the men. I lost sight of him, but didn't see any way he
could live."

We walked over to the pallet where he lay propped

up. Green summer flies were buzzing around the bloody bandage that swathed his head and eyes. A private soldier stood close by, holding a horse that provided shade for the wounded officer—the only shade anywhere around. The horse was stamping and swishing its tail at the biting flies.

I stood silently for a moment, not knowing if Guy Wellsey were even conscious. "Colonel Wellsey?"

"Yes?" He raised his head slightly.

"Sir, it's Matt Tierney and Robert McPherson. It's good to have you still with us."

"Ah, yes. It's good to be here." He seemed coherent.

"I saw you fall. I'm sorry. Do you have much pain?"

"Some. But it's nothing, really. Anyone can be a soldier in peacetime. You really ought to enlist, Matt. You'd make a good fighting man from what I've heard about your action today."

"Thank you, sir." In spite of myself, I grinned at the irony of this gritty battalion commander trying to recruit me while he lay severely shot up. I was glad he couldn't see my face. I had the feeling he was not joking.

"I hear there was one helluva fight over my body between the Sioux and the Crows. Wish I had been conscious enough to see it." He paused and took a deep breath of the lung-withering air, and then continued in a low, weary voice. "I think the doctor must have given me a shot of morphine or something. I'm starting to feel relaxed." His face, or what I could see of it below the bandage, was very pale and clammy. He had apparently lost a lot of blood. The flared mustacle was the only part of his face that had not changed. His head lolled back on the padded saddle that served as a pillow.

I motioned for Mac to move away. "Looks bad, but I can't tell with that bandage on his head."

"I know. Sure hope he makes it," Mac replied in a husky voice.

"Oh, I feel sure he'll make it, but his soldiering days may be over."

We turned to see Dr. Kenneth Donnelly, one of the

surgeons, plunging his hands and forearms into a bucket of river water and wiping them on a towel an orderly held for him. Donnelly was a short, stocky Irishman of about fifty, with a broad, ruddy face that was just now streaming with perspiration. His sleeves were rolled up above the elbows, revealing hairy, muscular arms. The front of his white shirt, between the galluses, was soaked with water and blood.

"How bad is he hit?"

"Took a slug through his left cheek. Came out just below the right eye. Shattered his cheek bone, and apparently severed the optic nerve. Won't know if he'll be blind in both eyes until the swelling goes down." He splashed some alcohol on his hands and arms quickly and turned to set the broken wrist of one of our buglers.

We moved off, my thigh still painful. A detail of soldiers was down at the water's edge, cutting and trimming big willows, while another group stood by to receive them and were fashioning travois to transport the casualties. In the slowly milling horses and mules of the corral, I spotted my still-saddled bay.

I pointed him out and a soldier caught his reins and brought him to me. I rubbed his head between the ears and spoke gently to him, trying to reestablish familiarity. Then I ran my hands down over his chest and legs, checking for any injuries. Luckily, he seemed unhurt. He had apparently only stumbled. I had not even named this horse, but after several weeks together, he seemed like an old friend as well as my means of transportation. And it was as a vital friend that I welcomed him back. Satisfied that he was all right, I slid my rifle into its scabbard and led the bay away for a drink in the river.

Wilder had come back along the riverbank and was talking to McPherson when I came up. ". . . transporting the dead and wounded. The general wants to bivouac here for the night so the surgeons can have a chance to treat the worst cases. And the men will have a chance to get some rest and get the travois built."

"What's up?" I inquired, dropping the reins and letting my bay thrust his muzzle greedily into the water.

"General Buck just had a staff officers' call and announced he was going to fall back on the supply train at Goose Creek."

"Some of these men look too bad to be dragged that far on travois."

"Can't be helped. The worst cases will be put on mule litters. And a detail of men has been assigned the job of lifting or carrying the ends of the travois poles of the others over the rough spots."

"Why aren't we following up and chasing those hostiles?" McPherson asked.

"The general says the command's pretty well exhausted, we're low on ammunition and food, and the wounded need care."

"He's not really a little afraid of Crazy Horse, is he?" Mac chided.

"In the mood he's in right now, I wouldn't ask that question to his face if I were you."

"Well, is he?"

"If you're planning to report this to your paper, make it your own opinion and not mine. But, off the record, I think he was just plain overconfident, and this battle was a real blow to his pride." He swept his arm in a half-circle. "Sure, we're in possession of the field, and I guess most military strategists might call that a victory, but what have we really accomplished?"

He removed his hat and wiped a soggy blue shirt sleeve across his brow. All of us had been up since three A.M., and the fatigue was showing in his reddened eyes and his sweat-streaked face. His dark blue cavalry trousers and black boots were gray with dust from the knees down. He put his hat back on and looked around. "No chance of surprising the village of Crazy Horse now, either, so General Buck is going to fall back and wait for reinforcements. I think he's realizing these Sioux and northern Cheyenne are a lot better fighters than he's been giving them credit for being—especially when they're cornered."

"What about the plan to close the pincers with General Terry near the Yellowstone?"

Wilder shrugged. "Don't know. No couriers have been able to get through. The general thinks we encountered only part of the total fighting force that's in the field between here and there. He wanted to make one fast thrust to capture that village. That's the reason we were detoured up that canyon. The scouts thought the village of Crazy Horse was about eight miles north of here. But we were called back because the rest of the command was so hard-pressed."

"So that's where we were going," Mac said.

"I believe this group of Sioux and Cheyenne were just fighting a holding action to prevent us getting to their village."

"If that's all they were up to, I guess they succeeded."

"Pretty enthusiastic holding action," I remarked.

"Big Bat and Grouard just rode in from a quick scout up that canyon. They reported that about a half-mile beyond where our column defiled out, they found evidence that a large party of Indians had been lying in ambush behind a jumble of boulders and wind-fallen timber."

Wilder paused and three of us looked at each other silently. Mac whistled softly. "God," he breathed, "the history of the world turns on such strokes of luck—or Providence."

"Got to go," Wilder said. "See you when we get camped."

"Right."

I started to mount until a sudden pain in my left thigh reminded me I couldn't lift my leg high enough to get my foot into the stirrup. So I went around to the right side and hauled myself up awkwardly. It was good to settle into the saddle and feel my horse under me again—and to get the weight off my injured leg. My clinging, wet pants and shirt were beginning to dry in the heat.

We went into camp about four o'clock and formed a

wide circle around our horses and pack train as we had done the night before. While the camp was being set up, the dead—twenty-six of them—were tied to the backs of horses and brought up to a level area near the camp. Most of the bodies were already turning black from the heat, so it was imperative that they be given a quick burial. A detail of exhausted, long-suffering privates had been set to work with short-handled shovels, digging the graves in the dry earth. The only thing that saved this chore from being even more onerous was the fact that the grayish soil was relatively loose and powdery. But they performed this service for their dead comrades without the usual soldier's grumbling. They were either too tired to talk or were simply grateful they weren't the ones going into the ground.

Each body was wrapped in an army blanket and lowered into a separate grave. While the burial detail and most of the men who were not occupied elsewhere stood bareheaded in the late afternoon heat, General Buck pronounced a brief eulogy. The general was tight-lipped and grim. He was apparently taking the loss of these men very personally. As soon as he finished, he stalked off and disappeared without a word to anyone. No bugler sounded taps.

To prevent desecration of the bodies by the Sioux, traces of the graves were obliterated by several companies of cavalry riding their horses repeatedly back and forth across the site. Their hooves raised a thick cloud of dust that drifted slowly upward and northward on some imperceptible breeze. Then, as the long shadows of the setting sun slanted across the valley, camp fires were built on top of the graves to further confuse any scavenging Indians later.

I turned my bay over to Corporal Schmidt to unsaddle and curry. Mac retired to his blanket to rest and begin writing up a report of the battle for his newspaper while the action was fresh in his mind. Captain Wilder and Lieutenant Shanahan were both still out on some duties, so I wandered back down to where the wounded lay, now in the shade of twilight.

It was Mr. Jenkins I was looking for. I found him
lying unconscious on his back on a folded blanket, his
feet slightly elevated and his bare torso now clothed in
clean, white bandages. He was near several of the other
seriously wounded, grouped so the surgeons could mon-
itor all of them regularly. Wiley and Cathy were sitting
at his side.

I greeted them and sat down on the ground close by.
"How is he?"

"Not too good, I'm afraid," Cathy replied, turning a
tear-stained face to me. "The doctor says the bullet
damaged a lot of muscles and may have clipped a rib or
the edge of his lung. He's lost a lot of blood." She
looked back at her father's pale face and I could see
her biting her lip and blinking back the tears. She
leaned over and smoothed his wavy gray hair with her
fingers. Wiley, aside from acknowledging my greeting,
had not spoken. He was still looking blanched and
shaken. "I just hope we can camp here awhile so he can
rest and start getting his strength back," Cathy continued.

I said nothing, not having the heart to tell her the
command was moving out early in the morning. Yet,
she must have seen the travois being built. Her words,
if not her manner, indicated there was no doubt in her
mind that he would recover. Maybe she had talked to
the surgeon. But, from what my layman's eye could see,
Mr. Jenkins might very well die from shock before he
could reach a hospital.

I sat with them a few more minutes, making small
talk, and discussing the Indians' retreat, but all the time
observing their faces, especially Wiley's. I didn't know
if he was grieving for his father, was feeling guilty about
freezing up at a crucial moment, or was still befuddled
from the trauma of first combat. "Well, I'll look in on
you later. If there's anything you need, I'm not in the
army, so . . ." My voice trailed off. I wasn't even sure
what I meant, and the words sounded so damn trite, I
could've kicked myself for even saying them. But Cathy
Jenkins, gracious woman that she was, thanked me with

her eyes. I got up, touched Wiley on the shoulder, and walked away toward my camp area.

I found Wilder, Mac, and Shanahan ready to eat when I arrived. Corporal Schmidt and one of the other orderlies had cooked up supper for our mess from the meager rations we carried. The four of us hardly spoke as we sat down on our blankets to eat. Apparently, no one had the energy or the inclination to discuss the battle. All Wilder said was, "I've seen considerable battle action but that was one of the hottest fights I've ever been in, including the war."

No one replied. Shanahan sat moodily throughout, his mind evidently occupied elsewhere.

Since we carried no tents, each mess and company was grouped around its own cook fire. As the deepening dusk obscured details, the camp became small circles of light from the fires. Even though the smell of bacon and fried corn tied my stomach into knots of sudden hunger, it was all I could do to fight off drowsiness as I ate. My heavy eyelids kept falling, even as I chewed my food. I jerked my head up for about the fourth time and opened my eyes. Mac was grinning at me across the fire.

"I know how you feel. Resting feels better and better as I get older. And I'm a darn sight older than you." He swallowed and continued. "I can remember the day when I could go all day and most of the night without even thinking about sleep. But that day's long gone. I guess that's why armies are made up of young men."

He began to cough—only a little at first. But this triggered a paroxysm of coughing that caused him to get up and walk away from the group, his handkerchief to his mouth. It seemed strange to me that I had not noticed him coughing at all today. I watched him carefully for a minute or two to be sure he was all right, before I resumed eating. I would have offered my assistance, but since there was nothing I could do, I didn't move. Mac wanted no well-intentioned sympathy from anyone.

CHAPTER
Twelve

No sooner was supper over and all of us had rolled wearily into our blankets than a mournful wailing started up from the Crow and Shoshone camps. In addition to their own warriors killed—how many, we didn't know—a young Shoshone boy had been killed and scalped while holding horses in the rear area. Some of the Cheyenne had ridden completely around the command and caught him defenseless near the river.

"It's not so much that he was killed," Wilder remarked, raising his head at the sound. "There's some superstition about his being scalped. They believe he can't get into the happy hunting grounds without his scalp."

Some of the men nearby were grumbling about the noise, but I was awake just long enough to notice that it prevented none of them from falling into an exhausted sleep immediately. I could have slept on a bed of nails myself.

Reveille sounded at four A.M. on a frosty Sunday morning, and we were all up and under arms quickly. But, as General Buck had correctly predicted, there was no dawn attack by the Sioux. The Snake Indians waited until sunrise to bury the boy they had mourned the night before. All the relatives appeared in hideous black paint, many of them weeping openly. The boy was buried in the shallow ford of the streambed, and afterward, several Indians rode their ponies back and forth across to be sure all traces were obscured.

Each seriously wounded soldier was carefully loaded onto a litter slung fore and aft between two surefooted mules. It was no spring ambulance, but it was the best that could be devised under the circumstances. The less seriously wounded were put on travois behind horses and mules and the entire command slowly began a withdrawal, its pace regulated by the slowest of the injured.

Instead of riding in formation with our Company B, Mac and I decided to ride off to one side of the column. We had gone only about a half-mile when I noticed some dismounted Crows clustering around something in the deep grass off to the right of us. Mac and I rode over and found them grouped around the stiff corpse of a Sioux warrior. The body had a bullet hole in its breast, but was otherwise unmarked. The Crow, chattering among themselves, gleefully started their mutilation. First they stripped the body of all clothing and ornamentation. Then they scalped it. One Crow sliced off the warrior's ears and put them in a pouch he carried at his belt. Others hacked off his fingers, toes, and nose. Mac and I protested, but they only laughed at us and pretended not to understand.

Finally, one big buck cut off the penis and held it overhead, a grin splitting his brutal features. He shouted something in broken English to the effect that there would be great distress among the squaws when they found out what had happened. They all cheered and laughed. Just then Captain Wilder, attracted by the commotion, rode up with a squad of men. He drew his revolver, and with a few hard words, put a stop to any further dismemberment.

I was sick with disgust. "Damn, Mac, that may be common practice among various tribes, but a sight like that sure makes me lose any respect I ever had for the Crows."

"Well, they talk a good fight around the camp fire,

but most of 'em would rather attack a dead Sioux than a live one." He pulled his horse's head around. "Probably why the Sioux have always bested them until the white man came along."

The command rode on up and out of the valley of the Rosebud following the easiest grades possible. Small bands of mounted Sioux or Cheyenne watched us from the hilltops but made no move to hinder our departure. Mac and I took the opportunity during the morning to ride back and forth along the column, observing the movement of the wounded.

I rode up alongside Colonel Wellsey to speak to him just as two men on foot were lifting the ends of his travois up the steep bank of a feeder stream. The foot of one of the soldiers slipped and he dropped his end. The injured man was pitched off and rolled over a few feet down the bank. The soldier cursed himself, and the other man sprang to help.

"It's okay, boys. I'm not hurt," Wellsey replied when the private began apologizing for his clumsiness as they eased him back onto his litter. The officer's cheerfulness under the circumstances amazed me. He still couldn't see because of the swelling and the bandages around his head. In spite of the laudanum, he had to be in pain. He acted as if he was sorry to be a burden to the soldiers who had to carry his travois poles.

"He has a better disposition, wounded, than most men do whole," Mac remarked, reflecting my own thoughts.

"Especially Major Zimmer."

"Speaking of the devil, do you suppose he'll be the C.O. of the 3rd Cavalry now that Wellsey is out of action?"

"Sounds likely. Reckon Wilder's thought of that?"

"Glad I'm not in uniform."

"Yeh. Wilder's the one who'll be catching hell if that happens."

We camped early that evening at a level spot where there was good wood, water, and grass. We were still a few miles from our wagon train at Goose Creek. After the camp had settled in and before supper, I got up the courage, at Mac's prompting, to seek out Surgeon Donnelly to get my hand and leg attended to. "Compared to these other cases, Doc, I feel like a fool coming to you with something like this," I said as I sat down on a campstool for the bluff Irishman to examine me.

"You let me worry about that." He took my hand and gave it a professional inspection. "Did you pour any whiskey on this?"

"No."

"Good thing you came to me when you did, then. It's about to become infected." He pressed gently around the jagged wound with his thumbs, and I caught my breath with sharp pain as the scabbing cut oozed serum and pus. He cleaned, and dressed the wound with clean bandages, and then asked if there was anything else, since he had seen me limping as I came up. I told him about my thigh.

"Drop your pants."

"Here?"

"Sure, here. By the saints, who's here to see you?"

I could feel myself reddening as I did as I was told. He took considerable interest in my left thigh, which was discolored about two-thirds from knee to hip and still very swollen. He pressed and punched here and there and then had me flex my leg, which I did with considerable pain.

"Step up and down off this stool."

I complied, with even more difficulty. I was sweating when I sat down again.

"How'd you say you did that?"

"Indian pony kicked me."

"Hmmm. It's one of the most beautiful bruises I've seen in over twenty years. You must not have caught the edge of the hoof, or you'd have a broken femur and some damaged muscles there. As it is, you've got a lot of small blood vessels broken and a lot of swelling. There wouldn't have been much I could have done for you even if I had gotten to it right away. About all I could've done would've been to keep the swelling down.

And I don't have any ice out here for that, so . . ." He shrugged. "Go ahead and put your pants back on. That's going to be sore and stiff for a week or two. When we get back to Goose Creek, I'd advise you to get off that leg and keep it elevated as much as possible. When it turns pure black, it's just before healing up."

"Thanks, Doc. Guess I'm pretty lucky. Especially compared to a lot of these other poor bastards. By the way, how is Mr. Jenkins?"

"Who? Oh, the tall slim fellow with the silver hair?"

"Right."

"Touch and go. If he lives through tonight, he *might* make it. *Might*, I said. I've done all I can for him in the field, but that's not too much. He needs hospitalization quickly."

"That's a shame." I shook my head at the thought of this man I had only met and spoken to once.

"It's all a shame, Matt, for humans to be doin' this to each other."

"Oh?"

"I'm a doctor, first and last. It just so happens that I'm in the uniform and employ of the United States Army at the moment. I'm along to pick up the pieces and try to put them back together. It's what I'm trained for, and I can help people here as well as in some city hospital, or private practice."

"Guess you're right. Well, thanks, Doctor." I stuck out my hand and he gripped it firmly.

When I got back to the bivouac area, I told Mac and Wilder about Jenkins. There was nothing much any of us could say about it, so the conversation drifted on to other topics, primarily the campaign. Shanahan, as he had the night before, remained mostly silent during supper. Curt returned my Colt which he had found. After the meal, Mac turned to writing his dispatches again while there was still some daylight. I knew I would have to be doing the same shortly, since couriers would be leaving for the telegraph at Fetterman soon after we reached Goose Creek.

While the mess gear was being cleaned and stowed away, I noticed Wilder fidgeting. It was not like him. Finally, he drew me aside. "Matt, can you show me where Cathy Jenkins is?"

"I think so." I didn't ask why. "Do you want to go now?"

He nodded.

I led him to the camp area of the miners and located Cathy at a small camp fire with several of the miners. The burly, middle-aged miner with the salt-and-pepper hair who had been with us on the miners' ridge, seemed to have taken her under his fatherly protection. Her face was wan and her eyes looked red-rimmed in the firelight from crying and lack of sleep.

I left Wilder and retired unobtrusively. Wiley was not with his sister. I guessed he was back with the mule packers, or, possibly, with his father. I didn't try to look him up. Wilder had not returned when Mac and Shanahan and I rolled into our blankets under the stars about nine-thirty. My leg was aching and I was still very fatigued.

Reveille came with dawn about five A.M. We stirred up the dead fire and put some coffee on. We were out of bacon, so breakfast was only black coffee with some hardtack dunked in it.

"Matt, would you do me a favor?" Wilder said as the horses were being saddled.

"Sure."

"We should reach the wagon train by noon. But I have to ride at the head of my company 'til then. Would you kind of keep an eye on Cathy Jenkins for me. Make sure she's okay?"

"Of course. Want me to keep the wolves away?" I grinned.

"No. Her father died late last night." His face was pale and grim in the gray morning light. "She was pretty shattered when I left her a little after midnight."

"Oh, no!"

"Yeh, he never regained consciousness."

I looked away from his eyes and stared down at my own scuffed, dusty boots. "Well, I can't say I'm really surprised. He took a pretty bad hit. The surgeon didn't give him much of a chance. I guess I was just hoping he'd make it in spite of the odds."

"I think she'll be okay. She's pretty gritty. I'm more impressed with her all the time. Well, perhaps that isn't quite the word I'm looking for. I don't know. I know I've damn well taken a strong liking to her, anyway." He seemed embarrassed by the admission.

"I'll ride by and check on her for you. How is Wiley taking it?"

"Don't know. Haven't seen him."

"I'll find him."

The command was passed along to mount, and we were shortly moving out in the now-familiar formation. I told McPherson what had happened. Then I rode back to the pack train and found Wiley Jenkins. He was slouched on his mule, head down, looking nothing like the cocky, cynical man I had first met. He barely acknowledged my greeting when I rode up alongside.

"Wiley, I'm really sorry about your Dad." I mouthed the standard words, trying to make them as sincere as I could.

"Don't patronize me. You think it's my fault, don't you?" he snapped, looking up at me.

I was taken aback.

"Not really. You had no experience in combat. The kind of reaction you had to have at that instant could've come only from instinct or previous exposure to such situations," I replied carefully.

With that his defenses seemed to crumble, and even though he was not looking at me, I could see him blinking back the tears. We rode along in silence for a minute or so, my torso swaying comfortably with the slow rhythm of my horse. The only sounds were the soft thudding of hooves, the squeaking of leather, and the rattling of gear. A slight breeze carried away the puffs of dust rising from the hooves of our animals.

Finally, he regained his composure and, when he spoke again, it seemed to come from deep reflections within him. "I didn't agree with many of the things the old man did and stood for, or appeared to stand for. But I'll have to admit he had his good points. I've been doing a lot of thinking, and I'll have to admit I'm in no position to judge his motives for the things he did. I'm beginning to have a lot of regrets for not coming to terms with him before it was too late. Or at least getting to know him better."

"Huh . . . If it's any comfort, about half the human race could probably say that, including me."

"Ah well, who knows? Maybe things work out for the best." His voice still had a forlorn note to it, but he straightened up in his saddle.

I didn't want to go into the details of his family problems; I was only interested in his own health of mind. I knew he was going through some rough self-recriminations but hoped he could pull through them with a minimum of damage. And I hoped it wouldn't drive him to escape in the bottle. Presently I said, "Cathy could use all the help you can give her, you know. She's not as tough as she makes out."

"Yes, I know. I'll go to her as soon as I catch up with myself."

With that, I left him and riding forward to find Cathy among the miners, I saw Mr. Jenkins's body wrapped in a canvas and tied across the back of a horse. He was the only unburied fatality in the command. The horse was being led by one of the miners, and Cathy rode a few yards ahead on her sorrel.

"Hi."

"Hello, Matt." She looked tired but otherwise composed. She wore jeans, and a soft cotton shirt with small green-and-white checks. Her doeskin jacket was tied behind the saddle. A broad, low-crowned hat shaded her eyes from the sun, and her brown hair was swept back from her face. The gun belt she had worn earlier was missing. She didn't seem disposed to talk, and I didn't know what to say, so I rode silently alongside her, hoping just my presence would show my concern.

"Why did it have to happen." she said plaintively, without looking my way. It wasn't a question. "He was a good man," she continued, speaking softly, almost to herself. "It seems so pointless. He had no business fighting. What did he accomplish by giving up his life?"

"You said he was a good man. I didn't know him except as a courageous man. But maybe, since he had asked for the protection of the army, he felt obliged to help earn it by doing some of the fighting, too."

"Maybe so. We've had several close calls and faced a lot of danger since I've been old enough to leave my aunt's place and school to travel with him. Maybe the law of averages just caught up with him. I guess it could have happened at a dozen other places at a dozen other times." She seemed to be trying to think the thing through aloud.

"Captain Wilder is feeling really bad about it."

"Curt's a compassionate man. If it hadn't been for having him to lean on last night, I don't know what I would've done. Wiley wasn't much help. He was in worse shape than I was. For some reason he feels it's his fault, but I don't know why. Can you tell me exactly what happened? I've kind of pieced it together from some of the miners, but you were there with them, weren't you?"

"Yes." So I started in and gave her a detailed account of the fight, downplaying Wiley's moment of panic.

"Well, I can see why he feels like he does. But he's never run up against anything like this before. I don't think he's ever shot a gun before. At least not that I know of."

"I know. I know. I tried to explain to him that it was just one of those things that can't be predicted or prevented."

She shook her head. "I feel sorrier for him than I do for Dad." She lowered her voice slightly. "Some of the miners are a little bitter about Wiley, too. I heard a few of them discussing it last night. They aren't so much sorry for Dad, since they've only known him about a month. But they were saying it could have been any one of *them* who got it. And there are some hard cases in that bunch."

"Have you thought of what you might do now?"

"Not really. We'll bury poor Dad when we get back to Goose Creek, although I wish I could somehow return his body to Kentucky to be buried near my mother. I'm not sure if I'll stay with the miners for now or strike out on my own for Deadwood. Or, I guess I could go back East and try to find work of some sort. But there's not much open for a woman. Haven't really thought that far ahead yet. Maybe Wiley will have some suggestions or ideas. I'm just too upset to even think just now."

I nodded, noting the absence of that flashing smile that had been so much a part of her since she came into camp that first day. It was easy to see how Wilder could be smitten with her.

"I've been crying most of the night. I must look awful!"

"Curt said we should be at Goose Creek by noon. You can rest there."

"Oh, if I only *could* sleep. I think I'd feel so much better."

"I'll ask the surgeon to give you a sleeping powder if you like."

"I think a shot of whiskey would do just as well. Wiley's got some. Thanks just the same."

"Okay."

She gave me a wan smile as I touched my hat brim and wheeled my horse away from her.

CHAPTER
Thirteen

WE reached Goose Creek right on schedule, and Major Duke and the troops who had been left behind to guard the wagon train were so glad to see us they all crowded around, wanting news of the battle before we were even out of our saddles. Their eagerness made me realize, with a start, that I was here to provide just such news for thousands of readers of my employer's newspaper. And since the battle, I had made only a few brief notes.

Before anything else was done, General Buck ordered the entire command to move about two miles up Goose Creek to a camping area that was both large enough and had sufficient grass for all our stock. It was almost three o'clock by the time we were all settled into the new campground.

Mr. Jenkins was buried in the shade of some large cottonwoods on the bank of Goose Creek. There was no wood for a coffin, so he was wrapped in a gray army blanket. Wiley stood at the foot of the grave, showing no emotion, and Cathy was weeping quietly as her father was lowered into the grave. At Cathy's request, Captain Wilder read some appropriate Scriptural passages, and the few of us who were standing there finished the brief service by saying the Lord's Prayer in unison. Then I retired to our tent and spent the next three hours acquiring a good case of writer's cramp. But I finally finished my despatches just before supper.

The next morning General Buck ordered the wagon train carrying the wounded, to return under the escort of most of the infantry to Fort Fetterman for supplies and reinforcements.

"Looks like this is going to be a longer and tougher campaign than anyone realized," I remarked to Wilder at breakfast, as the wagons were being readied with fresh grass beds for the wounded.

"Yeah. I hope we don't have to sit here until more troops arrive. But I'm afraid that's just what we're going to be doing. General Buck is a little on the conservative side. He's not about to take a chance on plunging us into another hornet's nest."

"What would you do in this situation?" Shanahan inquired somewhat irritably over his coffee cup.

Wilder shrugged. "Can't really say since I haven't given it much thought. He's the one who's being paid to make the decisions."

"Then why don't you let him make them?" He flung the dregs of his tin cup into the fire and went into the tent.

"What's ailing him?"

"Brad will go far in the army. Probably make Brigadier some day, with any luck at all. He's a company man down to his shiny boots." Wilder was obviously becoming less and less enchanted with his messmate. I wondered how much of it was connected to his not so obvious disenchantment with the army. But he was pursuing another thought. "Where's Mac this morning? He's usually first up."

I turned and saw Mac coming toward us.

"Why the long face?" I smiled at him.

He started to reply, but broke into a fit of coughing. It was a good thirty seconds before he was able to talk.

"Matt, I've been down to see Surgeon Donnelly."

"What about?"

"This." He tapped his chest. "It's worse. I was awake most of the night."

One look at his gray face and I knew he wasn't joking. For Mac to admit he was hurting, much less to go see the doctor, told me he was really having trouble. "What did the doctor say?"

"Advised me to return to Fort Fetterman with the wagon train. Said there was nothing he could do for me here." He reached for the cup of coffee I poured for him, and I noticed his hand shook slightly. His ashen skin and gray hair made him look much older than his fifty years. "Hell, Matt, he was just being nice. No doctor can help me—here or anywhere else. There's no cure for consumption. You know that. I'm not kidding anybody, let alone myself."

I put my arm across his shoulders, and gave him a quick squeeze. "I know, Mac, but with your guts, it won't get you 'til you're ninty-nine." He smiled and toasted me silently with his coffee cup. "Are you going?"

"Yes. I have a notion I've seen most of the action that's going to be taking place around here for a while. And I don't relish the idea of stagnating around camp, eating pig meat, beans, and the kind of hardtack that could replace the cobblestones on any street in America." He grinned. "Trouble is, if I report back in this shape, I'll probably lose my job. Maybe I'll stop over at the post hospital at Fetterman, or a civilian hospital at Denver before I head back to Los Angeles."

"Isn't there some other job you could do on your paper that would be less strenuous than this?"

"Oh, sure, plenty of them. And my editor is kind enough to work me in somewhere. It's sure going to be boring, though." He sighed. "Guess I'd better get my stuff together."

"Mac, it's been a real pleasure." I thrust out my hand. "Feel like I've known you all my life. Keep in touch. Write me at my paper when you get settled. I'll probably be back by then."

He went into the tent to pack.

Some of the wagons with our remaining provisions were to stay behind. Mac and I gave our news dispatches, wrapped in oilskins, to the courier who was leaving for the telegraph at Fort Fetterman. By traveling fast and light on a good horse, he would arrive several days in advance of our wagon train—assuming that he was also lucky and didn't get his hair lifted and become a carrion feast. But the speed of the news was paramount, and the closest link with the outside world was at Fetterman.

With Mac leaving, I felt an emptiness. He had become a close friend and confidant in just the short time I had known him. He had seen much of life and had the type of personality that went down easy with camp coffee, hard trails, and early dawns. And being fellow journalists, we automatically had something in common. There were four or five other correspondents scattered throughout the command, but I had only a nodding acquaintance with them.

The miners petitioned General Buck to be allowed to stay on with the command, even though we were going nowhere for the moment. They had most of their own provisions and could help hunt fresh meat for the troops, they argued. Besides, they couldn't get to the Black Hills without the army opening the way for them. The general readily consented, recalling the valuable firepower they had lent at the Rosebud. However, he was a little more reluctant to allow Cathy Jenkins to remain. But, after disclaiming any responsibility for her safety, he finally agreed. I think he was influenced by the fact that her father had been killed while voluntarily fighting with the troops, so he was more inclined to give in to the strong arguments of Wiley and a few of the older miners that they would look out for her.

"I let him know I could take care of myself," Cathy told us later, tilting her pretty nose defiantly.

"I'll bet you did!" Curt replied. "I have a feeling you usually get your own way."

After the wagon train pulled out with the wounded, escorted by most of the mule-mounted infantry, the camp seemed to get very quiet. And time suddenly hung heavy on my hands. Days and weeks of marching, fighting, trying to snatch some food and sleep in between, had conditioned all of us to almost constant activity. The sudden slump into the routine idleness of camp life seemed strange. But, before I had a chance to get bored, I was summoned to General Buck's headquarters tent. This was an unusual command. I had never attended a meeting or conference of any sort with the general without going along with Wilder. And, just now, Wilder was nowhere in sight.

The orderly who had conveyed the command led the way and lifted the flap of the white wall tent as I stepped inside. General Buck sat behind a small, folding camp table, his forearms resting on it. He was hatless and dressed in his usual dun-colored canvas field outfit. His hair was damp and tousled, as if it had been hurriedly dried after a swim in Goose Creek. His face was set and stern. On each side of the table, standing about eight feet apart and not looking at each other, stood Captain Wilder and Major Zimmer. I sensed the tension in the air, as my eyes took in the scene in a couple of seconds.

"Come in, Mr. Tierney," General Buck said, addressing me with a cold formality I had not heard in weeks.

I stepped closer to the table and stood, arms at sides, waiting.

"Major Zimmer, here, has preferred a serious charge against Captain Wilder for allegedly deserting his post under fire. As a preliminary matter, I need to get a few of the facts straight before this goes any further. That's why you're here. Major Zimmer says that Captain Wilder left his Company B while they were engaged in a running fight with the Sioux. Captain Wilder claims he saw you on foot being attacked and rode back to help you. Is that right?"

"That's right, sir. He did come back for me. My horse fell and an Indian on horseback just about got me. Luckily, I managed to kill the Indian before the captain reached me, but I was injured and he carried me riding double up to the ridge and left me with some of the miners who were fighting there."

"This man is his messmate. He would naturally support that story."

"You can check it with the miners," I retorted.

"Captain, did you leave your company leaderless during this time?" General Buck asked.

"No, sir. I delegated command to Lieutenant Shanahan."

"How was this done—by verbal command?"

"Yes, sir. I yelled at him to take over, that I would be right back."

"Did he hear and understand you in all the confusion?"

"Yes, sir."

"Well, we can check that with him later. Major, whether you or I agree with his action, we both know that a company commander has the discretion to use his own judgment in battlefield situations—within the framework of general orders, of course. So far, his story checks out, and I see no need for any charges to be filed."

"What he says may be true, sir, as far as it goes. But I didn't see him again for over an hour. Not until the battalion was withdrawn at your orders to circle around through the canyon toward the village."

"That's a damn lie!" Wilder was facing his accuser now, eyes blazing in his flushed face.

"That's enough!" The general's voice cracked like a whip.

I was feeling extremely uncomfortable, standing between the two of them.

"How long would you estimate it took you to rejoin your command, Captain?"

"No more than fifteen minutes, sir. I don't know exactly, since I didn't really have a chance to look at my watch and didn't figure anyone would be asking me to justify it later." This last he delivered with sarcasm and a glance at Zimmer.

"Could it be that, in all the fighting and confusion,

you just failed to notice his return until an hour or so later, Major?"

"Not a chance. In fact, I was looking for him to give him an order. The command was getting too strung out and scattered, and I was afraid some of the inexperienced men would be drawn out so far they would be surrounded and cut off. I wanted his company to dismount and form a skirmish line to hold the hilltop. But I couldn't find him and finally had to give the order to Shanahan. In fact, there were several casualties suffered by his company before I saw what was happening and ordered them back. If it hadn't been for his cowardice in the face of the enemy, those casualties might have been prevented."

"Cowardice has yet to be proven, Major," General Buck's voice was now icy. "And Lieutenant Shanahan is an able enough officer. He could command a company of men with no trouble."

He turned to Wilder. "It seems we have a considerable difference of opinion here. In any case, I don't think it would have made any difference in the outcome of this engagement. Major, if you insist on pursuing this, you have a right to file formal charges when we return to Fetterman. Then a Court of Inquiry will have to sit, and I'm sure enough witnesses can be found to establish the fact of whether Captain Wilder returned promptly to his command or not. But I'm somewhat at a loss as to what your motive is in all this, Major."

Zimmer's back straightened perceptibly as he came almost to attention. "I just hate to see inept, lax, and cowardly officers in the U.S. Army, sir. It gives all of us a bad name. And you know what kind of bad press we've been getting lately."

"Yes . . ." The general nodded thoughtfully. "But, just for that reason, and for morale, I caution all three of you to keep this to yourselves until we get back to the post. And I definitely don't want any of this to appear in your paper, Tierney."

"Yessir."

"Will he be confined to quarters or put under close arrest, sir?" Zimmer inquired.

"Absolutely not!" General Buck's blue eyes snapped and his braided beard quivered as his jaw worked. "Captain Wilder has not been found guilty. I remind you, Major, we are in the field under battle conditions, and we need every able officer. There is no place one man can go out here in any case. And I have just explained my reasons for not noising this incident around. That's all. You're dismissed."

"The bastard! What the hell is he up to, Curt?" I burst out as we walked back to our tent.

For a man who had just been outrageously accused, Curt was remarkably cool. "Don't rightly know. He outranks me so I don't believe I'm any threat to his possible promotion."

"Unless you're in a position to do something to make him look bad. Don't get in the way of ambition; it's deadlier than a .44."

"Yes. Could be he's trying this ploy to impress the general that he runs a tight outfit. Anything to keep himself the center of attention. It's a cinch we don't like each other, but a personality clash is no reason for an accusation like this that he'll never be able to make stick at a court-martial. Maybe it's just another form of harassment to eventually get me out of his battalion. I don't know. Then again, he may never file formal charges when we get back to Fetterman—just did this to give me something to think about. Even if a man is never tried or convicted, the suspicion of wrongdoing lingers in people's minds. It can be very damaging to an officer's career."

"The general didn't seem too impressed."

"You never know about him. He might think it over and decide in his own mind Zimmer is right. The general belatedly covered his own tracks last March by throwing the whole blame on Colonel Reynolds for that fouled-up operation. So the general's not above pulling something like this himself."

CHAPTER
Fourteen

SURPRISINGLY, no word of that incident leaked out, and for the next two weeks, the camp fell into a quiet routine, with everyone trying to find a way to kill time. Horse racing was popular. Some mended equipment or cleaned weapons, others sewed up damaged clothing, gave each other haircuts, wrote letters home, and read. Reading material was at a premium. Everything was devoured, from labels on cans to newspapers several months old that were found stuffed as packing in some of the supply boxes. One of the young lieutenants had a small library of dime novels that were in constant demand. After each volume had gone through a dozen hands, it began to look pretty limp and dog-eared.

The Crows and Shoshones, seeing what was happening, decided that it would be "good medicine" for them to go home. So they departed with many promises to return before the campaign was over. They also left their wounded to be cared for by our doctors. The weather continued clear and very hot with the temperatures from ten A.M. until four P.M. hitting the hundred-degree mark. But the nights remained very cool. Luckily, we were in an area where we had plenty of shade and water. Every couple of days General Buck ordered the camp moved two or three miles up Goose Creek, closer to the base of the Big Horns, to keep constant pasturage for our large herds.

One of the prime recreations was swimming in Goose Creek during the heat of the day. The stream made many lazy bends with some of its banks overhung by large cottonwoods. The water, coming out of the mountains, was always bracingly cold and refreshing. Running clear over a pebbly bottom, it was not only good for swimming and washing clothes but also supplied all our drinking and cooking needs. Best of all, though, the deep, shady pools were alive with trout. For one man to take thirty or forty trout a day out of there was nothing unusual. Fresh trout became a daily item on nearly everybody's menu.

General Buck took advantage of the lull to indulge in his favorite sport—hunting. He often left camp with one or two aides, or by himself, and disappeared into the mountains a few miles west of the camp. Most of the time he returned the same day. Other times he was gone overnight. Seldom did he return empty-handed. The fresh meat he brought back on his pack mule in the form of deer and game birds also helped to diversify the larder. Some of the officers were irritated that he did not allow them to do the same without special permission, which he himself seldom granted.

But Wilder was not a hunter and had no interest in this activity. A lot of his free time was spent in the company of Cathy Jenkins. I stayed discreetly out of the way but watched the two of them walking along the shady creek bank, deep in conversation. Wilder seldom spoke about her, but I could tell by the look in his eyes that he had been bitten hard.

One evening, when Shanahan was not with us, Wilder finally broached the subject to me. "Matt," he began hesitantly, obviously searching for the right words, "you know how I feel about Cathy Jenkins. She's friendly enough toward me, but there doesn't seem to be anything more to it than that—just friends."

"Hell, Curt, give her a chance to know you." I grinned. "You only met her two or three weeks ago.

And how much of that time have you been able to spend with her? Besides, she's come through a lot, losing her father and all. She needs time."

"I see what you mean. But I wanted to get my bid in early. I know there are several other officers seeing her, and I just feel awkward as hell around her. Feel as gawky as a schoolboy. Maybe I've been soldiering too much for the last few years and not socializing enough."

"Any girl friends in Philadelphia?"

"Oh, there are a few I've gone to parties with when I was home last spring, but of course, most of the gals near my age have long since gotten married or have given up and resigned themselves to spinsterhood—most of them with good reason."

"Maybe Cathy just looks better to you because you're seeing her in this setting where there are few women. Here she looks glamorous, but she might be insignificant in a city where there are plenty of women."

"I don't know, Matt. I just can't picture her in a drawing room, or even as a scullery maid. She's got an independent turn of mind that her father has apparently fostered all her life. I can tell from the way she talks that she's well educated. She tells me she was tutored some and also spent several winters attending school in Louisville, where she lived with an aunt."

"Is her mother dead?"

"Yes. Died when she was about five."

"Have you ever been married, Curt?"

"No."

"Ever thought about it?"

"Not seriously. But the thought of growing old alone doesn't really appeal to me. And I would like to have some kids of my own someday. And someday may be about here. I'm only thirty-three years old, but if I'm ever going to do it, it's time to start looking around. Most of my time the last few years has been spent in the West, where the only women I see are either married or prostitutes or are so damned ugly they'd hurt your eyes. Some are so coarse that you'd have a hard time figuring out that they're women under the dirt and buckskin. Cathy has managed to live out here and still remain a lady—capable and proficient, but still a lady."

"Well, like I said, it might not be the wisest thing to go after her with the idea of marriage in the back of your head. She probably seems more desirable because, for the moment anyway, she's unattainable because of her disinterest and your competition. And also because she's the only attractive female you've seen in weeks. Besides, she may not want to get married. As you said, she seems pretty independent and has a mind of her own."

My weighty words of wisdom seemed to help. At any rate, Curt cheered up some.

As the days passed, the wound on my hand scabbed over and began healing very well. My leg was also on the mend. The swelling in my thigh gradually went down. As the surgeon had predicted, the bruise turned an ugly black and yellow. Day by day it was limbering up and getting stronger.

The Fourth of July came and went, with no word from anywhere. Some of the men talked about what a celebration was probably going on back East for the Centennial. But our camp had become an oasis, completely isolated from the rest of the world. I often had to look at a calendar to be sure what day it was, since the days ran into each other with a monotonous sameness. There was no official observance of Sunday. I had never believed there could be such a thing as too much leisure for my taste, but I began to revise that assumption.

On July 6, General Buck issued a call for all his officers. I went along, eager for some news and a break in the routine. We couldn't all fit into his headquarters tent, so we congregated on a trampled grass and bare dirt area in front of the tent. It was ten o'clock in the morning and the daily heat was beginning to bear down on the camp. But we stood in relative coolness under the shade of several large trees. The dappled sunshine on the green and brown earth shifted its pattern continuously with the tossing of the treetops in the wind. General Buck stepped up onto a box in order to be seen and heard by everyone.

"Gentlemen, as you all know, I've sent for reinforcements. Frankly, I had expected to have them with us by now. I had hoped to take the field and be back in action. No couriers have gotten through to us, so there's no way of knowing what's happening with our counterparts on the Yellowstone. On June 25 Lieutenant Shanahan was hunting in the mountains and says he spotted what looked like a big cloud of dust or smoke rising many miles to the north. Of course, it might have been one of these lignite deposits we've seen smouldering before, or a prairie fire. But just in case it's not, I'd like to get an idea where the Indians are or if they have a village anywhere in this vicinity. So, while we're waiting for the troops I've asked for, I'm sending out a party to reconnoiter an area north and west of here. Major Zimmer will select an officer to head this detail. Big Bat Pourier and Frank Grouard will go along to scout. They'll take provisions for several days. I want them to stay out of sight as much as possible. They're to find out what they can and report back to me. They're to leave as soon as they can get ready.

"Also, I'm appointing Major Zimmer as acting commander of the 3rd Cavalry, due to the loss of Colonel Wellsey. If there are no questions, you're dismissed."

He gave no opportunity for questions, but no one seemed to mind as the officer corps dispersed. Wilder's face showed no emotion in regard to anything we had just heard.

"I guess you were expecting Zimmer to be made acting commander."

He nodded, grimly. "Won't make much difference, since he's been my immediate superior, anyway, except that there's no one to keep him in check now, except the general."

"Captain Wilder!" We stopped as George Zimmer approached.

"Sir?"

"I want you to head up this scouting detail. Select about twenty-five men to go with you. Report to me when you're ready to leave."

"Yessir."

Zimmer returned Wilder's salute and walked away.

"What d'ya reckon his motive was for that?" I asked.

"You got me."

"At least he's letting you pick your own men."

"Yeh. He might be testing me or trying to get me out of camp for a while."

"In spite of not liking you, he may just respect your ability."

"Possible, but I doubt it. There are plenty of good officers in this command. And it's normal for a lieutenant to handle an assignment like this." He shrugged. "But then, maybe I'm reading too much into it."

"Damn! I'd sure like to go with you, Curt. My leg's healed well enough so it doesn't bother me. And I'm just going to seed around here."

"I'd be glad to have you. But General Buck will have to give the go-ahead since you're a civilian. I can pick the soldiers myself. If you're dead set on going, I'll put in a good word for you. But it could be dangerous."

"I could use a little excitement."

"Okay. Start getting your gear together and I'll have a word with the general."

After Wilder returned and started selecting about two dozen men from the various companies to go on the scout, I went and talked to the general myself. He reluctantly gave his permission for me to go but warned me about the possibility of danger, and let it be known that the army would not be responsible for anything that happened to me.

I thanked him and left before he could change his mind. If I were killed, it would make little difference to anyone else. My parents were deceased; my brother and sister were both grown and married. If I were somehow hurt or wounded, my paper would stand good for any medical expenses. General Buck even authorized me to draw a hundred rounds of army ammunition, but it was the wrong caliber for my new Winchester. Besides, I assured him, I had brought along plenty of my own.

When I returned to our tent, I was surprised to find Curt sitting on the cot with his head down, looking as if someone had just kicked him in the stomach. "What now?"

He looked up and attempted a grin, but it didn't come off. "I think I just discovered the reason why I've been picked for this patrol."

"What are you talking about?"

"I was rounding up the men and calling for volunteers. And I saw Cathy walking down by the creek with Zimmer."

"Well." I shrugged, trying to put the best light on it. "She can't very well avoid talking to the man—especially the way he usually pushes himself. He's got more brass than a cannon. You know that."

"Yes, but he was helping her along as though she couldn't do a damn thing for herself. And she was letting him!"

I was jarred and could think of nothing to say. Cathy Jenkins had struck me as a sensible young woman. Was she really attracted by Zimmer? He could certainly lay on the charm and present a totally different side of himself around women. There had to be some explanation for it, but I didn't know what. And maybe Curt's jealous eyes were seeing something that wasn't there. I put my hand on his shoulder. "C'mon. Don't worry about it. Put it out of your mind. You've got a job to do now."

With an obvious effort, he pulled himself together. "You're right."

As he strapped on his Colt, a sudden idea struck me. "Curt, I know this may be against regulations, or whatever, but can Wiley Jenkins ride with us?"

"I don't know, Matt. He's too inexperienced. And he's shown he can't be depended on in a tight spot."

"I'll be responsible for him. He's a good packer and horseman. And I think he's a different man than he was before the battle. He'll do all right. Besides, he needs this. That thing about his father has really been preying on his mind—especially since he's had nothing to do to keep him busy."

Wilder stood, staring at nothing. I could see his jaw muscles working as he weighed the pros and cons, remembering this was Cathy's brother. "All right, he can come along. Just be sure he keeps up and follows orders. And don't let Zimmer or the general know he's going."

"Thanks." I wasn't at all sure that Wiley even wanted to go, but I looked him up and found him sitting dejectedly under a tree by himself in the packers' camp area.

"Hell, yes. I'm ready to get out of here and take a ride to anywhere for any reason. Thanks for volunteering me, Matt." He was up and reaching for his saddle before he even finished speaking.

In about forty-five minutes, everyone was assembled and ready. Wiley had borrowed a horse to ride in place of his own mule. It was getting close to noon, and I questioned Curt about the advisability of moving out during daylight, but he indicated the scouts were anxious to get started. Grouard and Big Bat had ridden fifteen or twenty miles from camp a couple of evenings before and had seen three small bands of Sioux, so we knew the area was fairly crawling with war parties.

Wilder reported to Major Zimmer as ordered. "Ready to move out, Major."

"Very well, Captain."

Nothing more was said. Wilder gave a hand signal, wheeled his horse, and led our detail out of camp.

We rode out about thirteen miles, generally following the base of the foothills of the Big Horns in a north-westerly direction. At sundown we stopped on the banks of Goose Creek to rest and let the horses graze. We finished a quick supper, taking care to build a small fire with very little smoke. Just at dusk we saddled up again. Big Bat was scraping dirt onto the fire. Suddenly his head jerked up and he stared intently toward a shallow ravine ahead and to our left.

"Saw something move over there. Just saw it for a second before it disappeared. Looked like a horseman, from what I could see."

Frank Grouard was in the saddle instantly and his horse plunged away toward the spot. We could hear his hoofbeats fade into the gathering darkness.

Less than ten minutes later he was back, reining up his horse and dismounting. "Got away. Too dark to follow him."

"Reckon it was a single scout, Frank?" Big Bat asked.

"Don't rightly know. Way it was movin', it might not have even been a horse."

"What, then?"

"Could've been an antelope, or a stray elk."

The guides discussed this possibility for a minute, and decided that's probably what it was. Nevertheless, as we started off again at a slow walk, they appeared very uneasy. I didn't know how the soldiers in the detail were feeling, but I felt that if men with as much Indian experience as Frank Grouard and "Big Bat" Baptiste Pourier were uneasy, it meant that there was sure as hell something to be uneasy about.

Details of the terrain were obscured by the darkness, but Grouard seemed to know exactly where we were. He constantly rode out ahead to keep lookout from every vantage point. The moon rose behind us about eight P.M. and bathed everything in a ghostly light. The detail rode in total silence through the long grass. Now and then we startled up sage hens, and the sudden commotion made our hearts jump into our throats. The crunching of our horses hooves over the pebbles in the shallow streams we crossed was the only sound we heard.

Finally, about two o'clock in the morning, we bivouacked in a grassy area among several small bluffs.

We were now about forty miles from camp, and according to the scouts, the valley of the Little Big Horn lay just a few miles farther on. Wilder posted pickets on the low heights around us to guard against any surprise attack, and the rest of us went to sleep.

By seven o'clock we were up and on our way. It was full daylight and we pressed on cautiously several more miles toward the valley. About ten, Frank Grouard halted our detail by silently lifting his hand and pulling up his mount. Then he rode on about fifty yards, dismounted and ground-reined his horse below the crest of a low ridge directly in front of us. We watched him quietly creep up the slope of the ridge, remove his hat, and slide his head up just far enough to peer over. He watched intently for a few seconds and then slid back down and signaled for Big Bat to join him. The two of them made a careful survey with their field glasses from behind some boulders on the summit. Then they came sliding back down the ridge, mounted and rode quickly back to us. They reined up in a swirl of dust, their horses dancing in a circle.

"Follow me," Grouard said over his shoulder, "and ride for your lives!"

He and Baptiste spurred away and we galloped off, single file, after them, the adrenalin pumping. There was no time for questions; we didn't know what they had seen. Grouard led us through red sandstone bluffs at a breakneck pace, but I never lost a sense of confidence in my big bay as we had to jump our horses down several ledges six or seven feet high. Jenkins rode right behind me, handling his cavalry mount skillfully.

My bay was barely breathing hard by the time Frank drew us to a halt on the westerly side of a bluff that was big enough to conceal our horses. The four of us with field glasses—Grouard, Pourier, Wilder, and I—dismounted and climbed up into the rocks to survey our backtrail.

"What did you see, Frank?" Wilder asked, as we flattened out in the crevices and focused our glasses.

"A big Sioux war party. I knew Sitting Bull's bunch

was in the Little Big Horn valley before we even started."

It was hardly two or three minutes before several small groups of mounted Sioux appeared on the low bluffs. They leapt into focus through the twin lenses, and I caught my breath at the apparent nearness of the savage faces and the lean, brown bodies. They were decorated in war paint, wearing eagle feathers, carrying shields, and armed with bows, lances, war clubs, and Winchesters. I could feel a coldness down my spine at seeing this dread sight again. More and more of them appeared every second and seemed to cover the bluffs to the north and east.

"I don't think they've seen us," Grouard whispered. "If they don't cut our trail, we're reasonably safe."

I held my breath as the loose line of warriors moved down the slopes, angling away to our right. Abruptly, one brave, attired in a red and black blanket, stopped and stared at the ground for a few seconds. Then he rode quickly around in tight circles, waving his blanket, indicating he had found something.

"Damn!" Grouard pounded his fist savagely into the earth. "We're in for it now. They've spotted our tracks."

"Maybe they'll think it's a few days old," I suggested hopefully, in spite of the sinking feeling in my stomach.

He dismissed this idea with a snort of contempt.

"Can't fool an Indian about a thing like that. They can read that trail like you can read a newspaper." As he spoke he was slipping his field glasses back into their case.

"What now, Frank?" Wilder asked calmly, deferring to the more experienced scout.

"We've got only one chance," Grouard answered, "and that is to ride straight up into the mountains and try to shake them or discourage them from following. If they catch us and we have to stand and fight, well . . ."

"Yeh, I know," Wilder finished, as we started our climb back down the slope. "I'm glad all these men are volunteers."

Wiley handed me the reins of my bay and I swung up. Curt Wilder and the scouts also mounted.

"The Sioux have picked up our trail," Curt announced to the two-dozen blue-clad soldiers sitting their horses around him. "Our scouts know these mountains and we're going to do our damndest to escape together. If we have to fight, I expect the best from every man. The Sioux give no quarter to prisoners, so there will be no surrender."

Several heads nodded solemnly.

"The Sioux run a close second to the Apache when it comes to torture," Grouard added. "Let's go, Captain. They'll be after us inside of five minutes."

We thundered off, charging straight up a steep, rough hillside. When we got above the level of the ridge, we could see the Indians to our right, almost a mile away. They had caught sight of us. A quick glance over my shoulder fixed a picture in my mind of clustered Indians pointing in our direction. Then I looked no more. It took all my concentration to stay closed up with the detail, which was really making time. I was leaning over my horse's neck, giving him all the help I could as he scrambled up the steep mountainside, kicking loose stones down behind him.

After about ten minutes Grouard pulled us up on a fairly level spot to let our horses blow a minute. "This is an old hunting path that leads into the high snow country," he said, indicating the faint trail that wound unevenly through the trees and out of sight along the face of the mountainside. "I hunted with the Sioux up here when I was a captive. We'll have to string out single file to follow it."

Without further talk he spurred his horse to a gallop, and the rest of us fell into line, Captain Wilder after the scouts, the soldiers next, followed by me and Wiley Jenkins bringing up the rear. The trail was fairly good for not being well used, but we shortly slowed to a fast trot to save the horses and to avoid their tripping on fallen timber. We rode this way for about five miles, as near as I could estimate. When Grouard saw no sign of any pursuing Indians, he again halted the column. I could see him talking to Wilder. Then the captain turned and called out, "Dismount and unsaddle. We'll rest awhile."

We were in a beautiful, grassy area with ample shade among scattered pines on a gentle mountain slope.

"You reckon this is safe, stopping here?" Wiley asked, glancing back along the empty trail.

"The scouts seem to think so, and that's good enough for me," I replied, pulling off the saddle and blanket and dropping them on the ground. The horses trotted off to graze and roll gratefully in the grass. Some of the men had already gathered a few handfuls of dry pine needles and sticks and were about to light a small fire to boil some coffee they carried in their saddlebags. Wiley and I joined Captain Wilder, Big Bat, and Grouard. We all stretched out in the grass to smoke our pipes and wait for the coffee to boil.

"That was close," I remarked to Frank. "It's sure good to be able to relax."

"They either weren't interested in chasing a small detail like ours, or they don't want to fight in these higher altitudes," he replied. "At least that was the case when I was livin' with them. They hunted up here, but they preferred to fight in the lowlands."

I lay back in the grass and closed my eyes, feeling the warm sun slanting between two trees. Gone was the heat of the valley; the air at this altitude was pleasant and fresh with the scent of pine.

"Ah, this is the life," Wiley said, with a trace of his old verve. "Sure beats sweltering around camp."

In a few minutes the coffee was done, and we got our tin cups and filled them from the smoke-blackened pot. Those who preferred sugar had brought along a little in tiny, drawstring sacks. The soldiers, in their dark blue pants with the yellow stripes and their light blue shirts, sat cross-legged on the grass with their hats off, sipping their coffee and chatting quietly. Handpicked and hardened veterans, they were all lean and toughened by many marches and skirmishes, even though most of them were still on the shy side of thirty.

When we finally saddled up and moved on, it was early afternoon, but the hour or so we had spent was well worth it, since both horses and men were rested and refreshed. The trail led us gently up and down, angling across the face of the mountains. For a time we passed through dense stands of pine and fir. Then, the trail would lead out into an open mountain meadow with plenty of grass. Then, for a while, we would pass a part of the trail that was bordered on the uphill side by massive slabs of rock and boulders as big as houses, with stunted pines clingling to the crevasses in the rocks.

We rode down into a wide, open mountain valley and could see a big range of snowy peaks towering above, an unknown number of miles ahead. At the bottom of this valley, we were forced to pull off our boots and sling them around our necks to swim our horses across a clear, cold stream. Grouard wasn't sure if this was one of the main tributaries of the Tongue or a tributary of the Little Big Horn. We rode up the opposite bank in single file, and soon the magnificent view of the snowcapped mountains was cut off by trees again.

A half-hour later we were riding along a level corridor bounded by woods on our left and in front, and by rocks and timber on our right. Wiley was lagging about forty yards behind me at the time, while the rest of us were spaced out in open order about ten yards apart.

"Indians! Indians!"

I heard Wiley's voice behind me and the next second he shot past me at a gallop, pointing over his shoulder. We looked back and saw a mounted war party riding parallel to us through the timber, less than three hundred yards away and coming fast.

"Stay close to the woods on the left!" Grouard yelled to Captain Wilder, and just as we spurred our horses to obey, a volley of shots cracked.

My bay stumbled momentarily from the shock of a

bullet but regained his balance and needed no further urging to make for the woods. More shots followed us into the trees, slightly wounding two or three of the horses. Just as we reached cover and slid to the ground, Wilder ordered several of the troopers to return the fire. This slowed up the charge and halted the Indians in the rocks across the open space, which at that point was less than a hundred yards away.

"Hobble some of those horses to the trees right on the edge here," Wilder ordered. "Then form a skirmish line in a semicircle."

Luckily, we had a lot of fallen timber that formed excellent natural fortifications, and we all began firing from the protection of these tree trunks. I gave Wiley my Winchester, figuring he could hit more with that than with the old Spencer he had, or a handgun. I was using my Colt.

After a minute or so of heavy firing, Wilder held up his hand. "Hold your fire, men." The heavy explosions of .45 cartridges died spasmodically and the crashing echoes faded into the mountain stillness. "No sense wasting ammunition. They're holed up in the rocks over there."

The Indians also gradually stopped firing, seeing we were well entrenched. Then, after a moment, apparently in the hope of stampeding us, they started firing volley after volley. Bullets came zipping and humming through the overhead branches like angry wasps. We made sure no parts of us were showing, as the bullets sent chips of bark flying and thudded into trunks of the big pines.

The shooting stopped again, suddenly, and we looked out cautiously to see our poor horses bleeding from several more minor wounds. One sorrel was down and apparently kicking in his last agony. The trooper closest to him, without exposing himself, fired a shot through the animal's head to end its suffering.

"Good thing most Indians are notoriously poor marksmen," Wilder remarked, "or it would be more than horses wounded."

"Since they can't hit us, they're probably killing the horses to set us afoot," Grouard said.

Using his binoculars, Wilder took a closer look at the savages who were moving among the rocks. "Well, they're not the same bunch we shook back aways. See that one with the big warbonnet and all dressed in white?" he asked Grouard.

"Yes."

"I believe that's White Elk, one of the Cheyenne war chiefs. I've had a run-in with him before, about two years ago down on Crazy Woman's Fork. He's a notorious white-hater—would kill any white on sight, just for the hell of it. No quarter given and none expected. And there's no doubt about his bravery. He was one of the leaders of the raids against Fort C. F. Smith a few years back. I hear tell he's got more scars on his body than the floor of the Elkhorn Saloon after a Saturday night brawl."

"Looks like they're getting ready to mount an attack," I said. No sooner were the words out of my mouth than they came charging out of the timber, yelling and shooting, led by White Elk, his long warbonnet flowing out behind him.

But our seasoned men coolly stood their ground. At a signal from Wilder, a sheet of orange flame erupted with a roar from our cover. The charge was instantly broken and two or three of the Indians fell from their ponies. White Elk went reeling in his saddle and two Cheyenne braves rode alongside to support him, as the warriors broke and ran for cover in the rocks again. We poured another volley at the few who were brave enough to circle around and drag off their fallen comrades. But it had little effect since they were careful to keep their horses between us and were moving at a pretty good clip.

There was no cheering from our men. We knew it was only the first round.

"Somebody got White Elk, I think," Grouard said. "Couldn't tell how bad he was hit, but he'll be out of action for the rest of this fight, if I'm any judge."

"That should dampen their enthusiasm for a while," Wilder said, turning the cylinder of his smoking Colt and working the ejecter with the other hand. "We're still in a helluva fix. A good fifty miles from camp. Cut off, and nobody knows where we are. Even if we could get somebody out after dark to go for help, it'd be at least two days getting back to us."

"Just in time for them to keep the wolves from eatin' the rest of our carcasses," Big Bat finished.

"I thought it was a little strange they charged us like that," Grouard said, "but I think I see the reason for it now." He pointed. "Here come some of their Sioux allies to join them. White Elk's band wanted to show their brothers their bravery and maybe rout us out before the Sioux had a chance."

More riders were arriving and dismounting in the cover on the far side of the clearing. Looking around, I noticed the men getting a little edgy as they realized the trap we were in was growing tighter.

Some shooting started again from the other side and was answered sporadically from our side, as the troopers spotted a target here and there. For this kind of sniping, they used their Springfield, breech-loading, single-shot carbines. These were accurate up to six hundred yards. But for rapid firing they had to fall back on their single-action Colts. During a lull in the firing one of the newly arrived Sioux recognized Grouard and yelled across at him. "Standing Bear, why do you bring the long knives here? Do you think the white eyes are the only people in this country?" The brave spat derisively.

Grouard's only answer was to draw a bead on the distant Indian and squeeze off a shot. The slug ricocheted off a rock about a foot from the Sioux's arm, and we laughed at the way he scrambled for better cover. But the laughter died quickly, and with the arrival of the Sioux, the battle settled down to a siege. The Indians seemed to have plenty of ammunition and kept up a more or less steady fire, along with a lot of yelling. The noise of the battle was attracting other Indians from several miles away. We could see the increasing numbers moving on horseback and afoot among the boulders and trees, spreading out toward our flanks. Like a bulldog who only shifts his grip to get a better one, they were consolidating their position and gradually working their way around us. Time dragged, agonizingly. Though no one as yet admitted it aloud, we all realized after about an hour that our situation was critical.

Sergeant Killard, from Wilder's Company B, stood on my left only a few feet behind the same fallen pine. I looked over at him. "Well?" I nodded toward the clearing. "What do you think?"

"When I left home to enlist, my mother told me there would come a day like this," he commented. "But she thought it would come about a week after I joined, instead of fifteen years later." He spat out his worn-out chew of tobacco and wiped his mouth with the back of his hand. The perennial twinkle had disappeared from his eyes. "I tell you one thing," he vowed, "they'll never take me alive. If need be, I'll save the last shot for myself."

The tone of his voice left no doubt that he was serious. Several of the other soldiers within earshot muttered their agreement. I saw one or two farther down the line bow their heads on their carbines. To be struck down in the heat of battle is one thing, but to have to sit and look death in the face and wait for its icy grip to close on your throat is something few men can do without some show of emotion. I felt a knot in the pit of my stomach. Wiley hadn't said a word. His lips were compressed in a grim line; his only display of feeling was the taut grip of his hands on the rifle I had given him.

At that moment, I would have given anything to be back safe and sound—and bored—in General Buck's camp. I had been a fool to beg to come along. And because of me, Wiley Jenkins, the one who detested violence probably more than anyone in camp, would die a violent death. None of us would ever see another sunrise. The sight of my mutilated body kept jumping before my mind's eye—and I knew a stark, cold fear.

My knees felt weak and I sat down on the ground. Life had never seemed so precious to me as now, when I was about to lose it.

To calm my sudden panic, I pulled out my notebook, opened it, and wrote some brief lines explaining our situation. Maybe someone would eventually find it and know what had happened to us. Just before I closed it, I impulsively picked some mountain crocus and forget-me-nots growing close by and flattened them between the leaves. I don't know why I did it, since I'm not particularly fascinated by flowers. Maybe it was just a last, desperate attempt to grasp and hold on to something alive and blooming.

The sun was sliding toward the west, and I watched the afternoon shadows growing longer, knowing it was the last sunlight I would ever see in this world.

CHAPTER
Fifteen

WILDER had not given up. He called the scouts over and asked for information on the surrounding area and whether there was any chance of sneaking out of there.

"Captain," Grouard began, brushing away the leaves and pine needles to expose a patch of bare earth, "the passes are cut off on the east, north, and west by Indians." He drew some markings on the ground with his Bowie knife, indicating our relative positions. "Even if our horses were all in good shape, we'd never be able to outrun them on horseback. If the grass was a little drier, I'm sure they'd try to burn us out—one of their favorite tricks. With all the resin in these trees . . ." He straightened up and sheathed his knife. "We're in a hopeless position here."

Wilder thought a moment. "Could we make it if we left the horses?"

"Possible. Just barely. But it's the only chance we got."

"That's right," Big Bat agreed. "They're just toyin' with us now. Takin' their time. They'll attack sometime before dark when they get in position. We gotta do somethin' now, or it's all over."

It was either an heroic stand to the death, or a slipping away to fight another day—if we could get away. I know at least some officers who would have stayed to make a fight of it, but thank God Wilder had more sense.

"Sergeant." He turned to Killard. "Pass the word for the men to quietly take all the ammunition they can carry out of their saddlebags. Then, in single file, I want them to follow the scouts."

I had heard the order, and Wiley and I moved to obey without a word. As I got the cartridges and stuffed my pockets with them, I patted my bay. He was bleeding from a wound, and I felt sorry to have to leave him. But it couldn't be helped.

Wiley and I filed past Captain Wilder who was waiting to leave last, to be sure all his men were accounted for. He kept four soldiers with him, and when we were about a hundred yards back into the rocks, we heard some random shots and then two or three volleys to fool the Indians into thinking we were all still in position. Our horses still stood in plain sight of the Indians. This, plus the fact that we had been holding our fire for short periods, allowed us to retreat into the thick timber and rocks without our absence being noticed right away.

We were moving quietly, but quickly, through the woods, filled with boulders and fallen pines. We were forced to crawl over, under, and squeeze through places no horse could ever follow. When we had gone about a mile, Wilder and his four marksmen caught up to us, panting hard, and we all forded a branch of the Tongue River, wading up to our waists in the icy water. Then we began climbing the slippery rocks on the other side.

"Damn mountain goat would have trouble with this," Wiley grunted, as his foot slipped and he grabbed for a handhold to catch himself.

A few minutes of scrambling up that steep incline was all we could do before we stopped and gasped for breath. Five or six volleys of sudden gunfire crashed and echoed and reverberated through the mountain canyons.

"They're probably charging our position," Grouard said.

"I'd like to see the look on their faces." Wilder grinned.

"I hear losing face is not one of the things an Indian does best," Jenkins added.

"Let's get some more distance between us while we have the daylight," Wilder said.

The big guide took off again. I tried to keep up as he leapt from rock to rock above me, sometimes grabbing a handhold on a bush. The man was indefatigable. He was about six feet two inches, slim-hipped, and appeared to be about two hundred pounds of supple muscle. He was hatless and dressed in shirt and trousers of soft, tanned doeskin. His feet must have been taking a fearful beating since they were protected from the rocks only by rawhide moccasins that had been further softened by a soaking in the river. But he kept up a half-running lope, uphill and down, that made us all strain to keep pace.

The late afternoon weather was sultry. There was no breeze and there had been a light shower earlier in the day. We were all sweating and soaking the rest of our clothes that hadn't been wet in the river. Climbing and crawling and scrambling, it was all we could do to carry our rifles and what was left of our ammunition. We kept up this pace until almost midnight, heading generally in a southeast direction. But then we were forced to stop from absolute exhaustion. We curled up to sleep near the top of a high ridge, protected a little by an overhanging rock ledge.

But we had hardly fallen into fatigued oblivion when a terrific crash of thunder woke us to a storm sweeping across the mountains. It was almost as if Nature had been waiting for us to doze in order to catch us off guard. A sudden blast of cold wind was followed by solid sheets of rain, driven almost horizontally.

"God! That's too cold to be rain," Wiley shouted into my ear, as we scrambled back with the rest of the troop to flatten ourselves against the granite wall that was partially sheltered by the overhang. And, sure enough, the rain quickly changed to hail. The pounding pellets of ice bounced and rattled off every rock around us, sounding as loud as someone throwing gravel onto a tin roof.

The wind began to gust even more strongly, and we heard crashing, banging, and popping explosions as the pine trees on the slopes below us were broken off or were uprooted and fell. Over the noise of the hail, it sounded like artillery fire. We clung to our pitiful shelter, freezing, shaking, and in awe of this fearsome display of power. But the storm finally passed over, and we huddled together for the rest of the night in a vain attempt to keep warm. The few matches among us were soaked and useless. And even if they hadn't been, there was nothing dry enough to burn. All blankets, tent shelters, and jackets had been left behind.

"Well, at least this should have pounded our trail to a mush," Wilder remarked cheerfully, and since we were eager to get started, we moved off again behind the scouts as soon as it was light enough for us to see.

Just after sunrise we reached the top of a tremendous canyon, cut through the mountain by a branch of the Tongue River. The scouts estimated we were still about twenty-five miles from camp. Most of us were not equal to the climb straight down to the river and up the other side, so Grouard took a chance and led us down a fairly open path to the riverbank. The walking was easy, but we were stepping pretty lively, since we would have been caught without a chance if any Indians had seen us. But we got across to the right bank with no trouble.

"Sure wish I could just walk along the riverbank right out there," Wiley said, indicating the river cutting its way through the lower foothills to the east and then reappearing to sight as a winding thread far out on the plains.

But Grouard had other ideas. He led us up a trail that narrowed to about a foot and a half in width as it angled diagonally across the face of the canyon wall. At several points we hardly dared look down since the rock face fell away almost sheer beneath our feet about five hundred feet to the river and went straight up above our heads another two hundred feet or so. Several times the trail was so narrow we had to flatten our faces to the perpendicular wall, and inch our way along for a few yards.

Wiley's hat brim was crushed against the sheer rock. The hat flipped up and off his head. He made a quick, backhanded grab at it, but missed. Out of the corner of my eye, I saw it sailing out into the dizzy space below our feet. "Damn!" he panted, the sweat trickling down his face. "We escaped getting shot or scalped just to have the fun of falling off a cliff and spreading ourselves all over the landscape."

"Shut up," one of the soldiers growled, without looking around.

It took us nearly an hour to reach the crest where we were able to see, in the distance, the mountain that overlooked our camp. Jutting up in the clear sunlight, it looked fairly close, but the guides assured us it was a good twenty miles away.

"Man, that looks mighty good," Sergeant Killard said.

"Might as well be the moon, for what good it'll do me," another soldier said weakly, sinking to the ground.

"I sure as hell didn't train in the infantry, or on an empty stomach," a corporal named Boyle added. "My folks came here from the heavenly isle because we were hungry, and here I am, thirty years later, performin' a starvation march in their honor. Disgustin'!"

After a short rest of about ten minutes, Wilder ordered us up and moving before anyone had time to get settled. The scouts wanted to move fast until we reached the eastern foothills before we slowed down. Then we could work our way southwest toward camp through a little easier terrain.

But thirst was the immediate problem.

The big scout led us down toward the river again for

a drink. The steep slopes were covered with slick pine needles and loose shale, so as often as not, we were sliding on our rumps or our hands and feet, since it was impossible to walk upright.

We slaked our thirst with the cold water and had just gotten about halfway back up the slope and into the cover of the trees, when the sharp-eyed Grouard said "Sshhh!" and threw himself flat on the ground, facing north. "Get down!" he hissed.

All of us obeyed instantly and without a word. In a few seconds we saw a party of Sioux come into view across the river and below us. They were riding leisurely in single file from around the point of the opposite canyon wall.

"By God, make every shot count if they see us," Wilder whispered hoarsely.

We were so tired we knew we couldn't run. At this point we were so irritated from fatigue and hunger, we were almost eager for a fight. We had the courage of desperation. Barely breathing, we gripped our rifles and carbines, froze as immobile as the boulders on the hillside, and awaited the outcome. The long, loose column came slowly on, apparently unaware of our presence. But they trailed on past, not looking our way, and went winding on down the river trail and out of sight toward the foothills.

As soon as the tension was lifted, we felt twice as tired as before. We could walk only a few paces back into the trees before we all, almost as one, flopped down and fell sound asleep. When I opened my eyes, the sun had disappeared and darkness was fast closing down around our bedraggled group of fugitives. The ever-alert Grouard and Big Bat were on guard.

"Captain, the men are pretty well used up," Frank said quietly to Wilder, as the rest of the men were being roused from their stupor. "I don't think they'll make it if we stick to the mountains."

"You're right. I'm about done in myself." He scrubbed a hand over the dark stubble on his lean

cheeks. "I'm leaving it up to your judgment as to how
we get back. But I think we have to sacrifice safety to
speed at this point."

"All right, Captain. We'll strike straight down out of
the mountains and head directly across the plains to
camp. We'll just have to chance the Indians seeing us.
If we push it, we can get most of the way before daylight."

So, with aching muscles and bruised feet and concave
bellies, we started once more. A deadly fatigue seemed
to drag at me like invisible weights. I no longer felt
hunger pains—just a constant desire to rest. After
stumbling along numbly in the scouts' footsteps for
what seemed like forever, we finally reached Big Goose
Creek at the base of the mountains about three A.M. We
forded the stream, wading up to our necks in the icy
water. Three or four men lost their footing on the slippery rocks and were carried downstream several yards
before they could swim to the bank and flounder out.

Two privates who couldn't swim absolutely refused
to cross. No amount of persuasion or coaxing or reas-
surance could move them. The fear of drowning in that
swift, black water, sliding by in the moonlight, overrode
any fear of Indians, starvation, or anything else. So we
finally left them there to hide in the underbrush and
promised we would send someone back for them. We
were all pretty far gone, so it was fortunate we were at
least walking on level ground.

Dawn broke early as the light spread up over the
plains. At five A.M. we spotted several Indians on
horseback to the east of us. I'm sure they saw us, too,
but they made no move in our direction. Even though
we were on foot, they may have mistaken us for outly-
ing pickets from General Buck's camp.

My boots were split at the seams, and the right sole
had partially separated from the boot, allowing stones
and dirt to be scooped in at every shuffling step. It was
aggravating to be walking on small, sharp pebbles, but I
was too tired to stop and empty them every few steps. I
just gritted my teeth and ignored the pain as Wiley and

I stumbled along, sometimes leaning on each other. We were all so exhausted, it took us four hours to cover about six miles.

About six-thirty we spotted two horses grazing on a little knoll. The carbines shining in the saddle boots told us they were cavalry horses. The two soldiers rose up out of the tall grass and went for their guns before they recognized us. They turned out to be men from the 2nd Cavalry who had been given permission to go hunting. They were working their way toward the Tongue River. It was just as fortunate for them as it was for us that we met before they got any farther. Wilder sent them back to camp for some food and transportation. He also instructed them to ask that an escort be sent to pick up the two privates we had left at Big Goose Creek.

Unable to walk anymore, we flopped down and awaited their return. About an hour and a half later they reappeared, along with Captain Stubblefield and Captain Anderson, leading horses for us and carrying what looked and smelled like cooked provisions.

"Have you ever seen anything that looked so good in all your life?" I asked Wiley.

He grinned wearily back at me. "Never."

CHAPTER
Sixteen

IT was a joyous homecoming. We were welcomed back into camp like returning heroes. And I can't even find the words to express the joy of living that overcame me on that sunny Monday morning, July 10.

After a good bath in the creek and a change of clothes, I felt almost like a new man, but still very tired as I sat down to eat with the rest of the detail. While bathing, I had caught a glimpse of my reflection in the waters of Goose Creek and was startled at the shimmering image that stared back at me. It was the gaunt, bearded face of a stranger. As soon as I had eaten, I borrowed a razor, scissors and Wilder's tiny mirror. I gave myself a good, close shave and then trimmed as much of my hair as I could see.

The rest of the day we rested and were besieged over and over by various members of the command to repeat the story of our narrow squeak. Most of our audiences whistled, shook their heads in disbelief, and looked at us like we were men returned from the dead. General Buck was out of camp on one of his frequent hunts in the adjacent mountains. But Colonel Peterman, who was in charge in his absence, was lavish in his praise of Frank Grouard and Big Bat for their cool judgment in leading our escape. He was also complimentary about

Captain Wilder for having the good sense to take the scouts' advice. That's why what followed later in the day came as such a surprise to me. In the general celebration, I had missed seeing Wilder for a time. But about three he came into our tent, where I was stretched out, dozing in the afternoon heat. He sat down heavily on the opposite cot and blew out a long, tired sigh.

I opened one eye. "Why the long face? I'm still giving thanks I'm alive and well, even though I'm pretty irritated that my only toothbrush was in my saddlebags."

"Well, I'm thankful too. But if the Sioux had scalped me, it would've deprived Zimmer of the pleasure."

"Oh, no. Not again."

"He called me into his tent and really chewed me out for leading my patrol into a 'trap.' Called me an incompetent nincompoop who wasn't fit to command troops. Said I ought to be court-martialed for being so lax. 'Course that was just bluff since Colonel Peterman has publicly commended the scouts, and me, too, indirectly."

"I don't think it was anybody's fault. But the scouts led us into that; you didn't. We were ordered to find the Indians, and we did."

"I know. But, as the officer in charge, I had the veto power over any recommendations of the civilian guides. Frankly, Matt, we both know that neither of us would be sitting here now if it weren't for those two scouts."

"Sounds like being acting C.O. of the 3rd has gone straight to Zimmer's head. Just throwing his weight around again."

"Unfortunately, he's not man enough for the job, in my opinion. Wonder why it is that the light-headed ones always seem to rise to the top."

"Well, give him enough time and he'll hang himself. His type usually does."

"I don't know if I can wait that long."

The strange tone of his voice made me glance sharply at him. But his downcast face told me nothing. "Were there any witnesses to this tongue-lashing?"

"No."

"Then forget it. If anything develops from it later, it's be your word against his. You heard what Colonel Peterman said about the 'Wilder Scout,' as they're beginning to call this action. Zimmer wouldn't dare write up an official reprimand after that. He's just trying to keep you rattled and let you know he's still the boss. But, without even trying, you've hit him in his most sensitive spot."

"Oh? Where's that?"

"In his pride. You've stolen the limelight from him for the time being."

"You're right." He grinned. "I hadn't thought about it that way. T'hell with him." He rose and stretched. "Man, I ache all over. I imagine I'll feel even worse in the morning. It's going to take a day or two for me to get over this."

"Have you seen Cathy since we got back?" I ventured.

"No." The smile disappeared from his face. "Think I'll let that matter rest, at least for now. She's apparently made her choice."

"Oh, don't be so damn stiff. You sound like somebody's maiden aunt. Go after her. I dare you to take her away from Zimmer," I challenged, "provided Zimmer even has the inside track with her. What better way to get the old bastard in his pride again?"

"I don't want to make a fool of myself running after some young girl who's not interested in me."

I shrugged. "Well, suit yourself. If you're not interested, I might try, myself."

"Really?"

I couldn't keep a straight face at his pained expression. "No," I laughed. "There's an Irish girl in Chicago I've got my eye on. Cathy's not really my type."

We heard some commotion outside as some horses

approached. We went out and saw General Buck and several of his aides riding in from their hunt. Their horses were loaded down with elk, deer, and mountain sheep, and the hunting party was being escorted in by two companies of the 3rd.

"Why the big escort?" I asked Wilder.

"Colonel Peterman sent them out to get General Buck right after we came in this morning. Apparently, some Crows came into camp yesterday with a garbled tale about a big battle where all the soldiers were killed. Couldn't make much of it through the interpreters, Shanahan said. But when we came in with our story, Colonel Peterman got mighty uneasy and sent for the general."

"Looks like all that game will take care of our fresh-meat problems for a while," I remarked, as the general's party dismounted, and several soldiers took charge of their mounts and began unloading the field-dressed carcasses from the pack horses. Just then the two privates we had left behind at Big Goose Creek were brought into camp and were greeted by everyone with a welcome like we had received earlier.

General Buck dismounted and went into his tent, followed by Colonel Peterman. The general took the news of our scout and the Crow story of another big battle with his usual stoic air. In fact, his reaction was the same the next morning when Louis Richaud and some half-breeds rode in from Fort Fetterman with official dispatches that confirmed the rumor about a big battle. Custer and five companies of the 7th had been wiped out at the Little Big Horn River only a week after and thirty miles north of our own encounter on the Rosebud. Richaud gave our shocked command the details of the disaster after delivering the official account to the general.

"Just like that damn Custer to take two hundred and sixty good soldiers with him when he departed," Wilder remarked to me. "Sounds like the arrogant bastard disregarded orders and tried to grab all the glory for him-

self without reporting back and waiting for reinforcements. Well, the army is better off without him, but I'm
afraid certain people will make a posthumous hero of
him, and we'll never really be rid of him."

"Y'know, that could've been us if we had gotten far
enough north to hit that big village we were after."

"Or that disaster might never have happened if we
had gotten through to Terry on the Yellowstone."

"Well, so much for the 'might have beens.' We know
where they're massed now. Our 'scout' confirmed it,
even if we hadn't heard about this. The question is,
what is the general going to do about it?"

We glanced toward our bearded commander, who
was just then scanning one of the telegrams Richaud
had delivered. General Buck snorted and stuffed the
paper into his pocket. He looked up and saw us watching him. "General Sheridan sends his regards and his
compliments on our action against the Sioux. He tells
me to hit them again—and harder. I wish he'd make a
trip out here from Chicago and show us how to surround three Indians with one soldier." With that disgusted comment he walked off to his tent with a fistful
of dispatches to digest at his leisure.

There was a lot of talk pro and con among the officers for the rest of the day about Custer's actions, with
Major Zimmer and Lieutenant Shanahan among those
who defended the unconventional cavalry leader. Wilder
said little on the subject to avoid any useless arguments
with his messmate and any further problems with the
volatile George Zimmer.

The next day the Snake Indians—213 of them—
returned as they had promised: They were still under
the command of their old chief Washakie and his two
sons. Their reappearance surprised me, but I kept it to
myself. I had long since reconciled myself to the unpre-
dictable whims of all Indians and never expected the
Shoshones to keep such a long-term promise. Nevertheless, General Buck was glad to see them since they had
proven themselves good fighters, and they swelled our
numbers.

The following day, the thirteenth, our wagon train arrived from Fort Fetterman, escorted by seven companies of infantry from the 4th, 9th, and 14th Regiments. A whiskey peddler came in, unobtrusively, with the train. Some of the men and officers, who had been in the field about two months without a drink, didn't waste any time giving the peddler all the business he could handle. And this was no moderate drinking. They were making up for lost time. A few of them, who had the money and the urge, got thoroughly drunk. In fact, one of the captains named Ryan, whom I had seen around but only casually met, got drunk on duty and failed to place his pickets properly. He was promptly arrested by Major Zimmer and tried in the field. He was relieved of his command and ordered back to Fort Fetterman with a choice of resigning his commission or being court-martialed.

"Isn't that penalty a little harsh?" I asked Wilder, as we watched the disgraced captain being escorted, under guard, out of camp the next morning after breakfast.

"Yes. Ryan's a fine, conscientious officer. I hate to see his career go down the drain like that because of one mistake. But I guess General Buck figures he has to maintain discipline by making an example of him. We are in the field under battle conditions, what with those braves sniping at us the past few nights."

"Placing those pickets wasn't really his job, was it?"

"Not directly. But it's his responsibility to see to it that his sergeants get it done. Of course, the noncoms don't, as a rule, need any supervision about something routine like that."

"Well, routine or not, the pickets have been keeping those Indians from making off with our horses these past few nights."

"You're right." He blew into his tin cup and sipped his coffee tentatively. "Those little night raids we've been getting aren't really dangerous. Just one or two Indians at a time using it for a little sport. Showing their bravery by trying to slip past the sentries, maybe run off a few horses, and keep us on edge, knowing they're close by."

"By the way, what happened to that whiskey peddler?"

"He was a civilian, so General Buck couldn't arrest him, but he confiscated all the whiskey and ran him out of camp."

"Those several barrels of whiskey'd better be well locked up, or somebody's sure to be into them."

"I doubt if anybody in uniform will try it again after seeing the punishment the men got, and what happened to Ryan."

"Zimmer's walking around like the King of the Mountain since he got rid of Ryan."

"I wonder if he really thinks he's enforcing discipline or is just one of those self-centered bastards who's not happy unless he's playing 'Lord and Master' and abusing his power?"

"God knows."

Breakfast was just over the next morning and the camp was settling into its usual dull daily routine when we were surprised by the arrival of a Sergeant Stark and two privates. They were attached to the 7th Infantry and had managed to get through with dispatches from General Terry on the Yellowstone by traveling at night and hiding by day to avoid the hunting and war parties that infested the country. But they reported they had crossed no large, recently made Indian trails. Sergeant Stark brought more details of the Custer disaster.

General Buck called his staff officers into his tent with the couriers, and they didn't come out for over an hour. I wasn't privileged to be part of this conference, but Wilder briefed me later at supper. The "Wilder Scout" that I had been part of, along with the news from the messengers, convinced General Buck that a huge village must still be somewhere near the Little Big Horn valley where Custer had been wiped out. Even though we had been reinforced by the infantry from Fort Fetterman, the general still planned to delay taking the field again. General Merritt's 5th Cavalry was on its way in from near Red Cloud Agency to reinforce us also. Even Lieutenant Shanahan, who had been a staunch supporter of General Buck, was growing a little irritated and impatient with the continued hesitancy of our commanding officer to go against the Sioux.

General Buck sent the three couriers back to Terry two days later with some message I didn't get. My own dispatches, with eyewitness accounts of the "Wilder Scout," had gone back to the telegraph at Fetterman by way of a paid courier a few days before.

The camp, with the additional infantry and our Snake allies, settled into the same boring routine we had known before. But, as the last half of July rolled away, blistering days following each other as alike as clumps of sun-browned buffalo grass, I kept my vow to myself that I would never again be bored with life, no matter what my circumstances. In fact, I remarked to Wilder, after about ten days, that our near-disaster in the Big Horns almost seemed like a bad dream—as though we had never really been there at all.

"Huh! Some dream," he retorted. "If it was a nightmare, I'm glad I don't have them often. I might not wake up from the next one."

During these peaceful days I entertained myself by swimming, fishing for trout, reading everything I could lay my hands on, sleeping, eating, and generally taking it easy. I also did some makeshift repairs on my wardrobe, and was allowed to requisition a pair of cavalry boots to replace the ones that had been torn up beyond repair by our march out of the mountains. Since I had lost my horse and saddle, I didn't venture much beyond the confines of the camp.

I spent a lot of my time with Wiley Jenkins, playing cards, fishing or just talking. We had been through a lot together, but we didn't really know each other. As he gradually learned to trust me as a friend, he opened up, and behind the facile exterior, I caught glimpses of his past, his personality, his fears and ambitions. I discovered he had been asked to leave the University of Kentucky at the end of his sophomore year, after he pursued parties and girls with greater vigor than he had pursued his courses.

"Couldn't get interested enough in any particular field of study," he explained, passing the whole thing off with a wave of his hand, even though I could see it bothered him more than he wanted to let on. Apparently, it was this failure at college that precipitated the final break with his father. He had left home, clerked briefly at a Cincinnati dry-goods store, but quickly tired of this. Then he was drawn by the lure of the steamboats passing up and down the Ohio. He collected his savings, and booked river passage for St. Louis. In St. Louis he worked for a time as a stevedore and then took another steamboat to the upper Missouri. It was in the Dakota Territory that he first encountered the Plains Indians and the postwar army. And in the next four years, he traveled back and forth across the West, with frequent visits home to Kentucky. He had worked at every conceivable job, from railroading to driving a freight team. And it was during this time that he had picked up his skill as a mule packer.

In his disjointed narratives, he played down his various escapades with women, but I knew his handsome face, easy smile, and athlete's body were probably an irresistible lure to most women. He was widely read and literate, his interests tending toward philosophy, literature, and history, rather than to the sciences. This was probably another point of divergence from his engineer father.

We gradually drew Wilder into our company and the three of us spent more and more time together when Curt wasn't busy breaking up fistfights and handling discipline problems among the bored troopers in his company. It seemed to me he was becoming increasingly fed up with army life—although he seldom voiced his dissatisfactions. Since we were in the field, the routine drill of garrison life was absent, and the soldiers had even less to occupy their time. Old animosities flared. Desertions were being reported at muster every day, as some of the men decided they'd had all they could take. Even the officers were getting on each other's nerves. For the most part, they were expressing the frustration of General Buck, who conveyed this down through his battalion commanders to the officers to the noncoms. And the crushing weight of all this frustration, in the form of excessive discipline, fell on the hapless shoulders of the privates.

But not everyone was on edge. The Indians, the civilian packers and miners, and quite a number of the troopers were relaxed and enjoying the respite from the tension of marching and fighting. General Buck kept the scouts busy almost daily reconnoitering the area within several miles of camp. Indian hunting parties seemed to be everywhere.

"Must take a lot of meat to supply a massed gathering the size of the one on the Little Big Horn," Wilder said one noonday during one of our frequent discussions over a delicious meal of fresh trout.

"I never thought about that. Somehow, I forget they have to go about the same business of daily living we do—since I've only seen the warriors in a battle setting."

"Speaking of battle, I wonder if we're going to spend the rest of the summer camped right here. Some of the men have hauled in several wagonloads of rocks from the foothills and built a few fireplaces and chimneys for cooking. They're really making themselves at home," Lieutenant Shanahan said. "Hate to say it, but General Buck seems to have had the hell scared out of him by the Sioux and Cheyenne. Our stand off at the Rosebud and that Custer thing . . . I believe they've got him buffaloed."

I was a little surprised at Shanahan's appraisal. But he impressed me as a climber type, and if someone else,

"Well, if this isn't an ambitious crew!"

I squinted up into a shaft of sunlight that was streaming through the overhead trees. Wiley Jenkins was standing there, one of his slim Mexican cigars in his teeth.

"Join us," Wilder invited, "we've still got a little trout and cornbread left."

"No, thanks. Just ate. I'm here on business."

"Business?"

"Yea. On a little mission for Cupid. Cathy wants to see you, Curt."

"What?" He started, reddening slightly.

"Seems you haven't been around to see her lately."

"S'cuse me, gentlemen." Wilder got to his feet, looking a little discomfited, and dusted himself off. "I'll see you later."

Wiley and I looked at each other significantly. "I'm sure glad she finally took the initiative," I remarked when Curt was out of earshot. "He's been mooning around ever since we got back from that 'scout.'"

"So that's what's been wrong with him." Wiley sat down and picked at a cold piece of fish. "I don't pretend to know what's in my sister's mind, but I'd rather she'd be attracted to Curt than to anybody else around here I've met."

"But I thought she was taking up with Major Zimmer."

He shrugged, stubbing out his cigar in the dirt. "Don't know. I don't pay much attention to what she does or who she sees. Unless she asks for my help, I let her alone. She's a big girl now. I'm just repeating the message she asked me to deliver."

We cleaned up the leftovers, washed the dishes and loafed and smoked our pipes for over an hour while the camp slipped into its usual midday lethargy. As we talked and laughed, I was gradually struck by the strange fact that this young man—so much a mixture of the idealist and the realist—could have so much in common with Curt Wilder, who was about eight years commander or not, didn't come up to his standards of perfection, then he was quick to denounce him. "Somebody else thinks he's been buffaloed, too," I added.

"Oh?" Wilder looked up.

"Have you seen some of those newspapers the courier brought in?"

"Just glanced through one or two of them to find out what was going on in the rest of the world."

"Well, some of the editorials I read did everything but accuse the general of cowardice. And these papers were two weeks old. I can imagine what they're probably writing now."

"Nothing will make the general hotter than that. He can deal with savages a lot more stoically than he can with criticism in the press." He grinned. "I wonder if those editors are actually reflecting the feelings of their readers or are just trying to keep some controversy going to help circulation. You can bet it would be a different story if they were doing the fighting.

"Seriously, no one can fault the man's personal courage. His record proves that. But these Indians are not like the Apaches or the tribes of the Pacific Northwest. I honestly believe he has his men's welfare at heart—unlike men like Zimmer and Custer. I know for a fact he's itching to move out and was planning to as soon as our infantry got here, but then he found out that General Merritt's cavalry was on the way to join us. Now Merritt's overdue, and General Buck is really in a stew that the Indians are going to disperse if he doesn't move soon. Yet, he's afraid he'll miss Merritt. And he feels it will strengthen our force if we wait."

Shanahan finished eating, excused himself, and gathered up his clothes to go do his washing. I stretched out comfortably on the edge of the canvas that formed our mess table on the ground. "Whatever the general decides is okay with me. Personally, I could stand a little more of this. As long as my newspaper is paying me, this sure beats working."

* * *

older, a military academy graduate, a man trained to take orders, trained in strategy and tactics and discipline. What was it that made them similar? They were both single, both well educated, albeit one in the humanities and one in the sciences, both had a sense of humor and a sense of history. Wiley was drifting, trying desperately to find himself, while Curt was already a veteran of the war and several Indian campaigns and unless his own feelings got in the way, would advance steadily down the road of a distinguished military career. Yet in Curt there was an echo of the restless dissatisfaction so evident in Wiley—for different reasons, to be sure, but that, it seemed to me, was where their personalities seemed to mesh.

Our conversation began to flag after a time and Wiley and I stretched out in the grassy shade, our stomachs full and the heat making us drowsy.

"Hey, Matt! Wake up!"

A toe in my ribs brought me awake and instantly alert.

"What's wrong?"

Curt Wilder was standing over me, hands on hips and grinning broadly. Wiley had rolled over sleepily and was flicking an ant off his shirt sleeve.

"Nothing's wrong. Everything's right." Curt stood there grinning and I glanced around, suddenly alarmed.

"Damn, Curt, you haven't been into that whiskey, have you?"

"No, but I wouldn't mind a little drink right now to celebrate. Everything's fine between Cathy and me now."

"Great!"

"Turned out she was playing up to Zimmer so that he wouldn't be offended. She knew we'd been clashing and was afraid that if she rejected him he'd take it out on me. But he was getting pretty aggressive at the least encouragement, so she finally quit seeing him altogether. The bastard! Cathy said he's been in a pretty foul mood since she's refused to see him socially."

"How can you tell when that man's in a foul mood?" I asked.

"When it comes to matters of the heart, you're about as much of an amateur as I am as a soldier, but put 'er there," Wiley said, thrusting out his hand. "I don't know where it's going from here, but congratulations, anyway. Cathy's good sense impresses me more every day."

The three of us stood there, grinning at each other.

"I tell you what," Wiley said finally, with an air of conspiracy, "if you'll meet me about a quarter mile south of camp on the creek in a few minutes, I might be able to find us a little nip of something to commemorate this occasion."

"Done!"

CHAPTER
Seventeen

"WOULD you look at that!"

"Whew! Like the gates of hell just opened up," Wilder replied as the five of us turned our faces toward the west. A line of forest fire had just burst over the top of a ridge several miles away and begun stabbing fingers of flickering red light into the moonless darkness around us.

It was a week later, August 7, and Wiley, Cathy, Curt, Brad Shanahan, and I were sitting together outside our tent, where we had just gone in to camp after dark. Curt had invited Cathy and Wiley to supper. We had seen smoke all day as we rode the twenty-five miles from our base camp on Goose Creek to our present rendezvous with General Merritt's cavalry here on the Tongue. The fire in the foothills of the Big Horns, whether accidentally or purposely started, was having the same effect—burning off much-needed forage for our hundreds of animals. But it was still an awe-inspiring sight as it spread down onto the prairie grass, fanned by a rising west wind.

"Do you reckon the Sioux fired that grass to starve out our animals?" I asked. "Most of the horses look like candidates for the boneyard already."

"Don't know," Wilder replied. "It's one of their favorite tactics. And if they're retreating somewhere up

172

ahead, they could've done it to slow us up. And they wouldn't care if it temporarily ran out most of the game. But then, it could've been started by lightning, too."

"The animals haven't had any grain since May," Wiley added. "And our mules and horses can't subsist indefinitely on grass like Indian ponies can."

"Isn't it pretty?" Cathy said, her features softened by the rosy hue from the western sky. And the fires did look harmless from this distance, winking and flickering on the far hillsides. But I knew they were actually a crackling line of flames, leaping forward through the trees and grass as fast as a man could run. As we turned back to our own tiny cooking fire, the faces around me took on a harsher look, all of them sharply etched in light and shadow.

"All that smoke is gonna make it tough on the scouts," Brad observed, handing a tin plate of beans and bacon to Cathy.

"You think it'll really make much difference?" Wiley asked. "With the size of the force we have now, we won't be catching up with any Indians, unless they want us to."

"Well, if you remember the Rosebud, they picked the time and place," I said.

"That's what I mean. They'll be the ones with the initiative again."

"They'll always be the ones with the initiative," Brad Shanahan broke in. "Much as I hate to admit it, they are the best cavalry in the world, they live off the land, and they have the best motivation—to defend their way of life. A deadly combination. But the American soldier whipped the British with the odds even greater."

"With Merritt's troops," Wilder said, "we now have about two thousand fighting men and a hundred and sixty wagons. I think General Buck sent a civilian courier through to Terry to try to make some definite arrangement for his moving south to meet us."

Sitting cross-legged on the ground, I tried to soften up some hardtack by dunking it in my coffee and wiping up some bean juice. I was so hungry, I had eaten the thick bacon half-raw. We had not paused to eat on the trail, so I hadn't eaten since dawn, even though I had lost my appetite during the heat of the day.

"But we'll be moving faster than you think," Wilder continued. We looked at him curiously. "General Buck and General Merritt have agreed to send all the wagons back to Fort Fetterman and Fort Laramie and go on with the pack train. We can't take anything but the clothes on our backs and a hundred rounds of ammunition. No tents; no stoves."

"Oh, no. Not again."

"Do you get the feeling we've been here before?" Wiley asked, grinning at me.

"Sure do. Have you got a good poncho?"

"No. But I'll see if I can round one up before we head out tomorrow. But Cathy and I are a little better off than you three in that regard. We've been living off the backs of our pack animals, anyway, instead of out of wagons."

"I understand some of the miners are going back with the train," Wilder said to Cathy. "It might be safer if you went with them to Fetterman."

"I'm safer right here in a camp of two thousand armed fighting men, than anywhere else. And even if I'm not," she continued, "I'm where I want to be." She gave Curt a look there was no mistaking.

Wilder glanced down, slightly embarrassed, but pleased.

"Besides," Cathy continued, "Wiley's the only family I have out here now since Dad's death. And I intend to stick close by him until this campaign's over. Then we'll decide what to do."

The conversation ran on, with everyone reasonably content. It was a relief just to be on the move again, with something positive to do, and some goal, however vague. Later, Cathy and Wiley returned to their own tents, and the three of us rolled into our blankets, knowing this would be the last night we'd be sleeping under canvas for some time to come.

But it wasn't to be. Sometime past midnight, the wind increased to gale force and flattened most of the several hundred tents in camp, including ours. I woke up to a roaring, popping noise, with the wind flogging the canvas. Before I could come fully awake, the guy ropes were wrenched out and the white shelter came billowing down on our heads. We crawled out to find the air full of blowing smoke from the forest fire. Rabbits and small deer were bounding through camp, terrified by the flames a little over two miles away. Everyone else seemed to be struggling to stake down the flapping tents or to calm the frightened horses that were rearing and plunging at their picket lines.

A group of the Shoshones had gone out several hundred yards windward of camp and were setting a backfire in the grass to halt the approaching flames. Between the stifling smoke, the gusting wind, and the general uproar, sleep was impossible for the rest of the night.

The backfire worked, but at dawn we didn't see the sun rise. Only a bloody red glow showed through the smoky pall that shrouded the countryside. The wind had died away to a gentle breeze from the southwest. The fire had gone on past us, burning away somewhere to the north. We ate breakfast, our eyes stinging and noses running from the irritating fog that surrounded us. Shortly after, the wagon train began to move out, amid a creaking and groaning of wheels, cracking of whips and shouting.

I watched them go with more of a sense of loss than I had experienced the first time we left the wagons on Goose Creek in June. Maybe it was because I could anticipate this time what hardships lay ahead. General Buck didn't need to detail any troops to protect the withdrawing train since there were enough discharged soldiers, civilian miners, and hangers-on—about two hundred of them—to form an adequate force. The last of the wagons had not even cleared the bivouac area before we got the order to move out in the opposite direction. And the powdery ashes from the blackened

grass were being churned up with the dust by the
horses, choking us and sticking to our sweaty skins. It
was much worse than the gray dust alone.

General Buck called a halt after the scouts rode back
in about noon to report that they were having no luck
seeing anything. Rather than risk an ambush, the general ordered us into camp immediately, using some
choice language to describe his luck and the murky
atmosphere. We lay in camp until about six when the
evening wind sprang up again and cleared the air beau-
tifully. We grabbed a hasty supper, anticipating a night
march to make up for lost time. And, sure enough, the
orderlies passed the word down the line to saddle up.

Dusk came about eight, as we struck the Rosebud
valley again about six miles above our battlefield of
June 17. We turned north up the valley without stopping to rest or graze the horses. We stumbled along, our
horses nose to tail in the sooty blackness, until about
two A.M. Then we were called to halt in order to snatch
a few hour's sleep under our single blankets. At least
we slept on deep, green grass that bordered the river; it
had not been burned. But the trees and grass on the
rocky ridges around us were ablaze. As I lay on my
back with my head on my borrowed saddle, the fires
looked like a dozen or more small volcanoes.

The next thing I knew, it was daylight—a chill, overcast daylight with a northwest wind. The scouts had
been out since before first light. They rode back to
meet us, after scouting about fifteen miles up the valley,
to report that they had cut a large, fresh Indian trail
heading from the Big Horn valley toward the Yellowstone. We halted as the scouts conferred with Generals
Buck and Merritt. Our horses put their heads down to
graze.

Then the rains started.

Gently at first. But they increased quickly into a
cold, steady drizzle that was whipped into our faces under our hat brims by a gusting north wind. Dreary and
uncomfortable as it was, I thought at least it would put
out the grass and timber fires and leave some good

grass for our starving horses. And it would also settle the dust.

I untied my poncho from the saddle, unrolled it and slipped it over my head, letting it fall over my shoulders and cover the saddle as well. The borrowed cavalry horse I rode was about average compared to what the rest of the command was riding, but he was sorry specimen when I thought of my bay. When the command started again, I rode back to find Cathy. She had taken to riding with her brother alongside the mule train, rather than with the few remaining miners. They were hunched down under their ponchos, looking as miserable as I felt.

"Still glad you decided not to go back with the wagon train?" I asked Cathy. She made a face at me and Wiley laughed. We rode along for a mile or two in silence, the cold drizzle increasing gradually to a steady downpour.

It rained the rest of the day and all night. And a more miserable night I had never spent. With no shelter, we were all soaked through by morning. The small fires we managed to start were only sufficient to steam our clothes—not dry them—before the fires fizzled out and we were drenched even more thoroughly.

The next day we made twenty more miles, still following the Rosebud valley. But the beautiful, grassy valley now looked like the bottom of an extinct volcano. The rain had started too late to prevent the retreating Indians from burning off all the grass. Late in the afternoon the scouts rode in to report that a large body of horsemen had been spotted in the distance. The column came to a halt, and a ripple of excitement went back through the command as the men looked to their arms.

But it was a false alarm. The approaching horsemen turned out to be General Terry's force moving south to meet us. It was nearly dark when our commands finally met and went into camp together. General Alfred Terry was a tall, distinguished-looking man with sad, basset-

hound eyes and a black mustache and goatee. Astride
his black horse and wearing his regulation uniform, hat,
and cape, he looked every inch the military man. I
couldn't help but notice the contrast as General Buck
rode up to him and the two men saluted each other.
General Buck epitomized our down-at-the-heels,
scruffy soldiers, who wore all kinds of nondescript clothing. Fighting men we may have been, but we looked
more like a group of underground rebels than we did
United States Cavalry and Infantry. General Terry's
men, on the other hand, were mostly in regulation uni-
forms, riding well-fed horses, and sported neatly
trimmed whiskers or were clean-shaven. And the reason was obvious—they were traveling with a train of
wagons to supply all their needs, including, I guessed,
grain for their horses.

Even from a distance of almost a hundred yards I
fancied I could read the disgust and disappointment on
General Buck's face. I'm sure he intended to operate
alone and had just met Terry more or less by chance,
even though the broad, general strategy was to form a
pincer and trap the savages between us. The fact that
we had come together without meeting any opposition
meant that the Indians had avoided us.

"Slipped through our so-called net like water," was
the way Wilder put it, dismounting and handing his
reins to an orderly. The rest of the command had broken ranks and gone about the organized confusion of
setting up camp. The men of the two commands mingled and greeted each other, but no one made any great
show of rejoicing.

"Whoooeee! If this isn't a raggedy-ass bunch o' hoss
soldiers, I ain't never seen any!" one of Terry's men
shouted near me, as he gripped hands with a former
barracks mate from our command. But we were all too
tired, cold, and wet for any general socializing. Bivouacking for our men meant finding a spot on the
ground that was a little higher than the surrounding
ground and had the least amount of mud and standing

water. Wilder and I sat down near each other, and
looked around gloomily at the scene. I noticed with interest the regimental guidon of the 7th Cavalry—or
what remained of the 7th. They were under the command of Major Reno, a short, stocky, dark-haired officer, who had survived the recent massacre.

We had stopped in a sort of amphitheater, almost
surrounded by rocky ridges and spires of fantastic
shapes and varying heights. The quickly fading daylight
still revealed columns of stone that looked like tall
stacks of thick flapjacks and sharp spires of rock that
looked like church steeples splintered off. Some of these
contained stunted pine trees clinging at angles to small
crevices in the rocks.

"Looks like we almost have adjoining suites tonight,"
Wiley Jenkins said, striding up, his boots squishing.
Cathy was beside him in a hooded poncho.

"Well," Wilder said, looking up, "the roof leaks a
little, but the price is sure within my budget. Welcome.
Pull up a chair."

Cathy sat down next to him and Wiley found a spot
of grass close by.

"Since fires are out of the question tonight, I brought
something from the pack train that might beat chewing
on raw bacon." Wiley produced some strips of beef
jerky and handed them around with some hardtack.

"Wiley, you're a wonder."

"It helps when you ride alongside the pack train all
day. Gives you time to ponder all the choice delicacies
we're carrying and to select a menu for the evening re-
past."

"Speaking of food, I wonder what the boys from
General Terry's command are eating tonight?" I asked.

"I don't even want to think about it," Wilder said,
trying to gnaw off a piece of the jerky.

"Now that we've joined commands, where do we go
from here?" I inquired. The question had a familiar
ring—I seemed to have asked it on several earlier occa-
sions.

Curt did not reply immediately. Eventually he said, chewing thoughtfully, "It's my guess the Indians have dispersed into smaller bands, packed their belongings and trailed off in about fifteen different directions. They're sure not going to stand and fight an army the size of this one. We have upwards of four thousand fighting men. The Indians may be encumbered by their families, horses, and all their worldly goods, but we're even more heavily encumbered by Terry's wagons, our own slow infantry, weak horses, and tired men. I'd say the Indians have the edge. They knew we'd be mad after that Custer thing, so they've gone elsewhere so they can fight another day."

"Looked to me like General Buck was deferring command to General Terry."

"Right. General Terry is his senior. More a matter of military courtesy, though. The next move is up to them."

We sat there in the deepening darkness, the rain running off our hat brims, and tested our teeth on the hard bread and beef. A gloom as dismal as the night was settling over us. But I noticed Curt's hand steal out to grasp Cathy's in the darkness. To be in love in such a place would take a lot of the misery out of this night. I thought of my own girl in Chicago and almost wished myself back there, sharing some warm, dry restaurant with her, enjoying a big steak, a salad, a glass of wine. My mental picture veered off the girl and onto the food, and my stomach growled.

CHAPTER
Eighteen

THE next several days blur in my memory like a bad dream. There was no question of writing dispatches or even of keeping notes. It was simply a nightmare of cold rain, mud, hunger, and fatigue, of riding and marching numbly, constantly soaked to the skin, unbathed and unshaved, infested with lice.

Horses staggered along until they finally collapsed and had to be shot or abandoned. All the spare mounts were in use due to the attrition of the line horses. Many cavalrymen led their horses to save what was left of the shambling beasts. The dozens of men who lost their horses either had to leave saddle and gear or pack it on a mule. Many of the cavalrymen who were set afoot straggled painfully along, far in back of the column, trying to keep up.

The infantry who had joined us recently from Fort Fetterman held up best, marching along easily and quickly, usually beating everyone else into camp. It was very unusual for infantry to outdistance a cavalry column, but we were averaging only about two miles per hour. Most of the new infantry were seasoned veterans. For many of the others, the recruits in particular, it was a different story. Their feet and legs swelled; many of them fell out of ranks and had to be carried on the backs of spare Indian ponies or pack mules, and some of the worst cases were dragged on travois. This was the only transportation available since General Terry had agreed with Buck that we could travel lighter and easier with only a pack train and, consequently, had sent all of the wagons back to Rosebud Landing under the escort of Nelson Miles and the 5th Infantry.

We traveled northward along the Tongue for two more days until we reached Pumpkin Creek. There we turned east toward the Powder River. Here we found the skeleton of a murdered miner, with bullet holes in his skull and shoulder blade. He had apparently been killed by Indians, since his skull and remaining hair showed the marks of a scalping knife. We judged by the state of his clothing that he had died in early June, and it appeared that coyotes had eaten his body and part of his horse that lay nearby in a suffocating stench of decomposition.

We finally struck the Powder River and slowly marched along its valley, full of deep, rich grass, until on the afternoon of August 17, we at last sighted the Yellowstone. And here we went into camp on the level area where the two rivers formed an angle. As if in welcome, the rain stopped and the sun actually broke through the heavy overcast. Quite a few of the men made for the river to bathe and wash the mud from their clothes.

About the time we were getting settled into camp, the steamer *Far West* came up the Yellowstone and the men rushed to see it like a bunch of children. It was the first sign of civilization they had seen in three months. Some neatly dressed infantry were on deck, and a young black girl who was the cook stuck her head out of a door. The fact that most of the men in the water were stark naked fazed her not at all. The men washed their clothes as best they could without any soap, wrung them out, and laid them on the riverbank to dry in the sun. Wilder, Jenkins, and I were among them. Cathy, however, had to wait until after dark.

The next day I went to interview General Buck. Since there were no tents, it was pretty hard to locate him. But I finally found him sitting on the wet grass under a cottonwood tree with several members of his staff. They all looked like tramps. I wasn't able to get much information from him and came away from the interview with a distinct feeling of frustraion. The vague plan seemed to be to follow the Indian trail to the Little Missouri, and after that, nobody seemed to know for sure. The theory was that most of the Sioux and many of the Cheyenne had headed for the sanctuary of the Canadian border. Many of the followers of the expedition began preparations to leave. The correspondents of several papers decided to give it up and take passage on the *Far West*. The general feeling was that this campaign was fizzling out, and we would see no more action for the rest of the summer. Chief Washakie, his sons, and the rest of the Shoshones also decided that this was a good time to leave us. And the next morning, with a few words of farewell to the general, they were gone, knowing they were safe from the Sioux who had left the area. All of our Crow allies were next to go.

As dirty and miserable as I was, I had no great desire to leave and return to Chicago and a stuffy office, even though I felt I had seen all the action this campaign was likely to produce. Besides, I hated to leave my newfound friends, the two Jenkinses and Wilder in particular. So I resolved to stick it out for the time being, wrote up my dispatches to go down with the riverboat on its next trip, and settled myself for whatever might come.

What came was more pelting rain and cold. It almost seemed that an early fall had set in. We were now paying for all those beautiful, hot, dry days we had enjoyed during June and July. The night of August 23 was one of the worst of my life. The rain had set in steadily again just before nightfall. Wilder and I lay down under our blankets to sleep with our ponchos over us. Just as I was falling into an exhausted doze, listening to the rain pattering on the gum coating of my poncho and the rumbling of thunder, something stepped on me that felt like an elephant. I gave it a shove and the next second a frightened mule kicked the saddle under my head.

Thunder and lightning had started booming and cracking like cannon fire, scaring the animals, who reared and pulled their picket pins out of the sodden ground and began plunging wildly through the camp. When most of them had been caught and secured again, we went back to try for some sleep. And I actually managed to doze off for about an hour but woke up with water running all around and under me. I looked over at Wilder, who was awake. I just shook my head and said nothing. To get up was useless, so we just lay there until morning.

When we finally got ourselves up and stirring, we packed fifteen days' rations at the order of General Buck. General Terry had decided to split from our command and cross to the left bank of the Yellowstone. At 10 A.M., with little or no fanfare, we moved out to follow the Indian trail to the Little Missouri, and however much farther it might lead.

And the misery continued, even with our smaller command. Every step of the way was painful for both man and animal. My horse's back was a mass of scabs and blood from the galling of the wet saddle. I had to walk and lead him about half the time to keep him from falling. Under normal circumstances I would have felt sorry for him, but he was in comparatively great shape; we had left dead horses and mules every mile of the way.

On the twenty-seventh we reached O'Fallon Creek and camped in the usual shower. As I unsaddled my horse, I caught sight of the lanky Sergeant Killard working on a lifted forefoot of his horse.

"Is he lame, Sarge?"

The tough noncom looked up, a lump of tobacco bulging in one whiskered cheek. "Naw, Matt. Just makin' a few repairs to my boots."

"What?"

"Yeh. Water's causin' the soles and heels to come loose. Just pullin' a nail here and there outa these horseshoes to fix 'em."

I left him to his work and joined Wilder, Shanahan,

and Jenkins, who were trying to start a fire. Shanahan straightened up with a groan as I walked up. A grimace twisted his pink, clean-shaven face. It suddenly registered on me, as I looked at Lieutenant Brad Shanahan, that somewhere along the route, he had shaved off his stylish mustache and goatee. I hadn't even noticed it before. I guessed he had done it for convenience in the field.

"What's wrong, Brad?"

"Back is killing me."

"How'd you hurt it?"

"My saddle's been wet so long, the wooden saddle-tree's warped. It's making me sit in an awkward position."

We finally got a small fire started, after several failures. It was just barely enough to warm our hands and make some coffee and heat up some bacon and beans. But it was heaven. I never knew coffee could taste so good. Cathy joined us for supper as usual. She looked pale and hollow-eyed—almost as bad as she did just after her father died. Her hair was stringy and damp, and she had it tucked back under her hat. Her shoulders sagged with fatigue. But her eyes were bright and cheerful, and she never let on that she was about done in. By her manner, one would have guessed this was the greatest place in the world and that she would rather be here than anywhere else she knew of.

As she stood staring, hypnotized, into the flames, her face went somber, and I could tell her mind was many miles away. Wilder noticed her reverie also and spoke up.

"Cathy, if you could have one wish for anything in the world right now, what would it be?"

She blinked, and her face became animated again, but there was no hesitation in her answer. "A hot bath," she grinned.

After supper I left the smoky fire to sputter out and walked around the camp to see how everyone else was faring. It was more of the same. Some of the men were wringing out shirttails and socks. Others, including me, were not able to get their boots off due to shrinkage from water and the heat of camp fires. One lieutenant was sitting on a rock, scraping several pounds of sticky mud from his boots with a knife. He was completely soaked, his nose was a bluish purple, and his teeeth were chattering. Some of our horses and mules were sinking up to their knees in mud, the earth was so thoroughly saturated.

Several of the men were beginning to show signs of sickness due to prolonged exposure, improper diet, and fatigue. Rheumatism, fever, and stomach problems were cropping up. But one thing was in our favor. Here, like manna from heaven, the men discovered wild plums, small black cherries, and buffalo berries growing in profusion. The buffalo berries were a lot like red currants but were more acid. All three of these fruits grew on bushy trees that were less than ten feet tall and formed dense thickets along the riverbank. Not only was this a help to our general health, but was also a good preventative for scurvy. I ate as much of the delicious fruit as I could hold and then filled my pockets for my friends. We made a feast of our fresh dessert when I got back. My body must have been craving something like this. Apparently the others had been feeling the same, judging by the way they were stuffing themselves. In fact, we all made another trip back to the thicket before dark to pick and eat.

"Haven't heard much from Major Zimmer lately," I remarked to Wilder, my mouth full of buffalo berries.

"No, thank God," he replied, licking his purple-stained fingers. "He's been keeping quiet, and I've been avoiding him as much as possible. Only speak to acknowledge an order, or troop movement—something like that. A couple of times, I could've sworn he'd been drinking."

"Is there anything around to drink?"

"It'd be easy enough for him to have a couple of canteens full in his saddlebags. I think he and General Buck were about the only ones, outside of the quartermaster, who had access to that peddler's whiskey while the wagon train was still with us."

"Why would he be drinking on duty and jeopardize his position and career?" I asked.

"Who knows? He's been doing it ever since I've known him. Maybe he's hooked on the stuff and can't leave it alone. Quite a few officers are."

"Think you could somehow catch him drunk on duty and turn him in?"

"Not unless I could catch him in some obvious violation. And then I'd better have some witnesses who would be willing to testify. When you accuse a superior officer of something, you'd better have the evidence to back it up, or it'll backfire on you. I've seen it happen a couple of times before."

"Would you do it if you could?"

He finished chewing some wild cherries and swallowed them before he answered. "If the circumstances were right, I would. But it would have to be to protect myself or some of my men."

"You wouldn't bring charges against him just for the good of the service? A man that full of hate and ambition can't be too good for the U.S. Army."

"No. It would have to be something specific. I could spend a career trying to get rid of hateful, ambitious officers."

We moved out early the next morning and marched another ten miles east before camping in a level area among many cone-shaped bluffs. Since General Buck thought a village might be located at the headwaters of either Glendive or Beaver creeks, he sent out the scouts under Grouard to investigate. They were gone over thirty hours, forcing us to lay over for an extra day. But then they returned to report no Indian village in either area, so we took up the march again, following the trail that was leading directly toward the Missouri.

On the 31st we halted on Beaver Creek after a short march of twelve miles, so the men could have their bimonthly muster for pay. We were in another beautiful, grassy area where all our animals fed to satiety. Timber was fairly scarce, but there was plenty of coal in the area. The men broke off chunks of it from exposed seams for camp fires. It made a great substitute for the wood and grass that was too wet to burn, anyway. The smell of coal smoke reminded me strongly of the smell of a city in the winter. And from where we sat, cooking our supper, we could see a smouldering seam of coal in the face of a small bluff, where the creek had cut down through it. No telling how many years this natural phenomenon had been burning.

We made two marches north on Beaver Creek for a total of about thirty-two miles, and, finding no Indians, turned east and marched about twenty miles along Andrews Creek. General Buck had convinced himself that the fleeing Indians had made straight for the Little Missouri, so we marched directly there, arriving on September 4. To our surprise, we found quite a lot of corn growing there, with stalks as high as four feet and more. We finally deduced that this crop had sprung up from the seed dropped by Terry's wagon train in May when they had passed this same spot. Some soldiers were put to work picking and shucking the ears to give our animals a little grain to eat.

The Little Missouri was running bank full and muddy from all the rain. We crossed the river at two P.M. at a fairly shallow ford, the water coming up to the waists of the infantry, and marched along the opposite bank until dark. The next day we made a long march of thirty miles to Heart River.

"Damn, Curt, where are we now?" I asked as we sat down, tired, to supper that night. "And how much longer are we going to be chasing around out here?"

"We're well into Dakota Territory now. In fact, we crossed over into it a few miles before we hit the Little Missouri. Since we left Fort Laramie last spring, we've made a giant semicircle around the Black Hills." He went over to his saddlebags on the ground and pulled out an oilskin pouch containing a map. Unfolding it, he held it up off the damp ground and traced our summer route with a forefinger.

Our usual group of Shanahan, Wiley and Cathy Jenkins, Wilder, and I were grouped around our small cooking fire. Wiley was feeding the flames with a bunch of twisted grass, which was about the only thing we could find to burn.

"Do you think the government or the people appreciate what we're doing out here?" I asked of the group in general.

"Only the few whites who live out here, and the miners we're protecting," Wilder answered. "Nobody back East gives a damn."

"The government knows what we're doing and are directing us in this effort for the benefit of all the people, whether they know it or not," Shanahan said. He sounded pompous.

"Just who *is* the government?" Wilder shot back. "Not the people, in spite of all this ballyhoo we're reading this centennial year. It's a bunch of fat politicians who are out to line their pockets and bask in the luxury of their own power."

"That's your opinion," Shanahan countered, evenly. "I believe everyone in Washington, from President Grant on down, is concerned, at least indirectly, with the welfare of this country. It's our manifest destiny to expand our boundaries to the West Coast, and we're a major part of that expansion. We, in this expedition, are a part of history."

" 'Manifest destiny'?" Curt repeated scornfully. "I wonder what genius thought up that term? The only thing that rivals it for pure horseshit is the idea of 'holy war.' This whole business of driving the Indians off the land—of making and breaking treaties when it's convenient. It's been going on for a hundred years or more, and I think we're seeing the last of it now. I think we're at the high point of Indian resistance right now. This has been the summer of the Sioux. It'll be all downhill for them from here on. There's really no place else for them to run—except maybe to Canada. The army will bring up more and more men, and I'd bet that in just a few more years, all the tribes will be herded onto reservations, and that'll be the end of it. All the useless killing of whites and reds—what does it accomplish? It secures more land and gold for greedy people who don't want to work and pay for it."

"I think I'll interview General Buck," I said, to break the strained silence that fell when Wilder stopped speaking.

It was a spur-of-the-moment decision, and I was tired and impatient, but I tried to keep my tone professional as I questioned the general where I found him finishing his meager meal.

"We're about one hundred sixty miles west of Fort Lincoln, and two hundred miles directly north of the Black Hills," he replied to my query.

"Are you going to send in a courier, sir?"

"Yes, to Fort Lincoln to carry some mail and telegrams."

"What are you going to do now?"

He paused, thoughtfully, looking away from me at nothing and stroking his beard. When he spoke, his voice was slow and deliberate. "We are five full marches from Fort Lincoln and at least seven marches from the Black Hills. We would lose about half our horses if we go to the Fort for supplies and return. We would also lose about two weeks of time. If we want to stay on the trail of the Indians in the hope of winding up this campaign successfully, I have only one choice—we will start for the Black Hills in the morning."

"What about rations, General?"

"We have only two and a half days' rations, but we have to make them last for at least seven days."

"What?" I was incredulous.

"It's got to be done. It's obvious now that the Sioux and Cheyenne have gone to the Hills and to the agencies. We've got to protect the miners and punish the Sioux on our way south."

"We're not really in shape to punish anybody, are we General?"

"We've got to toughen ourselves to it. You can be sure the Indians are feeling the effects of this march, too. We've got to keep the pressure on them."

"General . . ." I struggled to form the words, in my amazement. "Do you actually propose to march two hundred miles in this wilderness with used-up horses and dead-tired infantry on two and a half days' rations?"

"Yes. We'll go on half-rations immediately. I'm sending a telegram to General Sheridan for supplies in wagons to meet us at Crook City or Deadwood. If they don't arrive, the settlements will have to feed us. Besides, this country looks pretty good for game. We should be able to shoot something to supplement our supplies."

My face must have registered my doubts because, as he turned away, signaling the end of the interview, he said, over his shoulder, "If all else fails, we can always eat our horses."

This offhand remark sent a chill down my back. Eat our horses!

"I'd rather eat my brother," was Shanahan's reaction a few minutes later when I repeated what the general had said.

"Better cinch up your belts," Wilder said.

"If I cinch mine up any more, the buckle'll be rubbing my backbone," Wiley Jenkins observed.

"And I haven't been this thin since I was fourteen," Cathy added, hitching up her soggy Levi's. "Wish I had a set of scales to weigh myself."

"Well, if you don't relish horsemeat, it looks like your diet is going to last a few days more," Curt said. "Besides, I thought you needed to knock off a few pounds, anyway." He grinned and then ducked as she swatted him across the shoulders with her hat.

The soldiers had made a great effort to collect a lot of combustible wood and somehow managed to build up some large camp fires that night for warmth and cheer. I made a lean-to shelter of my blanket with some cut saplings and crouched under it to write up my dispatches to send out with the courier to Fort Lincoln. As I wrote, I could look out and see steam rising thicker than smoke from the entire camp. Then it began to rain again harder than it had rained all summer.

CHAPTER
Nineteen

THE weather did not improve for the next three days. Every creek, wash and arroyo was running full of water. The mud was unbelievable. In places it was so gummy that it sucked the shoes right off the infantrymen's feet.

Two to three hundred cavalrymen who had to dismount and lead their feeble horses were following up the infantry in the column. Every once in a while I heard the crack of a pistol or carbine as one of these soldiers put his poor horse out of its misery. Some of the horses simply staggered and fell dead in their tracks, while others just laid down and refused to move. Since I was walking most of the time anyway, I was tempted to abandon my horse to forage for himself, but I needed the writing materials he carried in the saddlebags.

In spite of General Buck's optimistic prediction, this section of the country seemed devoid of any kind of game. We didn't even see a rabbit. On half-rations, many of the men were so hungry they took to slitting some cactus they found along the line of march and roasting the pulp—when they could find any wood that would burn. But this diet promptly produced some type of dysentery. By September 7, we were out of hardtack,

193

low on coffee, and the little remaining sugar and salt were dissolved by the constant rain. That day I saw two soldiers by the side of the trail carving up the hindquarters of a horse they had just killed.

It was horsemeat or nothing, so the five of us who now messed together made an unspoken vote for horsemeat. That afternoon Wilder and I skinned part of a horse that had to be shot, and carved some steaks from his carcass. While we were at this, Wiley and Lieutenant Shanahan somehow managed to start a small fire with some wet grass and shavings from a few small sticks. We grilled the steaks on willow sticks, with no salt, and tore at it with our teeth and knives. I noticed Cathy only took a few small, tentative bites and left the rest, her face even paler than before. About all I can say for worn-out cavalry horsemeat is that it served to sustain our lives. It was the consistency of stringy leather and had the flavor of sweaty blanket. Maybe the meat would have been slightly better if the horse had been a little fleshier.

We were just finishing this early evening meal about four-thirty when General Buck finally decided the situation was getting desperate enough to send a detachment ahead to Deadwood to buy and bring back all the supplies they could find. He ordered that a picked group of a hundred and fifty men—fifteen from each troop of the 3rd Cavalry—be mounted on the best remaining horses, and put under the command of Major George Zimmer, Captain Curtis Wilder, Lieutenant Bradley Shanahan, and Lieutenant Emmett Crawford. They were to be accompanied by a pack train of fifty mules.

Of course I volunteered to go. Since my horse was worn out, I managed to trade him for one in somewhat better condition to another correspondent who was staying behind. Wiley would be going to help with the pack train and he saw to it that Cathy rode with him. Privately he confided to me that he damn well intended to see to it that she stayed in Deadwood. We moved out just after total darkness had set in. The rain had stopped, but a heavy mist was still obscuring everything.

For about two hours we rode in silence, with the mule train closed up and closely guarded by Wiley and the other packers to keep them from getting away or lost. Now and then, Frank Grouard, who was guiding us, had to stop and strike a match to check his compass. About nine-thirty the misty rain clouds cleared and the stars appeared overhead for a few minutes—just long enough for Grouard to check our course by the position of the North Star and the Big Dipper. Then the clouds obscured everything again. About midnight we stopped and tried to get some sleep in the rain and mud, but few of us, except the most practiced or tired, were able to do more than catnap before the order was given by Major Zimmer to move out as the first faint dawn showed about four A.M.

It was another terrible day of rain and mud and rough country. We rode only about twenty-five miles in eleven hours. Around three P.M. Frank Grouard, who had been scouting ahead, rode back and reported to Major Zimmer that an Indian village lay ahead. Zimmer twisted his square frame in his saddle and spoke to Wilder, a few yards behind him. "Captain, have the detail wait in that hollow over there while I take a look at this village."

Without waiting for a reply, he and Grouard rode on ahead. Wilder, with a low command and an arm signal, led the column into a shallow ravine about thirty yards away where he gave the order to dismount. We stood around, shivering in the chill drizzle, holding our horses. Nobody spoke. A sense of dread foreboding settled over the three companies. A few of the men wiped the clammy moisture from the barrels of their carbines and attempted to dry off the cartridges. Finally, Grouard and Zimmer reappeared, and the three officers rode up to meet them.

I was standing a few feet away.

"It's a Sioux village of about thirty-five tepees in a valley about a mile ahead," Zimmer said. "We're losing the light too fast to attack this afternoon. Have the men fall back about two miles, and we'll camp for the night and hit them at dawn." That was all. The three officers saluted and turned their horses to obey.

I was already in the saddle. Zimmer watched, stolidly, as his order was carried out. His usually florid face was pale and grim under the wide hat brim that was bent down in front with the dripping rain. His great cavalry cape was wrapped up close about him, revealing the heavy legs encased in the high boots and blue trousers. We rode back the way he had come and bivouacked in a gulch that was bordered with a scattering of trees. The soldiers had some hard bread and a few scraps of bacon in their saddlebags to eat. But Wiley shared the packers' supper with Cathy, Curt and me. It was a soup made of flour and grease, and when we heated it over our little camp fire, I've never tasted anything so good. The way Cathy spooned it up, she must have been half-starved.

We tried to get some sleep, but, between our nervousness and the discomforts, we didn't sleep much. The five of us wrapped ourselves in our wet blankets and lay down near the fire on some greasy canvas we had taken from the mule packs. I dozed off and on, and finally slept. I dreamed I was surrounded by hideous-looking Sioux and trying to fight them off alone. Then when I started to run, I couldn't move my legs because I was knee-deep in freezing mud and slush. Just as I was about to be cut down, someone was shaking my shoulder and I opened my eyes. The dim form of Curt Wilder was there. A wave of relief swept over me as the realistic dream vanished. I got slowly to my feet, feeling about a hundred years old—stiff and cold with gritty eyeballs and a bad taste in my mouth. I pulled my damp corduroy coat around me, shivering myself temporarily warm.

"What time is it?" Darkness still enveloped us.

"About two," Wilder replied, moving away to rouse some of the soldiers who had managed to fall asleep.

Cathy and Wiley were both awake. Shanahan was up and gone somewhere in the dark. I could hear muffled sounds of men moving around, coughing, rattling equipment. The few fires that still burned were only piles of dully glowing embers, casting very little light. We all moved like zombies as we saddled our horses. Wilder helped Cathy cinch up her mount, while Wiley replaced the canvas on the mule packs. Very shortly everyone was ready and Major Zimmer's voice came out of the darkness, ordering us to mount. Then the command was passed to move out. In less than an hour we were near the spot where we had halted the day before. The murky blackness was still thick with mist, and for the life of me, I couldn't tell how Grouard could find his way in such obscurity. Even a cat can't see in total darkness.

Suddenly the column halted and low-voiced orders were passed back for the mule train and twenty-five of the troopers to remain where they were. Then the order to dismount was relayed and the twenty-five chosen troopers were given charge of their own horses plus another hundred. One hundred dismounted soldiers were to attack the village on foot at first light, while twenty-five mounted men under Lieutenant Crawford were to drive off the pony herd so the Indians couldn't escape on horseback. Zimmer didn't want to risk taking our own horses or mules too close. At the scent of the Indian ponies, our animals were liable to whinny or bray, giving us away before we were ready.

Wiley and Cathy were left behind with the packers, the mules and the twenty-five horse holders, while the rest of us moved forward on foot to be in position by first light. Lieutenant Crawford and his twenty-five mounted troopers moved off slowly to our right in a wide circle to come up to the valley farther west. My heart was pounding so loudly in my ears from nervousness and exertion that I just knew it could be heard several yards away. I was more scared now when we had the advantage of surprise than I had been at the Rosebud when the roles had been reversed. When we had been attacked in June. I hadn't known it was coming, not had time to be afraid.

When we worked our way cautiously to the lip of the shallow valley and looked down we could only vaguely make out blurred shapes of the lodges in the murk. They might have been big rocks for all I could tell. I was beside Wilder as we spread out and crouched down to await daylight. I noticed that he seemed more uneasy than usual. I had seen him under stress before and he was always under icy control. But now he fidgeted, moving around, wiping his hands on the insides of his trouser legs. I heard him take a deep breath every minute or two, and realized he was probably trying to relieve the tension and calm a wildly beating heart, just as I was. A couple of times he turned to me as if to say something, but each time apparently changed his mind. Lights and talking had been forbidden. I desperately wanted to strike a match and look at my watch; it seemed we had been here for hours. We were all coiled as tight as a hundred individual springs, ready to snap as one.

Very gradually, imperceptibly, I was aware of dim outlines of trees nearby. Then the outlines became more distinct, and I could make out the forms of the men crouched along the tree line, gripping their carbines. The valley before us slid slowly from the grip of dim and dripping night and took on some substance. The hide-covered tepees looked gray in the early, misty light. The valley was bordered on three sides by picturesque, cone-shaped hills covered with trees. It was open to the east. We were on the north side. As the light gradually grew stronger from the open end of the valley, I looked in vain for a guard or lookout. The Sioux apparently felt they were secure. I could see no pickets anywhere. There was not even anyone with the pony herd that was grazing quietly west of the village. Our own horsemen were somewhere out of sight off to our right. I was shivering—not entirely from the cold—and had to grit my teeth to keep them from chattering. My loaded Winchester felt clammy in my hands.

Finally came the full light of an overcast morning. A grassy slope swept down out of the trees where we hid toward the first of the three dozen lodges about a hundred and fifty yards away. Just as Major Zimmer came down the line toward Wilder, a slight movement caught the corner of my eye, and I looked down at the village to see a woman emerge from one of the lodges, followed by two Indian children who appeared to be about three or four years old. The woman had a basket in her hand. Wilder's quick eyes saw them at the same time.

"Captain," Zimmer said in a low, husky voice, "when I give the signal, you lead the men in a charge on that village. We've got 'em completely by surprise. Shoot to kill. We'll get at least some revenge for Custer and the 7th," he added, bitterly. Suddenly he also caught sight of the woman and two children. "Damn! We've got to hurry. Somebody's up." He raised his arm and glanced along our line. "Ready?"

"Major, there are women and children in that village," Wilder said.

"So?"

"We can't kill them."

"They can kill you as quick as any warrior," Zimmer snapped impatiently. "If they get in the way, cut 'em down. Anybody in that village is fair game. They're the enemy. Are you ready, *Captain*?" He glared at Wilder.

"No. I'm not killing any women and children. This has the smell of another Washita or Sand Creek Massacre to me."

"What?" Zimmer turned a face on Wilder that suggested he couldn't believe what he was hearing. I swear his eyes positively snapped. He looked like a big cat who couldn't believe that a mouse had just walked into his claws.

"Are you disobeying a direct order, mister?"

"You're damn right!" Wilder shot back, his own face beginning to color above a week's growth of beard.

"Shanahan!"

"Sir?" Brad stepped forward.

"You'll lead the charge. As soon as this action is over, Captain Wilder is to be arrested and confined."

Just as he finished speaking, our twenty-five mounted men went charging down from the hill a few hundred yards to our right. The pony herd was startled and their heads jerked up. They thundered away, wheeling toward the village and racing toward the open end of the valley.

"Charge! Charge! " Zimmer was yelling beside me. The line of men sprang out of the trees, shouting, and raced down the slope, led by Lieutenant Shanahan. Major Zimmer was close behind them. I stood still with Wilder as the action and noise rolled away from us. He stood with his head down, his carbine hanging at his side. Without speaking, I reached out and put my hand on his shoulder. I was as stunned as anyone else, but I knew this was not the time to say anything to him.

When I looked up a few seconds later, the ponies had beaten the soldiers to the village by a good seventy yards and were stampeding among the lodges, seeking to escape. A few shots were popping as the soldiers got closer. The woman and two children had disappeared somewhere behind a tepee when the ponies raced through. I saw hunting knives ripping open the hide and canvas coverings of the lodges, as the Indians didn't wait to unlace the flaps. One or two of the braves, rifles in hand, made a grab for a couple of the ponies as they went by, but it was no use. The herd was suddenly gone, but the Indian warriors rallied quickly. They faced the soldiers and fired two volleys from their repeaters, point-blank. I saw at least three men fall. Then the Indians, young men, old men, women and children, all helping each other, were running. The cracking of rifles and the shouting grew more general, and the smoke began to mingle with the low-hanging mist, and I looked away.

Wilder was still standing beside me, composed, but with a faraway look in his eyes. He only glanced toward the battle now and then as if afraid of what he might see there.

It seemed only a few minutes before the village was captured—without most of its inhabitants. They had managed to escape, some of them to a rocky defile on a hillside south of the village, thanks to the slight warning they got from the stampeding horses. But some of the Indians would never flee again. Their bodies lay sprawled in grotesque positions where they had fallen. From this distance, a few of the forms looked smaller— women and children, perhaps, who couldn't run as fast as the others. I could see two of our own men lying on the ground, and two others who had been hit and were trying to crawl away.

It was amazing to me how quickly the Indians had recovered and reacted after their initial surprise. One big sergeant grabbed the long hair of a dead Indian, jerked his head up and, with a couple of quick strokes of his hunting knife, scalped him. The firing had died down to some sporadic popping and the soldiers were already looting the lodges. Some of the men came out chewing on something that looked like dried meat.

About this time a lone horseman came riding back up the hill where Wilder and I stood. It was Lieutenant Shanahan. He pulled up his jaded horse. "Curt, Major Zimmer has ordered me to put you under arrest," he announced, somewhat stiffly. "I'll have to ask you for your arms."

"Sure, Brad." He handed up the carbine, stock first, Then he slipped the Colt from his holster and gave it up.

"Sorry to do this, Curt," Shanahan said, sounding truly apologetic, "but I have no choice."

"That's all right. It's not your fault."

"C'mon and climb up behind me. I'll give you a lift down there. I think this horse can still carry double that far. It's Crawford's horse." Wilder took the offered arm and swung himself up onto the horse's rump. They rode off and I trotted on down the hill on foot after them.

The Indians who had escaped to a rocky defile on the far hillside were entrenched where our men could not get at them without exposing themselves to a lethal fire. When this was discovered, the fight settled into a seige. A few of the men were ordered to keep the Indians pinned down with a more or less constant fire, while others were sent to round up the Indian ponies that had stopped a mile or so away and herd them back into the valley.

When I got down to the village, I discovered that our troops had taken a half-dozen prisoners—four men and two women. From them, through sign language and the scout's interpreting, we learned that this was only one of several small villages in this area—an area known as Slim Buttes, named for a series of tall, unsupported rock spires around the valley, not far away. Slim Buttes had been a traditional annual meeting ground for the Sioux since before the white man came, the prisoners told us. Other small villages in the vicinity were all under the leadership of Crazy Horse. In fact, the stolid captives told Zimmer, they had already sent runners to Crazy Horse's camp with news of the attack. Zimmer countered by dispatching a courier to General Buck to hurry with reinforcements.

Wilder was not shackled, though a private was assigned to guard him. But the soldier had little interest in this duty when he saw all his comrades hauling out buffalo robes, corn, and dried meat from the tepees. Consequently, I was able to talk to Wilder with no restrictions. I saw the guard almost drooling as he watched his comrades eating.

"Don't worry about it, soldier," I told him. "Those Indians you captured were laughing a few minutes ago about our boys eating that meat. Turns out it's not buffalo—it's Indian pony and dog. They told the major we'd kept them on the run so much this summer, they hadn't had time to hunt."

The private grinned. "I don't feel near as hungry now," he said. "I wondered why we didn't see any dogs in this village. Never saw an Indian village without dogs."

The mule train and the rest of the men with the horses had been called up, and at that moment, they came riding down into the valley. It wasn't long before all of them had the story of the fight and of Wilder's insubordination. Wiley and Cathy were at Wilder's side immediately where he sat on a fallen log at the base of one of the conical hills. The private was standing guard respectfully, just out of earshot.

"Curt, I know you had your own reasons for doing what you did, but let me ask you one thing," I said as the four of us sat together.

"Sure."

"Couldn't you have done more to keep women and children from being killed by leading the charge and directing the soliders yourself?"

"Maybe. But there comes a time to everyone, sooner or later, when you just feel it's time to take a different fork in the road. I just felt this was the time for me." He looked up and saw the distressed look on my face. "Don't worry about it. This was not really a spur-of-the-moment decision. I've been doing a lot of thinking about things for the past few months."

"Is this the end of your military career?" Wiley asked.

"No doubt about it. But, in a way, I'm glad. I've been having trouble for quite some time squaring the idea of killing with my conscience. Wiley, you're the one who finally crystallized it for me. It's bad enough to have to fight soldiers or warriors, but civilian bystanders is another story. That's General Sherman's and Sheridan's whole philosophy of total war—kill the entire enemy population and destroy their property to undermine their will to resist."

"Is that really their attitude?" I asked.

"Not officially, but I've heard it expressed by them in private meetings and briefings. But where it really shows up is in their actions."

"How's that?" Wiley said.

"Apparently you never saw Atlanta during the war after Sherman got through with it. If he did that to white people—his own countrymen, really—do you think he's going to have any compunction about destroying some copper-colored aborigines who have a totally different way of life?

"Don't get me wrong. I'm not saying I'm an Indian lover. By our standards, they're dirty, dishonest, and brutal to their enemies. But they are human beings, and I've finally decided in my own mind that humans shouldn't kill each other—unless it's strictly a matter of self-defense." He shrugged. "It's as simple as that."

Cathy leaned over and silently hugged him.

A fusillade of shots rang out and I looked down the valley where the soliders were trying to storm the brushy, rocky fortress where some of the Indians were entrenched. As I looked, I saw a solider jump up, grab his chest, and pitch backward down the slope.

"Another useless casualty," Wilder said.

"What happens now? A court-martial?" I asked.

"Yes. Then disgrace, loss of my commission, maybe a prison sentence. The army just opened a federal prison a couple years ago at Fort Leavenworth. But sometimes they're a little easier on officers—especially ones with previously good records. But I don't plan to stay around to find out."

"Oh?"

"Buck and the rest of the command are on their way up. Should be here before noon. And, if I'm any judge, Crazy Horse will be here with his force before dark. There'll be a battle of some sort. During the confusion, I plan to escape."

"Just let me know what you want, and I'll help you," Wiley offered eagerly. "In fact, if you don't care, I'll go with you. I'm pretty tired of living like a starving groundhog and playing nursemaid to a bunch of ornery mules."

"Hell, Curt, if they catch you, you could be shot as a deserter."

"That's probably the least of my worries. This is a sick command—no food, no transport, no purpose really, except to get the hell back. They won't be chasing deserters. I think I know army ways well enough to outwit them, once I get clear. Getting loose from here may be the big problem."

"But even if you get away from here, where will you go, what will you do?" Cathy asked, plaintively.

"If I can get my hands on a good Indian pony, I'll head for Deadwood. Don't have any plans beyond that." He sounded relaxed, lighthearted, as if a great weight had slid from his back. "Have to put some distance between myself and the military so there won't be such a chance of being recognized by somebody. But there's always work of some sort in these frontier towns. I won't starve until I can find something better. I've got a good education, and I think I've paid the government back for that by now."

He stopped talking abruptly, and I looked around to see Major Zimmer approaching. "Who gave you permission to consort with this prisoner?" snapped Zimmer. "Get away from here. This man is under arrest."

Wiley started to retort, but I caught his eye and shook my head in warning and then motioned for him to move away without replying.

"Private, keep this man under closer guard!" Zimmer ordered.

As I looked back, he threw a gauntlet down on the ground in front of Wilder. "Take a look at that, you coward!" he almost shouted. "Just pick it up and take a close look!"

Wilder made no move to pick up the glove, which further infuriated his superior.

"The name of Captain Miles Keogh is marked on the cuff. He died with Custer. And we've found the guidon from the 7th Cavalry and a few horses with their brand. What do you think of your precious Indians now, *Captain*?" His voice dripped with scorn. "The squaws you were so damned anxious to protect were probably out looting and mutilating the bodies of the 7th before they were cold. And do you know what else we found in some of those tepees? We found letters of good conduct issued to this particular band by Indian Agents. A bunch of damned incompetent, Indian-loving civilian appointees! Good conduct! God Almighty! They'll be good when they're all exterminated, maybe— not before."

"What did the Sioux have to say about it— or did you bother to ask them?" Wilder asked, calmly.

His manner seemed to goad Zimmer. His face flushed even redder. "Sure, I confronted them with it. Of course they lied and denied they were at the Little Big Horn. Claimed these things were brought to camp by some other warriors."

"How do you know they weren't telling the truth?"

Even though he had turned his back to me, I could almost feel the withering look he gave Wilder. "We'll deal with you later, mister. You'll live to regret the day you ever crossed swords with me," he said grimly as he stalked away.

"By the way, George, what was the final count on the dead children?" Wilder called after him in his most familiar, insolent tone. Zimmer pretended he didn't even hear.

CHAPTER
Twenty

I got my hands on some of the dried pony meat and corn and, when no one was around, brought some to the guard and to Wilder. Then I secured some more for myself and the two Jenkinses. Dried Indian pony and corn was sure a lot easier on the palate than cavalry horse. It actually had a certain resemblance to dried beef.

"We've got to help Curt get away, if that's what he wants to do," Wiley said, as we sat together on the ground, gorging ourselves on the Indians' food. "We can't leave him in this mess."

"Well, like he said, his best chance would be on an Indian pony. And we've got to get one for him. All our horses are done in. And none of the soldiers would stand a chance of overtaking him on one of ours," I answered.

"Hey, what about one of those five or six horses from the 7th Cavalry?" Wiley said. "They're probably fresh. And they would be bigger and stronger and more used to a saddle and bit."

"It's going to be tough enough getting him a mount, much less a saddle. It's not that far to the Hills. He can ride bareback. Those ponies have a lot of endurance."

"You're probably right. If we get caught stealing army property, it would go tough on us."

"Huh! Not half as tough as it will if we're caught helping a prisoner escape. Were you serious about wanting to go with him?"

"Yes."

"What about you, Cathy?" I turned to her. She had been eating quietly and thoughtfully.

"If Curt and Wiley go, I'm going, even if I have to just walk out of camp on my own and meet them somewhere later."

"Why don't all four of us go?" Wiley suggested, his eyes lighting up. "If we're caught, what can they do to us? We're civilians."

The idea of going myself hadn't really occurred to me, but I turned the idea over in my mind. The more I thought about it, the more it appealed to me. The three of us might be able to help Wilder without endangering ourselves. General Buck might report the incident to my paper, but unless I was caught in the act of helping a prisoner escape, I could claim I thought the campaign was over and chose this time to leave without telling anyone. If it weren't for collecting my summer's wages, I might not even go back to my paper. It seemed incredibly dull by comparison to frontier life. There were newspapers springing up in the West that probably needed good, experienced men.

"Okay, I'll go."

"Good!" Wiley said, slapping his hands together.

"But we'll have to wait until later today or tonight to see what develops. There'll have to be a lot of commotion or darkness or both to cover our move. And we don't want to ride out of the clutches of the army into a nest of Sioux and get ourselves killed. Wiley, you're good with animals. Why don't you get some rope or leather straps and fix up some sort of hackamores or bridles—four of them. I don't think these ponies will take to bits. And we don't have time to persuade them. The Crow use snaffle bits, but I don't know about the Sioux. We'll have to watch our chance later to steal the ponies. Shouldn't be too difficult if they don't tether them. There are at least two hundred in that herd. We may need a pack horse. If we can manage it, we should take one of the mules. Either of you got any personal belongings you mind leaving behind?"

They shook their heads.

Shortly after eleven A.M. General Buck arrived with the column. If he was informed immediately about Captain Wilder's arrest, he gave no indication of it. With him, it was always first things first, and he ordered several companies of infantry and dismounted cavalry to surround the gully and flush out the barricaded Indians who had caused most of our casualties. They began blazing away until the cracking of rifle fire became almost a continuous roar, echoing from the surrounding hills. The squaws in the rocks became terrified and began singing their awful death chant. Then the babies began wailing and the combination could be heard even above the gunfire.

General Buck called for a cease-fire and then, through Grouard as interpreter, offered to allow the women and children to come out. The offer was accepted and the general personally went to the mouth of the rocky gorge, rain dripping from his dirty white hat and beard, and took the hand of the first squaw out. She was a tall, fine-featured woman who had a papoose strapped to her back. She was trembling all over and grabbed the general's hand in both of hers and refused to let go for fear of being tortured or killed.

In all, eleven women and six children were taken out, but the braves refused to come out and began firing again. The battle raged for almost two hours. Finally, General Buck called for another cease-fire and again asked the braves to surrender. He told them, through Grouard, that they would not be harmed further.

"No quarter!" yelled one man a few yards down the line. The general shot him a look that would have shattered marble, and the soldier clamped his mouth shut. A minute or two later, a big, broad-chested Indian showed himself and held out his rifle, stock first, to General Buck.

"It's Chief American Horse!" I heard one of the troopers exclaim.

He had been shot in the abdomen, and his intestines protruded through the hole. But he stoically walked forward, without help, holding himself together with both hands, in spite of the pain he must have been experiencing. Blood seeped between his fingers. Two surviving braves followed him out, and the three of them walked to a small camp fire about twenty yards away and sat down among some of their own people.

Surgeon Donnelly came forward and signaled to American Horse that he wanted to examine his wound. He needed only a cursory examination to see that it was mortal. He looked over at the general and shook his head, but proceeded to wind a clean, white bandage around the chief's midsection.

General Buck ordered all the dead and wounded taken from the gully. There were three squaws and one baby, and one scarred brave covered with Indian jewelry. One old squaw had been riddled with bullets, the second had the top of her head blown completely off, and the third had only a single small hole in her left breast and appeared to be merely asleep. The Indians, soldiers, and scouts all crowded around to view the bodies, showing various emotions, ranging from hate to disgust. But the Indians, strangely, showed no emotion at all. The largest tepee, belonging to Chief American Horse, was turned into a hospital tent, and the surgeon, Dr. Donnelly and his orderlies began work on wounded troopers and Indians.

Major Zimmer had Wilder confined in one of the tepees under guard of a different soldier. I saw General Buck go in to see him and stay about twenty minutes. I attempted to get in to see Curt, but was turned away by the sentry, who said he was under orders not to allow anyone else to visit. Several more of the starving cavalry horses, too far gone to recover, had to be shot. Wiley unobtrusively made away with their bridles and reins, detached the bits, and fashioned four bridles he thought the Indian ponies would tolerate.

About midafternoon Crazy Horse hit us.

It was during a burial service for two of the soldiers killed that morning. The sharp crack of Winchester repeaters from the western bluffs was the first indication that he and his band were anywhere around. The burial was quickly abandoned as bullets came whizzing around us. What looked like several hundred Sioux on horseback could be seen circling among the trees and rocks on tops of the rugged bluffs on three sides of the valley.

Even though the attack was a surprise, it wasn't unexpected and General Buck was quick to meet it. He deployed the troops under General Merritt, Major Zimmer, and two colonels. The various companies of infantry and dismounted cavalry swarmed up the bluffs on the north, west, and south, while Captain Wilder's company, under Lieutenant Shanahan, rode out the open east end of the valley to prevent the Sioux from cutting off our means of escape, should it be needed. Another mounted company was sent out of the valley to try to circle around behind the hills to the north and come in behind the Sioux.

The steady popping of the long infantry Springfields, as the men dropped to fire from one knee, was followed by the crackling of the cavalry carbines and then the rapid fire of the Indian repeaters. The horses, pack mules, and captured Indian ponies were completely ringed by our troops to prevent the animals from being stampeded by the Sioux. Nearly all the animals were accustomed to the noise of gunfire, and even though they milled around nervously, they didn't bolt.

Our men worked their way up the hills and bluffs little by little, firing as they went. The Indians fired from horseback as they rode among the pines and boulders. The puffs of smoke from the rifles rose slowly and blended with the low-hanging fog and mist until it got so thick it enveloped the lines of skirmishers as they crept up the bluffs. I could only tell where they were by the orange tongues of flame flashing from their muzzles.

"Nothing we can do about getting away while all this is going on," I said to Wiley and Cathy, as the three of us watched the action from a safe distance in the center of the valley. "I don't know about you two, but I'm exhausted. In spite of everything that's happened, I can hardly keep my eyes open. Guess it's finally catching up with me. I've just been running on nervous energy for days. And all that food I ate, plus this dreary weather . . . Whew!" I yawned.

"Yeh, me too," Cathy said, yawning. "Now that you brought it up, you've got me doing it."

"Think I'll pick out one of those empty, *dry* tepees, wrap up in one of those warm buffalo robes we found, and get some sleep. We'll see if we have a chance to make that break tonight."

"Good idea," Wiley agreed. "Let's go. Did you ever think you'd be taking a nap during an Indian battle?" he grinned as we headed for one of the nearby hide tepees.

"Hardly."

The three of us found a stack of buffalo robes inside; each grabbed one and found a smooth spot on the packed earth. My fatigue overcame me almost as soon as I wrapped myself, damp clothes, wet boots and all, into the warm, furry robe and lay down.

It was dark when I woke. I lay there a few minutes, enjoying the warmth and comfort I had not known for so many days. I finally rolled out and ducked outside. There was still some daylight, but it was fading fast. I consulted my watch: Five-forty. The battle was over, and the attacking Sioux were apparently gone. Even though I had slept only about two hours and was a little groggy from my deep sleep, I felt more rested than I had in a long time.

I went back into the tepee and found Wiley gone. I woke Cathy and just as we came back out, Wiley appeared. "I think tonight will be our best chance," he said, handing me my saddlebags. "I took the liberty of

taking these from your horse. Thought there might be
something in 'em you'd need. I got Cathy's too."

"It's gonna be good and foggy and misty tonight," I
commented. "And most of the troops should be dead
tired, including the pickets. Do you reckon it'd be better to ride out the open end of the valley or try to get
up into the hills and disappear?"

"I'd vote for the open east end. The Sioux are more
likely up in the hills for cover, and besides it'd be too
tough getting horses up into those rocks in the dark.
Also, we might get mistaken for Indians and shot. The
tepee where they've got Wilder is toward the east end of
the valley anyway."

"Okay. When do we start?"

"Better wait until at least ten or eleven. Most everyone but the guards will be asleep by then, and the camp
fires will be burning low. As I see it, we'll have three
guards to get past. First of all, the pony herd. They're
herded up farther in the valley and were guarded pretty
closely to keep the Sioux from getting them back. Then
there's the guard on Wilder's tepee. Then we'll have to
run the pickets at the open end of the valley. Of the
three, I'd say getting past the horse guards will be the
toughest."

"How many guards will be on the horses?"

"Don't know for night herding. They haven't set the
pickets yet."

"Think the Sioux will be back for another attack tonight?"

"I doubt it. I woke up just as it was ending about
five. They hadn't had any luck in two hours of fighting,
so they just faded away." He shrugged. "I don't know
enough about Indians to know if they'll be back tomorrow. For all I know, they may be lying in wait right out
there."

"No. The Apache, maybe, but not the Sioux.
They've gone back to their camp, wherever that is—at
least until tomorrow. If we can get out of this valley, we
can ride all night straight south for the Black Hills and

Deadwood. If we don't blunder into an Indian camp in the dark, we'll be all right on that score. Right now, let's find Lieutenant Shanahan, get some supper, and act as if everything is normal. Don't bring up the subject of Wilder unless he does. We'll work out the details of our own plan later."

At eleven-fifteen that night I was slicing a gash in the hide covering at the back of the tepee where Wilder was a prisoner as the guard dozed in the front. Wiley was acting as lookout for me as I slid the knife carefully down through the soggy hide, cringing at every slight noise it made. Finally the cut was three feet long, and I thrust my head inside.

"That you, Matt?" came a whisper in the blackness, not two feet from my head.

"Yeh. All clear. Let's move!"

In a matter of seconds he was out and the three of us were walking directly away from the lodge at a normal pace in the darkness. When we felt we were at a safe distance, we made a wide detour around the sleeping camp to avoid the still-burning watch fires, and met Cathy at a prearranged place. Then we started for the horse herd.

"Any trouble?" Cathy asked quietly, as we walked in the deep shadows.

"None so far," I replied, "unless that sentry wakes up and decides to check on his prisoner."

"Have you got the bridles and saddlebags?" Wiley asked her.

"Right here."

"Good."

"Here, let me carry those," Wilder said, taking them from her.

"How are we going to get past the guards?" Wilder asked.

"I've got a plan I think will work," Wiley said.

"How many guards are there?"

"I saw six ride out there earlier. May be more."

"Okay, all of you wait over there in the dark at the

base of that hill. I'm going on alone," Wiley said, taking the bridles.

We complied.

"What's he up to?" Curt asked as we crouched down to wait in the inky blackness.

"We knew we couldn't steal those ponies outright, so Wiley is going to try to convince one of the guards that he has to have four of those ponies to replace four played-out pack mules. Most of the soldiers have seen him with the command all summer and know he's one of the packers. And they also know our remaining horses are in too bad shape to carry any packs."

"Hope he's convincing."

"Me, too. Or we might have to walk to Deadwood."

"I feel like I've walked all the way here from Goose Creek," Cathy moaned.

I could hear Curt give her a quick squeeze behind me.

After a long wait, I heard the sound of hooves thudding softly on grass, and suddenly Wiley materialized a few yards away, leading four bridled ponies.

"You did it!"

"It wasn't easy. Couldn't manage a mule as well as this lot; they didn't get along. That guard sort of halfway recognized me as a packer, but he was suspicious of my story. Kept asking me why I was coming out this time of night to get the ponies instead of in the daylight when I could pick out some good ones. I told him with the battle going on and all, there was no chance. And besides, the general had told me to get the pack train in shape to move out early in the morning, and that if he wanted to explain to the general why I couldn't get the ponies, I'd be glad to go wake him up. That did it. He even helped me catch and harness them."

From what I could see of the ponies as we led them at a walk toward the open end of the valley, they were all about the same size, all smaller than our cavalry horses. But I had seen them run and knew they were fast and strong. We walked along in silence for a few moments.

"When we get down here another two hundred yards or so," Wilder said, "we'd better get mounted and slip out as quietly as possible." He had naturally assumed command again, even though he had shed his captain's bars for good. "The pickets will be widely placed, and we'll be past them before they know what's happening. Besides, they're watching for attack from without."

When we got to the approximate point Wilder had indicated, he called a halt. The misty night enveloped us in blackness.

"Mount up."

We shushed and patted the Indian ponies until they let us mount, but even then the animals danced and shied, unaccustomed to the strange smell. Eventually they quieted. We waited in breathless silence to see if their thumping and snorting had alerted any of the pickets to unusual activity. At last Curt leaned over, caught Cathy's bridle and led out, moving like a shadow in the misty darkness. We kept close, single file, holding the horses down to a walk until we were well clear. Curt finally halted and we all came to a stop around him.

"Well, my friends," his voice was pitched very low, although there was now no possibility of our being heard, "this is the last chance for you to change your minds. You've got me safely out of the camp, and believe me, I am grateful. . . . I can make it on my own from here. So if any of you are having second thoughts, now's the time to have them."

There was only the shortest of pauses. Then Wiley said, "Far as I'm concerned, there isn't anything's going to stop me from finding a drink and a dry bed in Deadwood—"

"To say nothing of a steak," I added.

"And a hot bath! Let's *move*!" Cathy's voice was positively gleeful.

Together, the four of us trotted briskly into the darkness.

About the Author

Tim Champlin was born in Fargo, North Dakota and grew up in Nebraska, Missouri, and Arizona. He lives in Nashville, Tennessee with his wife and three children where he is employed in the federal Civil Service. He is the author of SUMMER OF THE SIOUX, DAKOTA GOLD, STAGHORN, and SHADOW CATCHER.

A round-up of BALLANTINE'S best... Westerns by your favorite authors